Pru was sitting opp ~~table, sipping at a g~~ **her companion feas** **pickles she had pro** **was. How ordinary. The heroine of her novel** **would have fainted off to find an intruder in her** **house. She would not have *fed* him.**

"What do you find so amusing?" Her companion's voice cut through these wry thoughts. She looked up to find him watching her. He waved a knife in her direction. "You were smiling."

"Not intentionally."

"Perhaps not." He studied her. "I see now. Your mouth curves up naturally at the corners."

"Yes." She looked away. "It is a fault."

"It is as if you are always on the edge of laughter. How can that be a bad thing?"

Pru realized this was not a proper conversation to be having with a strange man and did not reply.

"May I know to whom I am indebted for this supper?" he asked her presently.

"To my aunt, Mrs. Clifford. This is her house."

His eyes narrowed. "It is your name I wish to know."

"I am Miss Clifford."

He raised his brows and she firmly closed her lips, determined not to tell him her first name.

"And who are you, sir?"

"Garrick Chauntry. Duke of Hartland."

Author Note

Prudence Clifford is a confirmed spinster, living a rather dull life in Bath with her aunt. Then a chance meeting with Garrick Chauntry, Duke of Hartland, turns her ordered world upside down. Not that she knows it at the time. She never expects to see him again, until her aunt receives an unexpected invitation to go to London for the summer.

In the capital she discovers that Garrick is a social pariah and her strong sense of justice means she cannot sit by while he is vilified by society. Garrick has lived with the scandal too long to care. He would be content to retire to the country, only he cannot allow an obstinate, headstrong young woman to fight his battles for him!

The Night She Met the Duke takes place in 1814 and the Allied Sovereigns have come to England to celebrate (prematurely) the downfall of Napoleon Bonaparte. It is also one hundred years since the House of Hanover ascended the British throne, which provides an excuse for even more festivities. The capital is bursting with visitors, all come to watch military reviews and balloon ascensions, to dance at balls and enjoy the celebrations taking place in the London parks.

It is not only the great and good crowded into London; ordinary citizens are there also, along with the mob. They are all there to watch the pomp and ceremony, to cheer the Duke of Wellington and the Czar of Russia, and to boo their favorite villain, the Prince Regent.

Pru and Garrick's story is played out against this dangerous, glittering background, where reputations are easily lost and occasionally restored.

SARAH MALLORY

The Night
She Met the Duke

HARLEQUIN®
HISTORICAL™

Recycling programs
for this product may
not exist in your area.

ISBN-13: 978-1-335-72383-3

The Night She Met the Duke

Copyright © 2023 by Sarah Mallory

For questions and comments about the quality of this book,
please contact us at CustomerService@Harlequin.com.

Harlequin Enterprises ULC
22 Adelaide St. West, 41st Floor
Toronto, Ontario M5H 4E3, Canada
www.Harlequin.com

Printed in U.S.A.

Sarah Mallory grew up in the West Country, England, telling stories. She moved to Yorkshire with her young family, but after nearly thirty years living in a farmhouse on the Pennines, she has now moved to live by the sea in Scotland. Sarah is an award-winning novelist with more than twenty books published by Harlequin Historical. She loves to hear from readers; you can reach her via her website at sarahmallory.com.

Books by Sarah Mallory

Harlequin Historical

The Duke's Secret Heir
Pursued for the Viscount's Vengeance
His Countess for a Week
The Mysterious Miss Fairchild
Cinderella and the Scarred Viscount
The Duke's Family for Christmas
The Night She Met the Duke

Lairds of Ardvarrick

Forbidden to the Highland Laird
Rescued by Her Highland Soldier
The Laird's Runaway Wife

Saved from Disgrace

The Ton's Most Notorious Rake
Beauty and the Brooding Lord
The Highborn Housekeeper

Visit the Author Profile page
at Harlequin.com for more titles.

Chapter One

Midnight, and Prudence Clifford was still wide awake. It was exceptionally warm for April and the drawing room curtains had not been drawn, allowing a welcome draught of cool air to come in through the open window, stirring the muslin under-curtains.

It had been a busy day. Pru had spent the morning assisting the doctors at the Bath Infirmary before joining her aunt to go shopping in Milsom Street. Mrs Clifford had retired soon after dinner, but Pru remained in the drawing room, reading the book she had recently chosen from the circulating library. The plot might be silly but she always enjoyed the adventures that befell the heroines of Gothic novels. Her own world seemed very dull in comparison. She was dull, too. She knew that because she had been described as such.

The incident had happened at the last assembly she attended before coming to Bath. It was almost four years ago, but she had never forgotten it. She had danced with a young gentleman who was visiting Melksham and later heard him talking about her to his fashionable friends: 'Ah, you mean Miss Prudence Clifford, a lady as dull as her name!'

Pru had just come out of mourning for her beloved brother, Walter, which somehow made the gentleman's words even more painful.

Walter had died following a riding accident shortly after his twenty-first birthday and it had been a blow to them all, but especially to Pru. Barely twelve months separated them and it was Pru who nursed Walter through the final weeks of his life. The pain and grief of his death had never left her. Also, with the loss of the heir, Papa's estate would now pass to a distant cousin and Pru's parents expected her, as the eldest of four daughters, to make a good match.

Prudence never shone in a crowd. Her height made her shy. She was too reserved, and the young man's words rang only too true with her. When, some weeks later, Aunt Minerva, relict of Papa's only brother and with no family of her own, declared she was going to hire a companion to live with her in Bath, Pru offered her services, thus giving her younger and far more lively sisters their chance to enter society.

Pru had never regretted her decision. Two of her sisters were very soon betrothed and she was genuinely happy for them. Now, at five-and-twenty, she had given up all hopes of marriage and life in Bath suited her very well. Aunt Minerva was kindness itself and a most undemanding companion. She made no objection to her niece's efforts for the Parish Widows and Orphans Fund or her other charitable causes. She even allowed her to spend two mornings each week helping at the infirmary. Now Pru was not only dull but *worthy*. A very lowering thought.

Deep in her book, an exciting point where the heroine is alone in a haunted house, Pru was disturbed by a sudden noise. The dull thud sounded very much as if it had come from Mrs Triscombe's house, a few doors away. The dashing widow was notorious for holding regular card parties that went on well into the morning. Pru would have dismissed the noise, except that the thin muslin at her windows moved with a soft sigh, as if an outer door had been opened.

She glanced at the clock. It was nearly one, but despite the hour she did not immediately conclude that the disturbance was intruders or a ghostly spectre. She thought, quite sensibly, that one of the servants had slipped in or out of the house. However, she could not be easy until she had been downstairs to make sure they had not left the door unlocked.

Lighting her bedroom candle, she made her way downstairs to the hall. The main door was securely bolted and she went on down to the basement. There was just one bedroom below stairs and that was allocated to their only manservant, Nicholas. Light spilled out from his open door and when Pru glanced in she saw the man lying fully dressed on the bed, one arm hanging down towards the empty brandy bottle on the floor.

She stepped into the room and shook Nicholas by the shoulder, but he merely shrugged her off and went on snoring gently. Pru felt a spurt of irritation. He must have come down the area steps and in through the kitchen. A quick glance showed her the ribbon of light along the bottom of the kitchen door and her irritation turned to anger. If the man had left the kitchen lamps burning, it was very likely that he had also left the door unbolted. Pursing her lips, Pru gripped the candleholder a little tighter and went into the kitchen.

The outer door was firmly closed, which would have been a relief, if there had not been a stranger sitting at the table.

Chapter Two

'What is the meaning of this?'

At Pru's outraged exclamation the stranger looked up. Her first thought had been that he was a friend of Nicholas, but she quickly changed her mind. A fashionable curly brimmed beaver hat lay beside him on the table and his dark coat was perfectly tailored to fit over his broad shoulders. His white silk waistcoat was exquisitely embroidered and as he raised his head, the candlelight glinted on the diamond nestling in the folds of his dishevelled neckcloth. Despite his craggy features and the dark stubble covering his face, this was no servant.

He did not get up, merely glowered at her from beneath his black brows.

'The gate to your area steps was open.'

'That may well be so, but it does not excuse your coming in here.'

'I fell down the damned steps! Since the door was open, I thought I might as well come in this way, rather than go back up to the front door.'

'But it is *one o'clock in the morning*!' she retorted.

'Aye. The night is still young.'

From the faint slurring of his words, she suspected

he was not quite sober. She blew out her candle and placed it on the table.

She said coldly, 'I would be obliged if you would leave the way you came. Immediately.'

'Oh, I don't think so. You see, I am in dire need of diversion.'

He pushed himself to his feet and Pru quickly stepped aside, keeping the full width of the kitchen table between them.

'Go,' she commanded. 'Get out!'

'Ah, you are thinking I have no money.' He glanced down at his clothes. 'I grant you I am a little dusty from the fall, but be assured, I can afford to pay for my pleasures.' He threw a heavy purse upon the table. 'There, does that make my presence more acceptable?'

'Not in the least,' Pru retorted. 'If you were a gentleman, you would go away this minute.'

'Well, I'm not. I am a duke—'

She gave a scornful laugh. 'Even worse!'

'For heaven's sake, ma'am, I have only come here to play.'

He took a step towards Pru and she snatched up the poker from the hearth behind her.

'Stay away from me!' she warned him. 'Get out now, or, or I will call my manservant.'

The stranger scowled. His black hair had fallen across his brow and he pushed it back with an impatient hand.

'Hell and damnation, woman, I have no designs upon your virtue! I want to play *cards*.'

'Cards!' Enlightenment dawned, but Pru did not lower the poker. 'Then you have the wrong house.'

His dark eyes stared at her. 'This is not Sally Triscombe's house?'

'It most certainly is not.'

'I'll be damned.'

She winced at his language but replied in chilling accents. 'Very likely, but not here. Now please, go away.'

He ignored her.

'This *is* Kilve Street, is it not?' He rubbed a hand across his eyes. 'And Sal Triscombe has a house here. A widow lady,' he added. 'Very attractive and…accommodating, I am told.'

'How dare you suggest I would know any such creature.'

'Are you telling me you don't?'

Pru bit her lip. She had heard rumours, of course, but no lady would discuss such matters with a strange man. He was looking at her, expecting an answer.

She said carefully, 'I believe such a person might live in the house two doors along.'

He nodded, but the effort seemed to weaken him. He staggered.

'I beg your pardon,' he said, leaning on the table to support himself. 'I am damnably drunk you know.'

'I gathered that much.' Good heavens, what was she doing, talking with this man?

'I have been drinking with my friends since dawn.'

'I have no wish to know about your celebrations.'

'Oh, I wasn't celebrating,' he told her, his lip curling. 'Drowning my sorrows. Although I didn't tell my friends that.'

But Pru was no longer listening. His head was bowed and he was clearly struggling to stay on his feet.

'When did you last eat?' she demanded.

'I cannot remember. Not today. We broke our fast with wine this morning…'

'Good heavens.' She waved him back towards the chair. 'Sit down.'

'What?'

'You need sustenance before you go anywhere.'

'Nonsense!'

'Believe me you *do*,' she told him. 'I would not wager on you getting more than a few yards in your present state. You are far more likely to collapse and be set upon by footpads. Sit down and I will find something for you to eat.'

With an effort he raised his head and looked at her. 'Why should you do that?'

'Because I would not want your death on my conscience!'

With a shrug he lowered himself gingerly onto the chair and Pru bustled about, fetching various foods from the larder. She set before him a knife, fork and a plate upon which she had placed the remains of a game pie. She found bread, cheese and a few jars of pickles and put them on the table before going off to retrieve a ham from the larder.

'Are you going to join me?' he asked, as she began to carve the ham.

'No.'

'But you are going to watch me.'

'I certainly do not intend to leave you alone here. Who knows what mischief you might make?' She placed two thick slices of ham on his plate. 'There. Make a start on that and I will fetch you a tankard of ale.'

'What, no wine?'

'I wish to make you sober, not more drunk.'

'Then at least pour a drink for yourself.'

Pru was about to make some cutting reply, but she stopped, realising that she would indeed like something to fortify herself.

Five minutes later she was sitting opposite the stranger

at the table, sipping at a glass of small beer while her companion feasted on the cold meats and pickles she had provided. How prosaic she was. How ordinary. The heroine of her novel would have fainted off to find an intruder in her house. She would not have *fed* him.

'What do you find so amusing?' Her companion's voice cut through these wry thoughts. She looked up to find him watching her.

He waved a knife in her direction. 'You were smiling.'

'Not intentionally.'

'Perhaps not.' He studied her. 'Ah, I see now. Your mouth curves up naturally at the corners.'

'Yes.' She looked away, saying with a faint sigh, 'It is a fault.'

'It is as if you are always on the edge of laughter. How can that be a bad thing?'

'My mouth is too wide.'

'I do not think so.'

Pru realised this was not a proper conversation to be having with a strange man and did not reply.

'May I know to whom I am indebted for this supper?' he asked her presently.

'To my aunt, Mrs Clifford. This is her house.'

His eyes narrowed. 'It is your name I wish to know.'

'I am Miss Clifford.'

He raised his brows and Pru firmly closed her lips, determined not to tell him her first name. However, after a few moments curiosity got the better of her and she broke the silence.

'And who are you, sir?'

'Garrick Chauntry. Duke of Hartland.'

'So, you really are a nobleman.'

'You did not believe me?'

'You are an intruder. And very drunk.'

'Yet you do not appear to be afraid of me.'

With a start Pru realised he was right. Even when she had snatched up the poker it had been in anger not fear. How foolish, when she had been warned since birth about the dangers of being alone with any man other than a relative. She should have been terrified and screamed for help. Although, what good would that have done? The only manservant was lying in a drunken stupor in the next room. She was clearly lacking in imagination.

...as dull as her name!

The echo taunted her and she replied with some asperity. 'Do you prefer females who fall into hysterics at the first hint of danger?'

'Not at all. I find them a damned nuisance.'

That sounded as if he had a great deal of experience in the matter. Pru wanted to ask the question, but quickly squashed the idea. It would be safer to change the subject.

'What happened to your friends? You said earlier you were drinking with them.'

'I had another engagement. Said I would meet them at Mrs Triscombe's.'

'And you are only now on your way there?'

'I decided to fortify myself in a tavern before my appointment, then realised I was too drunk to keep it.'

He paused, his mouth thinning to a grim line. Pru had the impression he was looking inside himself and did not like what he saw there. After a moment he shrugged.

'I dashed off a note, excusing myself and saying I would call in the morning. Then I broached another bottle. Or perhaps two, I can't remember. I thought the walk to Kilve Street would sober me. Clearly it did not work.'

'I am astonished you are not lying unconscious in a gutter!'

'I deserve to be.'

She was aware of a sudden stab of pity.

She said, 'Would it help to tell me about it?' He looked up at that, surprised, and Pru flushed. 'I work with a number of charitable bodies who deal with...distressed persons. Some people find it easier to talk to a stranger, someone they will never meet again. I assure you I am very good at keeping confidences.'

'Is that part of your good works, listening to other people's tales of woe?'

'Yes. Sometimes it helps them.'

'What a saint you are.'

He smiled unexpectedly, softening his harsh features and looking suddenly much younger. Much more attractive. Pru felt something contract, deep inside and she quickly pushed back her chair.

'Your tankard is empty,' she said, rising. 'Let me re-fill it.'

When she returned, he took the tankard with a word of thanks and glanced up at her.

'Do you really wish to know how I come to be in this state?'

No. Go back to your friends. You are no concern of mine!

Pru stifled her uncharitable thoughts, and the alarm bells clamouring in her head. She sat down, folding her hands in her lap.

'If you wish to tell me.'

Silence followed. The duke stared into his tankard for a long, long moment.

'I was celebrating my forthcoming betrothal,' he said at last. 'Yesterday—no, the day before—I spoke to the lady's father and received his permission to pay my addresses. I was to go back yesterday and make my offer to the lady.'

'That was the appointment you spoke of.'

'Yes.' A muscle worked in his cheek. 'I was too much the coward. I got damnably drunk instead.'

Pru hesitated.

'Forgive me,' she said slowly, 'but if you are so reluctant…'

'Why offer for her?' He huffed out a breath. 'We had an agreement. The poor girl has been waiting for me to propose these past ten years.'

'I see.'

The look he threw at her said he doubted it.

He went on. 'The match was arranged when Annabelle was in her cradle. It is a common enough tale, two families joined in a marriage of convenience. When she reached sixteen, I raised the matter with Miss Speke herself, to confirm she was happy with the arrangement.' He stopped to take a long draught from his tankard. 'We agreed I should propose on her next birthday.'

'What happened?'

'I was…*obliged* to go abroad.'

'And that was ten years ago?' Pru frowned. 'You have been out of the country for ten years?'

'Yes.' His shrug was eloquent of dejection, despair. 'I had nothing to come home for. I had been a damned fool and I assumed Annabelle's parents had dismissed any thought of an engagement between us. Viscount Tirrill was always a stickler for propriety. Then, two months ago, I received a letter from Lady Tirrill. She informed me that her daughter was still waiting for me to propose. That is why I came to Bath. The family are staying here at present. Do you know them?'

Pru shook her head. 'I know *of* them. The viscount is a subscriber to the infirmary.'

'The what?'

'The Bath Dispensary and Infirmary. It provides medicine and treatment for the poor and destitute of Bath. I am one of the volunteers there. However, I have never met Lord Tirrill or his family. My aunt and I do not move in such exalted circles.'

'No matter. The point is that Miss Speke thinks herself as good as engaged to me and, after talking with her father, we agreed the betrothal must go ahead.'

Pru could not help giving a little whisper of dismay. The duke flicked a derisive glance in her direction.

'You disagree, ma'am?'

'I think,' she said, choosing her words carefully, 'your behaviour this day shows you do not want this union.'

'It is not a case of what I *want*. The woman has remained single upon my account for the past ten years. At six-and-twenty it is highly unlikely she will receive another offer. I cannot in honour do anything *but* marry her!'

He dropped his head in his hands. Pru waited in silence. After a few moments he recovered. He sat up and straightened his shoulders.

'I have ignored my obligations for too long. It is time I faced up to them. Tomorrow I shall call in Royal Crescent. I will beg Miss Speke's forgiveness and do my duty.'

Pru thought that he was far more at ease now he had made his decision. He began to refill his plate and appeared to have forgotten she was sitting opposite. The food was also having an effect, for he looked much better than when he had first arrived. The harsh lines around his mouth had softened and that lock of black hair had fallen back across his brow, softening his rugged face.

It was easy to imagine him as a youth, wild and impetuous. Pru guessed that even now he was no more than thirty. Society would consider him to be in his prime, while a woman was unmarriageable by five-and-twenty.

'You look very serious.' He interrupted her reverie. 'What are you thinking?'

She smiled. 'That you have probably lived a very interesting life.'

'Not the term I would use for it!'

'But I have never left England,' she told him. 'You spend ten years on a Grand Tour—'

'It was hardly that! I was in France when the Treaty of Amiens ended in '03. Fortunately, I had good friends and sufficient funds to escape to Austria.' He grimaced. 'It was far from a pleasure jaunt.'

'Then why did you go abroad?' she asked, puzzled. 'And why stay away for so long?'

He pushed his empty plate away and raised his eyes to hers.

'Do you not know? I killed a man.'

Chapter Three

Garrick saw the lady recoil in surprise and horror. Confound it, he need not have told her that. He must be a great deal more intoxicated than he had thought.

He should finish his beer and quit this house. An apology for the intrusion, a word of thanks for the food and he could go. He could leave this peaceful room and the woman sitting so quietly across the table from him. Strange, he felt more at home here than he had anywhere else for the past ten years.

She said, quietly, 'Was it a duel?'

'Yes. No. Not exactly. It was my father.' His hand clenched hard around the tankard. 'I killed my father.'

He looked up to find she was regarding him with painful intensity. She looked very pale in the candlelight but it was not revulsion he read in her clear grey eyes, it was bewilderment.

Get out, man, now. No need to torture yourself with all that again.

'Go on, Your Grace.'

Her soft voice prompted him like a priest in the confessional and he found the words spilling out.

'I grew up like so many of my kind, too much money

and no occupation. At nineteen I was in town and living solely for pleasure. I took a lover. Or rather, she took *me*. I was too naive to see the trick.' He broke off and glanced at the woman sitting opposite. 'You are not married. I should not be telling you this!'

Her shoulders lifted a little. 'I have lived in Bath for almost four years and the gossipmongers here have no such scruples. I doubt your tale will be any worse than the salacious stories I have heard from them. Continue, sir.'

He hesitated but she nodded to him to go on and he wanted to do so. Odd, that he should now trust a stranger with secrets he had kept for a decade.

'Her husband found us *in flagrante* and challenged me to a duel. He hinted that we could settle the matter, for a large sum. Naturally, I refused.' His lip curled in self-disdain. 'I was too besotted to pay him off. I thought…' He took another draught of ale. '*All for love and the world well lost.* Ain't that the saying? I thought it was love. I knew the fellow was a crack shot but was determined not to back down. His wife begged me to pay. She said if I did not have the funds I should go to my father, but I could not do that. He was not in good health and I could not burden him. Even when she said she would rather give me up for ever than see me dead, I was not to be swayed from what I saw as a matter of honour. We met on the Heath and… I shot him. A freak chance, I suppose. I was certainly no expert in those days.'

Garrick stopped, reliving the chill of that misty morning, the bone-melting fear that had almost crippled him as he faced his opponent. His stupefaction when his bullet found its mark while he was unscathed.

He went on. 'Word was all over town within days.

The fellow was not expected to live and my father insisted I fly the country. I delayed only long enough to beg my mistress to come with me.' He stopped. 'Damme, but this is a sordid business!'

'Having heard thus much I should like to know the rest,' she replied placidly. 'Did she agree to go with you?'

Her calm, melodious voice was like balm upon his spirits.

'No. I found out *la belle* Helene was nothing but a—' He drew in a breath. 'I discovered the whole affair had been a sham. I was a credulous fool, besotted by a scheming woman. She was not unhappy in her marriage, but she was damned furious with me for wounding her husband! It turns out they had been filling their coffers for years by duping young men and then allowing the young fools or their families to buy them off.'

'That is dreadful. But why were they allowed to do it—did no one stand up to them?'

'No. Most preferred to pay up, or they asked their families to do so. Those who did agree to a duel paid a heavy price. At best they were wounded, at worst... either way no one wanted their humiliation made public.' His lip curled in disdain. 'And the devil looks after his own, it seems. The husband recovered. He inherited a baronetcy a few years ago, and a fortune to go with it. He and his lady live in London now, the height of respectability.' He scowled. 'On the surface, at least.'

'Never mind them. What did *you* do after the duel?'

'What could I do? I fled to Paris. I had intended to return if the fellow survived, but by the time my mother wrote, telling me the fellow was expected to make a full recovery we were at war with France again and I was stranded in Austria. Also.' He swallowed, forcing the words out. 'She told me my father was too ill to suffer any more worry. She said I should remain abroad. I was never more to darken their doors.'

'But surely that was written in the heat of the moment,' she exclaimed. 'She could not mean it.'

'Oh, she meant it.' He ground the words out between clenched jaws. 'After that, all my letters were returned unopened, and when the old duke died two years ago, I learned of it via the lawyers, who also informed me of my mother's wish that I should not return to Hartland Hall before she had removed to the Dower House. It is clear she blamed me for the old duke's death.'

'Forgive me, but you said he was already in poor health when you left the country,' she pointed out, adding gently, 'It was not your fault, sir.'

'I should have been there.' It was the first time Garrick had spoken of his regrets to anyone. He went on, 'Rather than raising hell in town I should have been a more responsible son.'

'You were very young—'

He interrupted her sharply. 'Pray do not try to excuse my actions, madam. You know nothing about it!' He saw her eyes widen and it sobered him a little. 'I beg your pardon, I should not have ripped up at you like that.'

'No, but it is understandable.' She replied calmly. 'Pray go on. What did you do, after you received the letter from your mother?'

'What could I do? I took her at her word and remained in Vienna. Although I confess it suited me to stay.'

He fell into a brooding silence and Pru observed the play of emotions flickering across his countenance. She guessed his memories were painful and her heart went out to him.

'And now you are in Bath,' she prompted him.

He started, as if he had quite forgotten her presence.

'Yes. I came to England after receiving the letter from Lady Tirrill and now I am in Bath to do my duty.' He picked up his ale. 'There, now you have the whole, unedifying tale.'

'I am so very sorry.'

His lifted a hand, as if to brush away her words.

'It is your turn to talk, Miss Clifford. Tell me about yourself.'

She shook her head. 'There is nothing to say that would not bore you.'

'Humour me.'

'I have done nothing of interest.'

He looked at her over the rim of his tankard.

'Come now, having given you my life history, it is only right that you should do the same! Let us begin with your name.'

Realising he was trying to lighten the mood, she capitulated.

'It is Prudence.'

'And why are you unwed, Prudence?'

'I am too old for marriage.'

He sat forward in his chair, frowning at her. 'That I will not allow.'

'I think you must, Your Grace. I am five-and-twenty.'

'Positively ancient.' His eyes gleamed with gentle amusement.

'Yes. I am but a year younger than Lord Tirrill's daughter.'

He acknowledged that with a nod. 'You have no family, save your aunt?

'On the contrary. My aunt needed a companion and I was happy to fill that role, leaving my parents to concentrate upon finding husbands for my three younger sisters. There are no living sons, you see, and it is imperative that the girls should marry. Or at least, that one of them marries well.'

'And has it worked?'

She smiled. 'Yes. The older two are married and the youngest, Jemima, is now betrothed to a very respectable gentleman of good fortune.'

'Well done, Jemima. And well done you, Miss Prudence Clifford, for your noble self-sacrifice.'

'It is nothing of the kind,' she retorted. 'You are not to think I am unhappy. Aunt Minerva is very good to me and we go on extremely well. There is plenty to entertain one in Bath, you know. We visit the theatre regularly and go to the Pump Room, where my aunt drinks the waters.'

'And do you attend the balls at the Assembly Rooms?'

'Yes, occasionally.'

'Then I do not understand why you are still single.'

Her chin went up. 'Not every young lady is looking for a husband.'

'That has not been my experience, whenever I have been obliged to attend a ball.'

'But you are a duke,' she replied sweetly. 'And therefore *extremely* eligible.'

'That's put me in my place!' he retorted, grinning. 'But tell me truthfully, do you not want to marry?'

'Why should I? My aunt and I live here very comfortably. I have my friends, plenty to entertain me. I have no wish to be paraded like a brood mare before every man on the lookout for a wife. Besides that, I have a little money saved and my aunt has made me her heir. I need not fear the future.'

The duke was frowning at her. Pru met his eyes steadily, refusing to admit that she did sometimes hope that life had more in store for her than dwindling into a lonely old maid. When at length she did look away, she noticed that the darkness outside the window had lightened to grey.

'Goodness, it is almost dawn! You should go, before the maids come downstairs.' She jumped to her feet, gesturing towards the table. 'And take your purse with you.'

'Keep it. For your trouble.'

'I have no need of your money.'

'Then give it to one of your charities,' he retorted, rising. 'It would have cost me a great deal more than that tonight, had I reached Mrs Triscombe's house.'

'You do not intend to go there now?'

'No, I am going back to the Pelican.' He straightened his shoulders. 'I need to make myself presentable for my interview with Miss Speke. I cannot change the past, but I can put right the ill I have done her. Once the knot is tied, I can go to Hartland and set my estates to rights.'

'Then I wish you good fortune, Your Grace.'

'Thank you. And I beg your pardon.'

'For what?'

'Burdening you with my story.'

Pru said lightly, 'It is forgotten already.' She walked over to the outer door and opened it. 'You may trust me, no one shall ever hear of it from my lips.'

He took her hand and held it, causing an unfamiliar fluttering in her breast.

'You are a remarkable woman, Miss Prudence Clifford.' He grinned suddenly. 'If I were not about to propose to another woman…'

The teasing glint in his eyes turned the fluttering to a drumbeat, robbing her of breath. In the early morning light, she could see that his eyes were not black, but a deep green, like the light in a forest at the height of summer. She wanted to stand there for ever, with him holding her hand, smiling down at her.

The fanciful thoughts unsettled Pru and she shook her head to dispel them.

'Goodbye, Your Grace,' she said, exerting every nerve to keep calm.

'Farewell, ma'am.' He brushed her knuckles with his lips. 'And yet, Bath is a small place. It is possible we may meet again.'

The kiss on her fingers made her heart leap most alarmingly and she hastily pulled her hand free.

'It is better we do not,' she told him. 'How would we explain our acquaintance?'

'Yes, that could ruin everything, could it not? However, you do not have much to fear. I shall not be in Bath long. Lord Tirrill has already drawn up plans for the marriage. He wants a quiet ceremony, as soon as possible, at his country seat in Hampshire. Understandable, when my reputation is so badly tarnished.'

'And you have no say in the proceedings?' asked Pru, unable to stop herself.

His mouth twisted. 'It matters little to me when or where we marry. In fact, the less pomp the better! But I should not be troubling you any further with my concerns. Goodbye, Miss Clifford.'

With that he jammed his hat on his dark head, ran lightly up the area stairs and disappeared.

Prudence stood in the doorway, looking up at the now empty pavement. A single star was visible in the morning sky, a tiny spot of silvery light. She pressed the back of her hand to her cheek, remembering the soft touch of his lips on her skin. Then, with a sigh, she stepped inside and closed the door.

Chapter Four

Garrick strode back to the Pelican feeling much better than he had any right to be. He had spent a whole day drinking as a way of avoiding an unpleasant duty. He had felt like a scoundrel, the heartless rogue his mother accused him of being. By the time he reached Kilve Street and fell down those steps he had concluded it would be better for everyone if he jumped off Pulteney Bridge and put paid to his existence.

Then he had been visited by an angel, a tall, graceful woman with kind grey eyes and a warm smile. He should have known immediately this was not the house he sought. The lady's demure gown covered her from neck to ankle, although the thin green muslin could not disguise her excellent figure. Did she know that? he wondered. No, Prudence Clifford used no arts to attract a man. She wore her light brown hair wound neatly about her head. It was a plain, no-nonsense style, but he had noticed how the candles sparked the occasional glint of gold from those soft tresses.

He thought back to the way she had defended herself. By heaven, she had wielded that heavy poker in fine style! Her outrage at finding a strange man in her house was understandable, what was not so clear was why she had then sat him down and fed him. Did she not know what a dangerous situation she was in, alone with a drunkard in the middle of the night?

'Damned foolish,' he muttered, casting his eyes up to the single star twinkling in the lightening sky. 'That was not very sensible at all, despite your name, Miss Prudence Clifford!'

Prudence. A smile tugged at his lips. Was there some morally uplifting tale about Prudence and Despair? If not, there should be. She had listened to him patiently, not judging, and by the time he had finished telling her his woes he realised just how pathetic he sounded, and what he must do about it. He had not only wasted ten years of his life but Annabelle Speke's life, too. It was time to face up to his responsibilities.

As he reached the end of the street he slowed, wondering if he should go back and check that Prudence had bolted the door against any further intruders. No, he decided. The best thing he could do for Miss Prudence Clifford was to keep away from her.

The maids were already at work in the Pelican when Garrick returned to this room. He locked his door and went to bed, expecting to sleep at least until noon. However, by ten o'clock he was awake again, refreshed and eager to get on with what must be done.

An hour later he was on his way to Royal Crescent, dressed in a new coat of Bath superfine over fresh white linen with tight-fitting pantaloons and glossy Hessians. His curly brimmed beaver had been brushed clean and now sat on his head, which was still a trifle heavy from yesterday's excesses. How much worse it would have been, had he not been rescued by the angelic Miss

Clifford. He wanted to thank her in some way, but reluctantly dismissed the idea, knowing that any communication risked being misinterpreted.

He was admitted to Viscount Tirrill's house by a harassed-looking footman who escorted him up to the drawing room. As he crossed the hall, Garrick was aware of voices coming from His Lordship's study. He could hear the shrill tones of a female and felt a trickle of apprehension run down his spine. Was his non-appearance yesterday the cause of such discord?

The footman left him alone in the empty drawing room. Garrick walked across to the mirror, running a nervous finger around his collar. Having assured himself that his cravat was unsullied and that his countenance bore no sign of his drunken revelries, he moved restlessly across to the window, unable to shake off the feeling that something was amiss.

At that moment the door opened and Viscount Tirrill came in.

'My lord Duke. Good day to you, sir!'

Garrick bowed, trying to ignore the obsequious formality of the greeting.

'Thank you, although I do not deserve such a warm welcome after my failure to present myself yesterday. I am sure you must be wondering—'

'Oh, no, Your Grace, not at all. Your note explained everything. Urgent business…unavoidably detained.' The viscount gave a nervous laugh. 'Happens to us all. Think nothing of it.'

'But I do think of it, sir. It was very wrong of me to disappoint you. And your daughter.' He forced his stiff lips into a smile. 'I trust I can persuade Miss Speke to forgive me, if I might have the honour of a few words with her.'

'Yes, yes, all in good time,' replied his host, clearly ill at ease. 'Will you not sit down, Your Grace. A glass of wine, perhaps?'

'Thank you, but no.' Garrick hesitated, then he said bluntly, 'My lord, has Miss Speke changed her mind?'

'Changed her mind? No, no, Your Grace. Nothing like that, I assure you.' The viscount gave a nervous laugh and there was no doubting his relief when the door opened and Lady Tirrill entered the room. 'Ah, there you are, dear lady. Do come and greet His Grace!'

The viscountess was a sharp-faced woman of decided opinions and Garrick had always considered her the stronger of the two. Now, however, she came towards him twittering nervously. He refused her offer of refreshment but allowed himself to be persuaded to sit down. She was clearly labouring under some strong emotion and began to chatter on about the weather. In this she was diligently assisted by her husband and Garrick felt a traitorous flicker of hope in his chest as he interrupted the flow of inanities.

'Forgive me, but is something amiss? Could it be that Miss Speke no longer wishes to receive my addresses?' The look that passed between them confirmed his suspicions and he nodded. 'If that is the case, then it may be easily remedied...'

'No, no, we are all eager for the match, Your Grace, believe me,' cried Lord Tirrill, jumping to his feet. 'I am sure it can all be resolved in a twinkling, just as soon as Annabelle returns.'

'Returns?' Garrick pounced on the word. 'She is not here?'

The viscount glanced nervously at his wife, who was glaring at him. Garrick frowned. He had been very drunk when he wrote that message crying off from the first appointment, but he was sure he had said he would be calling again today.

'She—she was obliged to go out,' stammered Lady Tirrill, twisting her hands together. 'Quite, quite unexpected, but if you could call again tomorrow—'

Garrick said gently, 'Ma'am, are you quite sure Miss Speke is not avoiding me?' She made no reply and Garrick rose. 'I see. Then I shall not detain you any longer.'

The viscountess gave an angry cry.

'It is all your fault,' she shrieked at him, hunting for her handkerchief. 'If only you had called yesterday, this would not have happened. Everything would have been well!'

'My dear, hush.' Lord Tirrill cast an uneasy glance at the duke.

'I will *not* hush! Annabelle understood what was expected of her. She was perfectly resigned—I mean—'

Garrick interrupted her. 'I beg your pardon, ma'am, but I understood Miss Speke was expecting my offer. That she was very happy to accept it. I think it will be better for me to return again and speak to your daughter myself.' He added firmly, 'Alone.'

'That may not be possible!' snapped my lady, two spots of angry colour appearing on her thin cheeks.

An ominous silence followed and Garrick looked from her to the hapless viscount.

'Do you mean,' he said slowly, 'has she run off with another man?'

'No, no, Your Grace, nothing like that,' Lord Tirrill made haste to assure him, although he had to raise his voice to make himself heard over his wife's angry mutterings. 'She, um, she has gone into the country. With a friend.'

'Emily Undershaw!' Lady Speke fairly spat out the

name. 'I knew that woman would be trouble, leading poor Annabelle astray with her independent ways!' She turned her angry countenance towards Garrick. 'She followed us here from Hampshire, Your Grace, filling Annabelle's head with silly notions!'

'A rich spinster,' explained her husband. 'Quite eccentric, of course.'

'And now they have gone off to W-Wales!' cried his lady.

'Wales!' Garrick's brows snapped together. 'Is she so anxious to avoid me?

'Yes!' Lady Speke buried her face in her handkerchief. 'And now they have some silly notion of setting up home together.'

'Hush, hush, my dear, it is all nonsense,' put in Lord Tirrill, hovering anxiously around his wife. 'It is all a tarradiddle designed to vex us.'

'Yes, yes, of course.' Lady Speke dried her eyes and turned to the duke. 'You have no need to worry, Your Grace, all this can be hushed up. We will fetch her back and beat some sense into her.'

'You will do nothing of the sort on my account, ma'am,' Garrick retorted. 'If Miss Speke is not minded to wed me then so be it. We shall say no more about the matter.'

He took his leave with the viscount following him down the stairs, repeating his ever more desperate assurances that it was all a misunderstanding.

'Please! My lord Duke, will you not reconsider?' he begged when they reached the entrance.

A wooden-faced footman handed Garrick his hat and gloves before jumping to open the door. The fellow must have heard every word his master had uttered. If Lord

Tirrill had no qualms about speaking plainly in front of his servant, then neither did Garrick.

He said, 'I am very sorry, my lord. It is evident that Miss Speke has no wish to receive my proposal and there's an end to it.'

'But I have already drafted the announcement, Your Grace. What will people *say* if you cry off now?'

'How many have you told?'

The viscount wrung his hands. 'No one!'

'Then you may rely upon my discretion, sir. If word gets out it will not be from me. I shall not mention what has occurred here today to anyone. Good day to you, my lord.'

Garrick set off down the hill to the Pelican, feeling as if a heavy weight had been lifted from his shoulders. He did not doubt there would be some gossip, but it mattered little to him if everyone in Bath knew his prospective bride had run away rather than accept an offer. The main thing was that he was not obliged to marry a woman he did not care for.

He would go to Hartland, as soon as he had concluded his affairs in London. Once he had ascertained that his mother had removed to the Dower House, he could take up residence at Hartland Hall and begin to put the place in order. Heaven knows it needed some attention, if the reports he had received from his steward were correct. His other properties, too, must be inspected. There must be enough work to keep him occupied for years to come and, suddenly, he relished the challenge.

When he passed the end of Kilve Street he thought of Miss Clifford. He would dearly like to see her. To tell her what had happened, but it was impossible. He had given Lord Tirrill his word that he would not speak of it. Besides, Miss Clifford would not want to see him again. Much better that he leave Bath immediately and forget all about this sorry interlude.

Chapter Five

Green eyes, smiling at her. Green eyes in a rugged face and an unruly lock of dark hair that insisted on flopping over his brow…

Prudence sighed as the dream faded and she opened her eyes to face another day. Not quite a dream. She had actually met such a man just a few short hours ago. A duke, no less. She smiled at the memory. A very brief encounter, no more than a few hours. They had done nothing but talk, and yet she felt that something had shifted inside her. She felt lighter, somehow. As if the cloud that had engulfed her since her brother's death had lifted a little.

Pru told no one about the duke's visit to the house, although her conscience was sorely tried when she sat down to breakfast and Aunt Minerva launched into a diatribe against the errant footman.

'Nicholas left the kitchen in *such* disorder last night, Pru, Cook was most put out! The best part of the ham was gone, as well as the last of the game pie and some of the cheese. To say nothing of the small beer, which is seriously depleted! Nicholas denies it, but since he does not remember anything, we cannot set any store by that.'

'Oh, dear,' murmured Pru.

She had done her best to tidy the kitchen, but clearly not well enough for her aunt's eagle-eyed cook, and there was nothing to be done about the missing food. She listened as her aunt continued.

'Cook also told me she found Nicholas unconscious on his bed this morning, having drunk the best part of the bottle of brandy we keep for medicinal purposes! He has begged her to give him a second chance but, really, Cook is adamant that he should go and I agree with her!'

'If he is truly repentant, then perhaps we might give him the benefit of the doubt this once,' suggested Pru, stifling a stab of guilt at not confessing the whole. 'We could impress upon him that he must mend his ways or be turned off.'

'No, no, Cook has the right of it. Why, what is the good of having a manservant if he is too drunk at night to protect us?'

'There is that,' agreed Pru, with feeling. After all, Nicholas had left the outer door open, which had resulted in the whole sorry business.

'Yes,' Aunt Minerva went on. 'We might have all been murdered in our beds and Nicholas none the wiser.'

Prudence could not refute that argument, but her conscience insisted she defend the man. She suggested they should keep him on as long as he promised not to drink anything stronger than small beer in future. It took her some time to persuade Aunt Minerva, but eventually she succeeded. After that she tried to put the events of the night out of her mind, but it was difficult, because it was the most exciting thing that had ever happened to her.

* * *

For the next several days Prudence was constantly looking out for the Duke of Hartland. She went about her business as usual but when she accompanied Aunt Minerva to the Pump Room or strolled with her along Milsom Street, Garrick Chauntry was constantly on her mind.

She was torn between wanting to see him and hoping they would not meet. If anyone should guess they were acquainted and discover the truth it would be disastrous for her and it might also jeopardise the duke's betrothal to the Honourable Miss Speke. Not that there had been any news of that, but she recalled the duke had said the family did not look favourably upon their future son-in-law's reputation.

At the end of the week Pru bought the latest edition of the *Bath Chronicle* and took it off to the morning room, where she scanned it carefully.

'At last!'

She found a small paragraph announcing that Viscount Tirrill and his family had quit Bath and returned to their home in Hampshire. There was no mention of the Duke of Hartland, but she thought that was by design. From everything he had told her, she guessed that Miss Speke was determined to have him but, given his scandalous reputation, her loving parents were far less eager for the match, despite his rank. It was not an ideal situation, but she truly wished him well.

'Oh, my dear Prudence, such news!' Aunt Minerva came in, waving a letter. 'You will never guess!'

Smiling, Prudence laid aside the newspaper. 'No, so you must tell me.'

'I have this minute received a letter from my dearest friend, Jane Borcaster.'

Pru raised her brows. She knew of Lady Borcaster, a friend her aunt had known since girlhood, but she had never heard her mentioned in such glowing terms before. Aunt Minerva glanced at the letter again, as if reminding herself of its contents.

'She has invited us to London! You will recall that her daughter is married to a diplomat, Sir Timothy Flowers, and they are gone out of the country until at least the spring of next year. Jane is therefore alone in town and thought we might like to join her, to see all the celebrations that are planned to take place in the capital this summer.' She hurried across the room to sit down on the sofa beside Pru. 'As you know, a host of foreign dignitaries is coming to London in June to celebrate the defeat of that monster, Bonaparte. And then there is the Grand Jubilee in August, for the centenary of the House of Hanover! Dear Jane has invited us to remain with her for the duration!'

Pru smiled politely. Privately she thought London in summer would be even more uncomfortable than Bath, where the streets could be white-hot. Aunt Minerva went on.

'I quite understand when she says that she does not want to be rattling around in her London house all alone. She lives in Brook Street, you know. The western end, of course, almost Grosvenor Square!'

She stopped, clearly waiting for a reaction from Prudence, who murmured a few words which she hoped would indicate that she was impressed.

'Well, Prudence, what do you say, shall I accept?'

She fixed her niece with a look in which excitement and hope were clearly mingled and Pru shook her head, laughing.

'My dear aunt, this must be your decision, you have no need to consult with me!'

'But I do so want you to come, and dear Jane has kindly mentioned you in her letter, begging me to bring my little niece with me.'

That made Pru laugh. 'Hardly *little*, Aunt, I am taller than most females in Bath. However, if you want me to come with you, then of course I should be delighted.'

'Thank you, my love.' Aunt Minerva sighed and patted Pru's arm. 'You have been such a godsend these past few years. I do not know how I would go on without you.'

Pru disclaimed, blushing, 'My dear, ma'am, I do very little.'

'Nonsense, you virtually run my household, organise any journeys I wish to make, to say nothing of bearing me company with patience and good humour. In fact,' she went on, dabbing at her eyes with a wisp of lacy handkerchief, 'you are like the daughter I never had!'

Pru was touched by her aunt's words, and a trifle guilty. She knew she was very lucky to have such a comfortable home with very few duties and a generous allowance. Yet sometimes she felt stifled by her life in Bath. She had been more aware of it recently. Even with all her charity work she was conscious of a creeping boredom that was making her restless. Perhaps a visit to London was just the tonic she needed.

She said now, 'My dear aunt, pray do not cry. You have been exceedingly good to me and if you want me to come with you then there is no question. I shall accompany you, and enjoy myself prodigiously!'

Mrs Clifford's tears were banished. After hugging Pru and announcing that she was the kindest, most obliging girl, she went off happily to pen her acceptance of Lady Borcaster's invitation.

* * *

Prudence was anything but bored for the next few weeks; there was far too much to do. The house in Kilve Street would be shut up for the summer months, which gave her the opportunity to give notice to most of the staff, including the hapless Nicholas, who was failing miserably in his attempts at sobriety. Then there was the arranging of their journey to London. A post chaise must be hired, and accommodation found along the route. On these points Mrs Clifford's many friends in the Pump Room were invaluable, recommending the best posting establishments and inns to ensure their comfort and security throughout the journey.

There was also the very pleasurable task of buying new clothes and for that the ladies needed no advice. They spent many hours browsing in Milsom Street and it was only Prudence's gentle reminders that they would have the pick of the most fashionable modistes once they reached London that prevented Aunt Minerva from buying far more than could be transported, even allowing for the fact that she had been persuaded to hire a second vehicle to carry Norris, her very superior lady's maid, as well as extra baggage.

Pru's final task was to withdraw from her charitable work. She gave notice at the infirmary that she would not be available to help them for the rest of the summer. After that she turned her attention to the task of packing everything needed for a prolonged stay in London.

At last, all was in readiness and one late May morning the little cavalcade left Kilve Street, waved off by Cook, the two maids and the scullery maid, who had been retained to look after the house until their mistress's return.

Prudence sat back with a sigh as the carriage bowled

out of Bath. Her view from the front window was somewhat obscured by the bobbing figure of the postillion
but that did not matter. She had done everything required of her and now she was going to enjoy a holiday.

Mrs Clifford was not a good traveller. They spent
three nights on the road, arriving in London on the first
day of June and pulling up in Brook Street in the late
afternoon. Prudence, who had thoroughly enjoyed the
journey, looked out eagerly at their home for the next
three months. Lady Borcaster's residence was a handsome, three-storey house with a stone pediment around
the freshly painted door.

It was clear they were expected. A servant ran out
to open the carriage door and by the time they had
alighted, Lady Borcaster herself had appeared on the
front step.

'There you are at last! Come in, my dears, come in!
Cotton will see to everything.'

They were shown into a spacious hall where Mrs
Clifford presented her niece to her hostess.

'Delighted to meet you at last, Prudence—I may call
you that, I hope? It is how Minerva always refers to you
and I feel I already know you so well from her letters!
Now, as soon as you have shed your coats, we will go
upstairs to the drawing room. Come along.'

As they followed their hostess up the sweeping staircase, Pru glanced back. An army of footmen was carrying in their luggage, overseen by Lady Borcaster's
butler, Cotton, while Norris, Aunt Minerva's dresser,
darted around giving instructions as to where each
trunk should be taken. With so many servants in the
house, Pru thought there would be little to do here, save
enjoy herself. She followed the other ladies into the el-

egant drawing room, where two long windows looked out over the street.

'Well,' declared Lady Borcaster, once they were all seated. 'I cannot tell you how delighted I am to have you here! I hope you are not too tired to take a little wine and some cake with me?'

'No, no, not at all,' murmured Minerva, her eyes widening at the sight of the laden table.

Pru had to admit it held more cakes, biscuits and sweetmeats than her aunt would order for a week of dinners. While they were served with wine or cordials from a selection of decanters standing on a side table, she took the opportunity to observe her hostess. Lady Borcaster had been a widow for many years and a generous pension allowed her to indulge her love of comfort and fashion. She was a large, handsome woman and, like Aunt Minerva, she was nearing her fiftieth year. Unlike Mrs Clifford, who was neatly dressed in a plain gown of sober colours, Lady Borcaster clearly favoured ornamentation.

Gold tassels shimmered from the short sleeves and bodice of her red-and-cream-striped gown while an elaborate gold necklace filled the space between her throat and the low-cut bodice. Rings sparkled on every finger and her improbably dark curls peeped out beneath a large turban fashioned from the same cloth as her gown.

A greater contrast to her aunt Pru thought it would have been hard to find. She could understand why Minerva preferred to live in quiet, genteel Bath rather than the bustling metropolis, but as she listened to the two ladies chattering she realised that there was indeed a strong bond between the two. Lady Borcaster had a ready laugh and was clearly very fond of Aunt Minerva. She seemed determined to make their stay an enjoyable one.

'And what about you, my dear?' Pru's wandering thoughts were recalled by the question from her hostess. 'What would you most like to see while you are in town?'

'Really, ma'am I am happy to join in with whatever you and my aunt wish to do,' she replied. 'I have never been to London before, so everything will be a novelty.'

'What, never?' the lady sat forward, her pencilled brows raised in astonishment. 'But this will not do! Minerva, we must produce vouchers for her for Almack's!'

'Oh, no, no,' cried Pru in alarm. 'Truly, Lady Borcaster, I have no wish to make a spectacle of myself!'

'Nonsense! Every gel likes to dance.'

'Not at the Marriage Mart!'

'Ah, so you do know of it, then.' Lady Borcaster gave a fat chuckle. 'Very well, if you are set against it, let us forget the matter. There are enough young debutantes vying for attention and another country miss could find it difficult to make an impression.'

'Unless she is head and shoulders taller than all the rest, as I am,' said Pru bluntly.

'That would make it difficult to ignore you, of course,' conceded her hostess. 'Although under my *aegis* I think we might achieve something for you. A pretty gel like yourself shouldn't be hiding away in Bath.'

'I have tried to tell her as much, very often,' put in Minerva with a heavy sigh.

Realising the two friends were uniting against her, Prudence knew she would need to assert herself.

'I am not hiding away, ma'am. I enjoy my life in Bath, very much.' She raised her chin and added firmly,

'I assure you, Lady Borcaster, I have no wish for a husband so I pray you will not try to find one for me!'

For a moment she thought she might have offended her hostess, but instead the lady put back her head and laughed.

'Well, well, I think we would both agree that life is much better without a husband, ain't that so, Minerva?'

'Oh, no, no, how can you say so, Jane?' protested Aunt Minerva in her mild way. 'I was devoted to Pru's uncle. Such an excellent man, so kind. I will not hear a word against him!'

'Aye, well, that's all very good, but I believe neither of us would want to marry again,' said Lady Borcaster, not a whit abashed. 'Of course, it helps that we both have sufficient pin money to do as we please. And to buy whatever we fancy!' She turned her twinkling eyes towards Prudence. 'And even if you don't want me to find you a husband, I hope you will let me to buy you a few trinkets, Miss Prudence. It will not take much to give you a little town bronze, and you will look all the better for it when you return to Bath, take my word!' Her smile faded and she gave a gusty sigh. 'I do miss my Susan. She is gone off to the Continent now with Sir Timothy and I have no one to spend my money on, save myself.'

Pru caught a glimpse of the lonely woman behind the glitter and felt sorry for her. It was impossible to dislike her hostess.

'My dear ma'am, I am very willing to be spoiled a little, if it makes you happy,' she said, reaching for a biscuit. 'Although you must grant me permission to say nay, if I think you are being too generous.'

'Excellent! That is capital! 'The smile returned and the dark eyes regained their twinkle. 'Oh, we shall have such a pleasant time of it together, although it will be such a sad crush in the streets, I fear, with so many people driving in to see the spectacles that have been arranged in the parks for the Jubilee. There is to be a Temple of Concord, and a re-enactment of the Battle of the Nile…oh, all sorts of excitement, including fireworks!'

'I do so love fireworks!' exclaimed Minerva, her eyes shining.

'And, before that, we have the Allied Sovereigns,' declared their hostess. 'They have finally arrived in London!'

It was Minerva's turn to sigh. 'I confess I have a great fancy to see the Russian emperor. I hear he is very handsome!'

'Ah yes, Tsar Alexander.' Lady Borcaster nodded. 'He is here, and what a fuss there has been! He declined to stay at Cumberland House, which had been refurbished for his stay, and instead chose to put up with his sister at the Pulteney! Quite a snub to poor Prinny.' Lady Borcaster's chins wobbled as she gave another fat chuckle. 'I am told he is very gentlemanly, quite unlike our Prince Regent. But you shall see for yourself, Minerva, for we are all invited to the levée he is holding on tomorrow.'

'Heavens, what an honour,' gasped Mrs Clifford. 'Pru, do you hear that? A levée!'

'I do, Aunt,' said Pru. 'I am sure we shall find it vastly interesting. But, Lady Borcaster, I am amazed that you were able to obtain the invitation for us at such short notice.'

Their hostess smiled and preened, just a little.

'Well,' she said, straightening one of the gold tassels on her sleeve, 'There is no point in having a diplomat in the family if he cannot be of some use! Sir Timothy arranged the whole before he and Susan went off. Of course, *then* I did not know who I would be taking with me, but that was a minor detail. It is quite a coup, my dear Minerva. We shall be the envy of all my acquaintance! Now, let me tell you what else I have in mind for your visit!'

Prudence let her thoughts wander while the two older ladies gossiped. It occurred to her that the Duke of Hartland might be in town with his bride. If that was the case then she would see him again, as it was very likely that the newlyweds would attend some of the grand parties Lady Borcaster was presently describing.

Garrick Chauntry had often been in her thoughts since their brief meeting and she was curious to know how he would look, without the dark stubble and his deplorably dishevelled clothes. Not that he would acknowledge her, thought Pru, reaching for another macaroon. It would not be right, and she did not wish for it, but that did not prevent her wanting to see him. After all, a cat might look at a king.

Chapter Six

'Good heavens, this is impossible!' Mrs Clifford stepped off the path to avoid the bustling throng coming towards her. The tracks and paths of Hyde Park were overflowing with sightseers and Prudence was already walking on the grass. After attending the levée at Cumberland House the previous day she was not surprised by the crowds. The Russian emperor was immensely popular and it seemed everyone in London was eager to catch a glimpse of him.

'The world and his wife are out today,' she remarked.

'They are indeed, my dear. I am sorry I suggested leaving the carriage!' declared Lady Borcaster.

'We had no choice, my dear Jane, with the roads so crowded and everything at a standstill. Besides, it is a lovely day, and everyone is in such good spirits, I am very happy to be out of doors!'

'You are always so cheerful, Minerva,' observed Lady Borcaster, moving her parasol to avoid hitting a rough-looking man who surged past with a small child on his shoulders. 'I never thought there were so many people in London!'

'Word is out that Tsar Alexander will be riding in

the park today with the grand duchess,' said Pru. 'They have come to see him. As have we, ma'am.'

'Yes, but the emperor does not want to be troubled by all the scaff and raff of the town,' declared my lady, eyeing the crowds with disfavour. 'If we did not have Thomas with us, I should be afraid to be walking here.'

Pru glanced behind at the tall footman who was following at a respectful distance. She had to admit it was comforting to have such an impressive manservant in attendance.

'It is the price the Tsar must pay for being so popular, ma'am,' remarked Aunt Minerva. 'But it is not only the scaff and raff,' she added, seeing a colourful group of fashionably dressed ladies approaching. 'Jane, did we not meet that lady at the tsar's levée?'

'Where?' Lady Borcaster looked up. 'Ah yes, it is Lady Applecross. And her sisters, the Countess of Fauls and Mrs Johnby! They were all there last night, but I had no opportunity to introduce you. Well, well, the morning has not been wasted after all. These ladies are most influential in town, my dears. It will do you a great deal of good to be acquainted,' she added before looking up and hailing the approaching ladies with a cheerful, 'Good morning.'

The two parties stopped, greetings were exchanged and Pru and her aunt were introduced. The countess graciously extended her hand to Mrs Clifford while Mrs Johnby asked Prudence how she was enjoying her visit to town.

'It is not always like this, Miss Clifford, and thank goodness,' she went on. 'We were planning to go to the Ring, to see the emperor, but it is impossible in this crush. We have abandoned the attempt and are going to stroll by the river instead. Perhaps you would like to join us?'

Pru, who had no burning desire to see the emperor again, or to fight her way through the crowds, decided to speak up.

'I for one would like to do that. I believe the Serpentine is a fine body of water, and it might be a trifle cooler there.'

It was agreed and the two groups walked away together to the riverbank. It was by no means deserted but only a few people were strolling there and the ladies could talk uninterrupted. They had reached the eastern end of the Serpentine and were making their way back towards the park gates and their waiting carriages when the conversation turned to last night's levée.

'It was a most glittering occasion,' declared Lady Applecross. 'Such a prestigious beginning to your visit, Mrs Clifford. You will be received everywhere now.'

'Which reminds me, Elizabeth,' remarked Mrs Johnby, turning to the countess. 'Have you invited them to your musical soirée tomorrow evening?'

'I was about to do so, my dear.' Lady Fauls beamed. 'My dear Lady Borcaster, you must bring your delightful guests with you to Fauls House tomorrow night.'

Lady Borcaster speedily agreed, and Pru listened as her aunt expressed her gratitude for the honour bestowed upon them.

'Just a small, select gathering, of course, Mrs Clifford,' said the countess. 'I assure you there will be no one there you would not wish to introduce to your niece.'

'Indeed not,' declared Mrs Johnby. Something caught her eye at that moment and she added, in quite a different voice, 'There is *one* person who will not be crossing the threshold!'

'Oh, who?' asked Minerva, as all eyes turned to follow Mrs Johnby's stare.

'That creature over there.'

A sudden chill ran down Pru's spine. She did not know if it was caused by Mrs Johnby's words, uttered with such revulsion, or the sight of the large, athletic man striding across the grass in their direction. He was too far away to be sure, but he looked frighteningly familiar.

'Well!' Lady Fauls actually huffed. 'The nerve of the man!'

Minerva turned to Lady Borcaster, who shook her head. 'I do not know him.'

'Nor should you. It is Hartland,' declared Mrs Johnby, confirming Pru's suspicions. 'He may be a duke but no respectable persons will recognise him now.'

Mrs Clifford stared at her, eyes wide. 'Oh, goodness, what has he done?'

'What hasn't he done!' declared Lady Fauls. 'He was banished for his scandalous behaviour as a youth, but even now he has returned he is no better!'

'Why?' Pru could not help herself. 'What is his crime?'

The duke was still a considerable distance away, but she recognised him now. The rugged features and broad shoulders, the powerful body and long strides exuding energy.

'Oh, I do not know where to start.' Lady Fauls waved a hand. 'He narrowly avoided being hanged years ago and was disowned by his family in consequence, I recall. It quite broke his poor father's heart. Then, when he became duke, he did not take up his responsibilities, but left his estates to go to rack and ruin while he enjoyed himself on the Continent.'

'Yes, a true rakehell.' Lady Applecross lowered her voice and Pru strained to hear. 'I have heard he spent his time abroad *conspiring* with Bonaparte!'

'Then why is he at large?' asked Prudence. 'Why has he not been arrested?'

'There is not sufficient evidence, but it is all over town. Heavens, what else is one to think when the man has been living in France for the past ten years? And here he is now, walking around in public, as arrogant as you like!'

'And that is not the least of it,' added Mrs Johnby, with obvious relish. 'He is the very worst of jilts! As good as offered for a poor gel before he went off to the Continent and kept her dangling for ten years. *Ten years*, can you imagine? She was faithful as a nun all that time although he quite ignored her!'

Minerva gasped. 'That is outrageous.'

'Aye, ma'am, never a word, I'm told! But that is not the end of it. Earlier this year he called upon the poor lady and jilted her most cruelly. Cried off. Just like that!'

'But…can it be true?' asked Prudence slowly. 'Could this not be merely conjecture?'

Lady Applecross shook her head. 'No, no. You may ask Mrs Burchell. She knows the family and had it from the mother herself. Naturally she would not divulge the gel's name, poor innocent, but she was happy to denounce the duke for his wicked behaviour!'

Pru thought back to that night, sitting at the kitchen table with Garrick Chauntry. He had been resolved to act honourably. She could not believe he had changed his mind, he had been so determined to do his duty. Surely there must be some mistake.

Lady Applecross exhaled, a long sigh. 'It is so very distressing for the lady. The family know there is little chance of finding her a husband after all this time. They are bereft and have withdrawn from all society. The young lady herself has gone off to the country to live in seclusion, her life and her prospects quite, quite ruined. I wouldn't be surprised if she went into a decline and perished before too long.'

'But that is scandalous!' exclaimed kind-hearted Minerva. 'Such villainous behaviour should be punished.'

Pru was more cautious. 'Certainly, if it is true.'

'My dear Miss Clifford, how can it be otherwise?' cried Mrs Johnby. 'Mrs Burchell had it from the poor gel's mother.'

'And the information about his activities,' said Pru, 'the accusations of his conspiring with the French?'

'You know the saying,' put in the countess. 'There is no smoke without fire. And if there is no truth to any of this, why does the duke himself not refute it? No, I believe Hartland is a rogue. And you may be sure, Mrs Clifford, that although his rank ensures he continues to be invited everywhere, all *respectable* society has shunned His Grace. He may be a duke but none of *my* friends will receive him!'

'No, nor mine,' declared Lady Applecross. 'Pray, Mrs Clifford, do not look at the man. We must pretend we have not seen him and give him the cut indirect.'

The conversation moved on to other matters but Prudence did not join in. The picture they painted of Garrick Chauntry was nothing like the opinion she had formed of his character and she felt a growing sense of injustice on his behalf. Be he a prince or a pauper she would not judge a man on mere hearsay.

The duke was almost within hailing distance now and he had seen them. She noticed a change in his countenance. It was very slight, but enough to convince Pru he had recognised her. His gaze flickered over her companions, who all studiously avoided him. His brows dragged together and Pru noticed how his lip curled in scorn. He gave her the briefest nod before looking away again.

Something in Pru snapped. She stepped across and blocked his way.

'Good day to you, Your Grace.'

He stopped, his frown deepening, but he touched his hat and gave her a polite bow.

'Perhaps you do not remember me,' she persisted. 'I am Miss Prudence Clifford.'

'How could I forget?'

'I should like to introduce you to my aunt, Mrs Clifford.' She ignored his cold tone and beckoned to Aunt Minerva who hesitated, glancing at the outraged faces of the ladies around her, before stepping over to join her niece.

'The duke and I met in Bath,' said Pru, once the introduction had been made. Mrs Clifford stared at her in amazement and Pru was forced to improvise. 'You will recall that occasionally I went to the Pump Room with Mrs Haddington.'

'Did you, my love?'

Aunt Minerva looked startled, the duke sardonic.

'Such a good-natured soul,' Pru trilled. 'She knows everyone!'

'I do not…oh, yes…' murmured her aunt, edging away to rejoin the other ladies.

Pru smiled at the duke. 'Mrs Haddington will be so delighted when she learns we have met again, Your Grace. I must tell her too, that I have formed the habit of walking in Green Park with my maid every morning, as she suggested.' She fixed him with a stare and added, pointedly, 'Before breakfast.'

There. Surely he would understand that she wanted to meet, to talk to him.

'An admirable idea, ma'am.'

He appeared to ignore her hint. Pru carried on with determined cheerfulness.

'Allow me to introduce you to the rest of my friends.'

'No need,' he cut in. 'I am acquainted with them all.'

He touched his hat in their direction and received only the chilliest of nods in return. Pru battled on gamely.

'Well, it—it was such a pleasant surprise to see you today, Your Grace. I am sure we shall meet again.'

'I doubt that. I am extremely busy. And I do not go into society.'

Oh, pray do not be so vexing, you odious creature!

Pru's smile never wavered, but she hoped he would get the message her angry gaze was trying to convey. She held out her hand to him, daring him to refuse it. That would be a very public humiliation. To her relief, he did not, but as he bowed over her fingers he muttered, so that only she could hear.

'Enough, madam. Stay away from me. For your own sake!'

Then, with a cold look and a nod, he strode away.

Pru rejoined her party. They were all regarding her with varying degrees of disapproval. Lady Fauls was tapping her foot and looking positively outraged.

'Well, how unfortunate that you should be acquainted with His Grace,' declared Lady Borcaster, two pink spots of indignation on her cheeks. 'Not that you were aware of his reputation, I am sure.'

Aunt Minerva rushed into speech: 'I was just saying, my dear Prudence, that your sense of propriety would not allow you to ignore the duke, however slight the acquaintance.'

'I quite appreciate that Miss Clifford might be a little awed by such a personage,' replied Lady Applecross in repressive accents. 'However, if she will allow me to offer her a word of advice, she would do well not to encourage the Duke of Hartland. Especially after all we have said of the man.'

Pru was silent, but did not look convinced.

'My dear Miss Clifford he is not to be trusted, believe me!' declared Lady Fauls. 'No respectable lady will go near him. Not only is his reputation in tatters, it is well known that his estates are mortgaged to the hilt. He has moved out of Grosvenor Square, you know, and is now living in Dover Street.'

'Yes, he is planning to sell the house, even though his family have been in the Square for generations!' exclaimed Lady Applecross.

'If his affairs are in as sad a state as you say, then that would seem a wise course of action,' argued Pru, refusing to be cowed by these fashionable ladies.

'Most likely he had no choice,' remarked Mrs Johnby. 'But the others are right, my dear Miss Clifford. No good can come of setting your cap at Hartland. Trust me, it won't be marriage he offers any woman without a fortune.'

'And his new bride is unlikely to be uniformly welcomed into the ton, whatever her rank,' added Lady Fauls.

'I have no wish to *marry* His Grace.' Pru laughed, genuinely amused by the idea. 'I would greet any acquaintance in a similar manner.'

Lady Borcaster stared at her. 'After all we have learned about him?'

'It does sound shocking, ma'am, but it is all hearsay. He may turn out to be no worse than any other nobleman. I will not condemn him out of hand.'

'But you cannot continue the acquaintance,' Lady Fauls advised her. 'For a young lady in your situation that would be quite disastrous for your reputation.'

Prudence looked at the shocked faces around her and thought it best not to say anything more. She merely inclined her head and the ladies, taking this for acquiescence, were satisfied. They turned the conversation to the far more agreeable subject of fashion. This lasted until the parties separated, but as soon as they were alone, Lady Borcaster lost no time in expressing her unease at Pru's friendship with the Duke of Hartland.

'Championing such a man is a credit to your good nature, Prudence my dear, but it will not do, you know. Will it, Minerva?'

'No indeed,' Mrs Clifford answered her, although she was distracted. 'But, a *duke*, Prudence! I cannot believe you made the Duke of Hartland's acquaintance and did not tell me!'

'Why, were you aware of the gossip surrounding him?' asked Pru, all wide-eyed innocence.

'No, no. I did not even know he was in Bath! And what Elvira Haddington was thinking of, I do not know, to introduce you to such a man. But then, she is an inveterate matchmaker.' She huffed in exasperation. 'As the countess said, my dear, you must be careful of your reputation.'

'And so I shall, but to cut an acquaintance because of mere tittle-tattle would surely not be right. I shall reserve my judgement until I have the story direct, from one or other of the parties.'

Mrs Clifford squawked in horror. 'Prudence! Pray do not tell me you intend to speak to His Grace about it!'

It was exactly what Pru intended, but she knew better than to admit it.

'I am merely saying I refuse to be swayed by gossip.'

'Happily, there is little chance of our meeting Hartland amongst my circle of friends,' remarked Lady Borcaster, taking a more sanguine view. 'There is the White's Club Fête at Burlington House, of course, but I am told there will be thousands in attendance for that ball, and I distinctly heard the duke say he does not go into society.' She sighed. 'It will be such a crush, and nigh impossible to get near the Prince Regent or his honoured guests, but nevertheless, I am sure we shall enjoy it.'

Mrs Clifford agreed absently. She was still thinking of the recent encounter and said, 'We can only hope Prudence has not offended your friends, Jane.'

'Well, I hope that too, Minerva. Lady Applecross and her sisters are amongst the most influential hostesses in London. I was concerned they might take umbrage at your niece's rather forthright speech, but I think I managed to smooth any ruffled feathers.'

'I beg your pardon, ma'am, for putting you into a difficult situation,' said Pru, sincerely. They had reached their carriage and, as they stopped to wait for the footman to scramble down and open the door, she added, 'I shall endeavour not to do so again. It would be very wrong of me, after all your kindness.'

'Well, well, let us say no more about it, my dear,' said Lady Borcaster, patting her cheek. 'It shows you have a kind heart, does it not, Minerva?'

'Yes, it does, Jane.'

Mrs Clifford was eyeing her niece doubtfully and

Prudence gave her a reassuring smile as she followed her into the carriage. However, behind her cheerful expression her mind was working feverishly on how to meet with the duke.

The gossip she had heard did not tally with what she knew of the man. Pru considered herself a good judge of character, and she refused to believe Garrick Chauntry was as black as he was now being painted. She needed to know the truth and there was only one way to find that. However, she knew she would get no help from her aunt or her hostess, and even the duke himself had warned her to keep away from him.

This was going to be far more difficult than she had first thought.

Chapter Seven

Meeting the Duke of Hartland in Hyde Park caused Lady Borcaster no little dismay. She was still worrying over it at the end of the day and pleaded with her young guest to cut the acquaintance. Pru steadfastly refused to do so, although she agreed it was unlikely they would meet socially and the subject was dropped. Pru did not wish to upset her kind hostess further and decided to say nothing of the note she had penned as soon as they had returned from the park. Nor did she mention the reply she had received by return.

The next morning the subject of the Duke of Hartland appeared to be forgotten. Pru went down to breakfast to find her aunt and her hostess discussing plans to visit Mrs Bell's establishment to buy new gowns. They invited her to join them and she readily agreed, declaring herself eager to meet the celebrated modiste.

The three ladies set off in the carriage for Charlotte Street and spent an enjoyable morning looking at dresses of all styles and colours. Lady Borcaster and Mrs Clifford both purchased several new gowns and, after some cajoling, Pru allowed her hostess to treat her to an evening gown of apricot blush crepe over a white satin slip. It was impossible not to be tempted by so many delectable creations and Pru also used some of her savings to purchase two new outfits for herself, although she was sorry that Mrs Bell was unable to deliver them until the following week. She would have dearly liked to wear her new walking dress when she sallied forth later that afternoon, rather than her rather dull green kerseymere.

After such a busy time in Charlotte Street the two older ladies retired to their respective bedchambers to rest until it was time to change for dinner. They were a little surprised when Prudence told them she was going out again, but raised no demur when she expressed a desire to visit the British Gallery in Pall Mall.

'To see the paintings,' she explained, observing her aunt's blank look. 'I am told it is very interesting.'

'I am sure it is, although I have never been there myself,' replied Lady Borcaster. 'I will order the carriage to be brought around again.'

'Oh, no, ma'am. Thank you, but there is no need for that. I am very happy to walk. Indeed, I should enjoy the exercise. With the Tsar and the other dignitaries out of town for a few days, the streets will be a little quieter today.'

Lady Borcaster was surprised, but Mrs Clifford, knowing her niece's energetic nature, merely bade her not to go out alone.

'No, of course not, ma'am,' said Pru cheerfully. 'I thought Meg could come with me. The maid Her Ladyship has so kindly assigned to me for the duration of my visit,' Pru explained to her aunt.

'Yes, an excellent young woman,' nodded Lady

Borcaster. 'Bright, too. She is London born and very obliging.'

'She is indeed,' replied Pru, her eyes twinkling in a way that should have made her Aunt Minerva suspicious.

An hour later Prudence had reached number fifty-two Pall Mall, where the British Gallery was situated. However, she did not go in but carried on, walking past St James's Palace and into Green Park. There were a few people walking in the park, as well as the park's famous milch cows which roamed freely, but Prudence paid no heed to any of them. She saw a small hillock topped with straggling trees and quickly made her way towards the lone figure standing amongst the gnarled trunks. As she drew closer, she could see that the fashionably dressed gentleman was resting on his cane as he gazed out towards the Queen's House.

Pru stopped a short distance from the hillock and turned to the maid.

'Now, Meg, you will wait here for me, if you please, while I talk to the gentleman. If we move off, you may follow, but at a distance. Is that clear?'

'Yes, ma'am.' The girl bobbed a slight curtsy, her face alight with excitement although she asked no questions. Pru had given her a silver coin for her compliance and there was the promise of more to come, for her discretion.

'The first duty of a lady's maid is loyalty to her mistress,' Pru had told her. 'You are doing nothing unlawful, but I would ask you not to gossip about our little outing today.'

And Meg, who had ambitions to work her way up

to become dresser to a fashionable lady, was only too pleased to oblige.

Prudence went on to the top of the rise alone. The gentleman was staring moodily at the ground but as she approached, he looked up, his dark brows drawn together.

'Well, madam, what is so urgent that you must arrange such an improper *tête-à-tête*?'

'And a very good day to you, Your Grace.' She ignored his irritable tone. 'I am very grateful that you agreed to meet with me.'

'I had little choice, since you threatened to come to Dover Street and hammer on my door if I refused! What do you want?'

'To talk to you.'

'You had much better stay away from me.' His mouth tightened. 'Your friends will have warned you about me.'

'Yes, they did, but I want to hear the truth for myself.' Prudence unfurled her parasol. 'Shall we walk? I think we will look less conspicuous.'

After a brief hesitation the duke nodded and they made their way out of the trees, following the meandering path.

'What happened in Bath?' asked Pru, when she realised her companion was not going to volunteer any information.

'Nothing.'

'When you left my aunt's house you had determined upon a course of action. Did you go ahead with it?' He did not reply and Pru's certainty wavered a little. 'I am curious to know how you fared with Miss Speke.'

'I didn't,' he said shortly.

She stopped and turned to stare at him in dismay.

'I do not understand,' she said at last. 'You told me

she was expecting your visit, that her father had given his blessing. Surely you did not...'

He gave a short laugh.

'Oh, I called upon her,' he said, indicating that they should walk on. 'I was determined to put right the injustice I had done, but it seems it was her parents who wanted the match, far more than the lady. When I arrived at the Royal Crescent, she had fled.'

'What! She, she *eloped*?'

'Oh, no. A rival suitor I might have understood.' He swiped at a thistle with his cane. 'She left Bath. With a Miss Undershaw.'

'Emily Undershaw?'

'Yes, do you know her?'

'I met her when she first came to Bath, although my aunt did not encourage the acquaintance. A strange creature, given to wearing mannish clothes and smoking cigarillos, although her idiosyncrasies are overlooked because of her fortune. Now you mention it, I saw her in company with Miss Speke on several occasions.'

'They are bosom friends, apparently,' said the duke, beheading an errant dandelion with a slash of his cane.

'But how can this be?' demanded Pru, bewildered. 'Miss Speke waited all these years for you...'

'It would appear that it was Lord Tirrill and his wife who were waiting for me, not Annabelle. I gather they had cajoled the poor girl into accepting my offer but when I didn't turn up on the appointed day, her courage failed her. She ran away rather than meet me.'

'Oh, I am so sorry!'

'Are you? I am not.'

Pru looked up, surprised. The shadows had fled from his green eyes and he was smiling. She quickly pushed aside a sudden, alarming jolt of attraction.

'You are not angry?' she ventured. 'The lady has scorned your advances. Many men would be mortified.'

'I am more relieved.'

'But the gossip. Everyone thinks it was your doing.'

'Let them. The family has put it about that it was I who broke the agreement, rather than their daughter.'

Pru stopped.

'That is despicable,' she exclaimed.

'No, it is understandable. There is no denying Annabelle would fare much worse if it was known she had jilted *me*.' He shrugged. 'I have broad shoulders, a little more censure will not hurt me. Besides, I shall not be in town much longer.'

'You are leaving?' she asked, as they walked on.

'Tomorrow. I am going to Hartland. God knows it is time I attended to my business there.'

'And...will you meet with the duchess?'

She waited in silence for him to speak.

'I shall write to her,' he said at last. 'But I shall not call without permission.'

'But if she has heard the rumours...'

His lip curled. 'Oh, I have no doubt some well-meaning friend has already written to inform her of all the new calumnies laid at my door! It will give her even more reason to shun me.'

Pru heard the bitterness in his voice and it tore at her heart.

'But how could any mother not wish to see her son?' she exclaimed.

'Quite easily, it would seem.'

'Surely she will not believe such things without talking to you, as I am doing.'

He exhaled and said impatiently, 'That is just the

point, you should *not* be talking with me! You are risking your reputation being here with me, Miss Clifford.'

'There are very few people in the park to see us.'

'It would only take one to gossip.'

'I needed to hear the truth.'

'And you have done so. I rely upon you not to tell anyone else.'

'You have my word, sir.'

'Thank you.' He added, after a pause, 'And thank you for helping me. That night in Bath.'

'I did very little.'

'I really believe you saved my life.' He sighed and glanced about him. 'I should like to kiss your hand, but in such an exposed spot that would not be wise. So I must wish you adieu, Miss Clifford. It is best we do not meet again.'

'You are leaving town tomorrow.' Why did the thought make her feel so empty?

'Yes, that is my intention.'

'And the other rumours?' She hesitated, but this was her last chance to ask him. 'Forgive me, but there is talk that you are a spy for the French…'

'Ah, yes. I had heard that.' His countenance assumed that familiar grim look.

'People think you lived in France for the past ten years, but you said you were in Vienna.'

'And you believe everything you are told?' He threw her a mocking glance. 'What a trusting soul you are!'

She turned and fixed her eyes upon him. 'Not always, but I did believe what you told me in Bath.'

Garrick felt his heart contract when he met the steady gaze of those clear grey eyes. She trusted him and it pleased him more than he could say.

'Hmmph! That night I stumbled into your kitchen I was in no fit state to dissemble, was I? In this instance your trust is not misplaced. I was in Vienna, some of the time. For the past ten years I have been many things, traveller, explorer, wanderer, but never a traitor to my country.'

'But why would anyone spread such a wicked falsehood?' she asked him. 'Could it be the lady's family, trying to blacken your name further?'

'No, I am sure it is not. These rumours began in quite a different quarter.'

'You cannot know that.'

Garrick hesitated. It would be a relief to share his suspicions, but it would not do. He had told this woman far too much already. What was it about Pru Clifford that made him want to confide in her? She was no beauty, her green pelisse was not new and far from fashionable, but he liked her open countenance, the honesty in her steady gaze. He liked *her*.

He said, 'True, I have no proof, but it is not important. There is no foundation to the rumour. Once I have left town it will die down and some other poor soul will become the subject of gossip.'

'But—'

'Enough, madam.' She was looking at him, her eyes full of concern. He said harshly, 'Leave be, Miss Clifford. You must not become embroiled in my affairs.'

'But you need help.'

'Not from you!' He needed to convince her how serious this was. How dangerous it would be for her to become involved. 'If someone really is trying to implicate me in a traitorous plot then the last thing I need is a damned woman getting in my way!'

That did it. She took a step away, her eyes widening

in shock at his brutal language. Garrick regretted the necessity of speaking so sharply, but it had worked. He touched his hat and strode away, leaving her standing alone on the path.

Chapter Eight

'My dear, you are looking decidedly pale this evening, are you sure you are well enough to go out?'

Mrs Clifford peered in concern across the drawing room at Prudence, who straightened her shoulders and forced her lips into a smile.

'I am perfectly well, Aunt, thank you.'

'It is no wonder you are fatigued, my dear, going off again on a jaunt the moment we returned from Mrs Bell's,' declared Lady Borcaster, coming in at that moment. 'And to a picture gallery, too. Nothing could be more tiring! But there, you young people will go your own way. Ah well, a quiet dinner here at Brook Street will perk you up before we set off for Lady Fauls's soirée, I am sure. And here is Cotton now, come to tell us it is ready. Shall we go in?'

Prudence silently followed her hostess into the dining room and took her place at the table. The serious business of eating would preclude any conversation for a while and she was glad of it, because her mind was still going over everything that had occurred in Green Park earlier.

She had been shocked by the duke's language and

the way he stormed off but, upon reflection, she was not surprised he was angry with her. The fact that she had fed him when he had stumbled into the basement kitchen did not give Pru the right to pry into his concerns. He was a grown man and quite capable of looking after himself. But Pru could not shake off the nagging anxiety, and even the diversion of the countess's soirée was not enough to banish it completely.

Lady Borcaster had impressed upon Prudence how fortunate she was that the countess had not withdrawn her invitation, following the lamentable scenes in Hyde Park, and as they set of for Fauls House she begged her young guest to be on her best behaviour. Mrs Clifford added her entreaties and Prudence, knowing how much she owed to both ladies, promised to do nothing to draw attention to herself.

Lady Fauls greeted them politely, but their arrival coincided with that of an august group of lords, ladies and visiting foreign diplomats. The countess hurriedly moved off to welcome these important personages, leaving the ladies to make their own way into the elegant salon set up for the evening's entertainment. A pianoforte took pride of place in one corner of the room, with numerous chairs and sofas arranged to face it. However, the entertainment had not yet begun and all the guests were chattering and laughing while silent-footed servants walked between the little groups with trays full of glasses.

Lady Borcaster appeared to be acquainted with nearly everyone present. She moved around the room, assured of her welcome, making Mrs Clifford and her niece known to Lady This and Lord That until Prudence thought her head would burst with so many names to remember. She was quite relieved when Mrs Johnby drew her away to join a party of her own particular friends at the far side of the room. When that little group dispersed, Prudence moved over to the pianoforte, admiring the polished mahogany and rosewood casing with its gleaming brass inlay. It was far grander than the little Pohlman pianoforte that Aunt Minerva owned. Her hand was reaching out to touch the keys when a voice at her shoulder made her jump.

'It is a fine instrument, is it not? A Broadwood, no less.'

Pru look around at the speaker. He was a stranger to her, but fashionably dressed in a dark blue coat over white silk breeches and waistcoat, the whole embellished with a number of fobs and seals hanging about his person.

He went on, 'Will you be delighting us with a recital later, ma'am?'

She shook her head. 'Sadly no, I am too much out of practice, but I should very much like to hear it played by a proficient.'

His appearance was very sleek, the short dark hair was oiled into place and greying at each side of his lean face, while his brows had been carefully plucked into neat arches. The heavy gold ring on his finger suggested a man of means, but she had no idea who he might be.

'Allow me to introduce myself,' he said, as if reading her thoughts. 'I am Sir Joseph Conyers. May I be very forward and ask you to tell me who you are? I know only that you are a guest of Lady Borcaster.' When she hesitated, he said quickly, 'Pray, ma'am, let us not stand upon ceremony! The recital will start soon and there isn't time to find a mutual acquaintance to introduce us.'

The playful look that accompanied his words made Pru laugh.

'Very well. I am Miss Clifford, sir.'

'Miss Clifford. Hmm, then why have we not met? I thought I knew all the pretty young ladies in town.'

Pru felt herself withdrawing slightly. Perhaps he thought he was being avuncular, but his words and tone were not what she had been expecting. Until that moment she had been prepared to be friendly, to overlook the impropriety of a man introducing himself, but now she was on her guard. His smile had not changed, but she could not like the gleam in his hooded eyes and she stepped away a little.

A sudden flurry of activity broke out. Everyone was moving towards the chairs, taking their seats for the recital. Pru quickly excused herself and hurried across to join her hostess and Aunt Minerva.

'My dear Prudence, who was that man talking to you?' asked Mrs Clifford.

'Sir Joseph Conyers,' she said, sitting down with them. 'Do you know him, Lady Borcaster?'

The lady shook her head. 'I am not acquainted with him. Although, I do recall Lady Applecross mentioning him. He has recently come to town with his wife. I am told they hold the most entertaining card parties, and routs full of lively wit and lavish refreshments.'

'Really? How interesting,' remarked Mrs Clifford.

There was no time for more. The audience hushed as Lady Fauls announced the first of the musical entertainments of the evening.

For over an hour Lady Fauls's guests listened to any number of ballads, airs and duets performed with varying degrees of success. Then there was a break for refreshments, a light supper to be taken in the dining room. As Lady Borcaster shepherded her little party out of the room, Pru saw that their hostess was standing near the doorway with Sir Joseph at her side, and as they passed Lady Fauls put out a hand to detain Lady Borcaster.

'I am glad I have caught you, ma'am. Sir Joseph has begged me to make him known to you.'

The gentleman stepped forward.

'I made Miss Clifford's acquaintance earlier and could not let the opportunity pass to meet her friends,' he said, bowing over their hands in turn.

Pru watched, appreciating the man's elegant manners and address. He charmed her aunt and Lady Borcaster but she thought him a little too polished and was relieved that he did not offer to accompany them downstairs to supper. She said nothing to the others, unwilling to disparage a gentleman upon such little acquaintance. She was unused to society and was probably reading far too much into the situation.

The second part of the soirée was far more informal. Several guests took their turn to sing or play, but only a few hardy souls occupied the chairs around the pianoforte. Wine was flowing freely and most of the guests were now mingling, talking amongst themselves.

Prudence was on the edge of one such group when she heard gasps and stifled laughter coming from the nearby window embrasure. A quick glance showed her that Sir Joseph Conyers was at the centre of a cluster of guests who were hanging on his every word. Across the room, someone was playing a particularly lively sonata but during a short pause in the music, a lady's shocked voice uttered a word that caught her attention.

'...*spying*...'

Pru stepped aside to take a glass of wine from a passing footman and sauntered away, supposedly inspecting the delicate watercolours ranged along the wall but all the time moving closer to the window. She had reached the final painting, a rather depressing depiction of a ruined castle under a lowering sky, before she could hear anything.

'Shameful!' exclaimed one lady. 'But can we be *sure*, Sir Joseph?'

The gentleman's voice was lower, more muted, and Prudence moved closer until she was able to pick up various words and phrases.

'...*vengeful*...*villainous duke*... *Years in exile*... *Hartland*.'

A chill ran through her at that last word. There could be no doubting the subject of Sir Joseph's disclosures. Pru sipped her wine, straining to hear more.

'He should be exposed,' declared one gentleman with his back to Pru. 'I presume there is proof?'

'Oh, there is, sir, there is.' Sir Joseph replied. 'Naturally, I cannot reveal my sources, but I assure you they are most reliable...'

The silky complaisance in his voice was unmistakable. Others were exclaiming now but Sir Joseph said no more, allowing the gossip to run on without him. Pru moved away, her thoughts racing. This was far more serious than mere tittle-tattle and Sir Joseph Conyers was the source. He was deliberately stoking the fires of speculation and she considered that to be quite wicked behaviour. All pleasure in the evening had been destroyed and she hurried back to her party, eager to be gone. However, Lady Borcaster showed no signs of tiring and Prudence was obliged to curb her impatience as the evening dragged on.

It was approaching two o'clock when at last Pru fell into her bed, but even then, sleep would not come. She did not know quite why it should matter so much to her, but she knew she would not rest until she had seen the duke and told him all she had learned.

'What is it, Stow?' Garrick said, putting the finishing touches to his cravat when his man came in.

'Begging your pardon, Your Grace. There is a visitor for you.'

'At this hour of the morning?' He glanced at the clock. It was not yet seven.

'A female, sir.' Stow allowed a tiny note of disapproval to creep into his usually impassive voice. 'She would not give her name, but said I was to mention Bath to you, sir.'

Garrick frowned. He said brusquely, 'Show her up.'

By the time he had shrugged on his coat Stow had returned, followed by a tall figure enveloped in a red cloak. He nodded to his man to leave them and, as the door clicked shut upon them, two dainty hands came up to push back the hood.

A soft, melodious voice said, 'I beg your pardon for coming so early.'

'Early!' he exploded. 'Miss Clifford, you should not be here at all.'

'But I needed to see you. You told me you were leaving today and I thought it most likely that you would be making an early start.' She glanced down at the red cloak. 'I thought if I wore this I would look like a servant and be less conspicuous.'

'You came here *alone*?' Garrick raked a hand through his hair. 'Of all the hen-witted things to do!'

'No, no, my maid is waiting below. I am not quite lost to all sense of propriety.'

'You are sailing dashed close to the wind, madam!' He glared at her. 'Very well, the sooner you tell me what you have to say the sooner you can be gone.'

Pru took a deep breath. He was very cross with her and it was important he realised she was not here on any trivial matter.

'I heard someone spreading rumours last night. About you being a spy. He said he had proof.' She bit her lip. 'That is far more than mere gossip, Your Grace. I thought, if you could find him, you could make him tell you his sources. Then you could put a stop to it.'

'Who was the man?'

'Sir Joseph Conyers. I met him at Lady Fauls's soirée last night.'

He stared hard at her for a moment. 'Was Lady Conyers with him?'

Pru blinked. 'Why, no, he came alone. It was after midnight that he gathered a little crowd about him and I heard him accusing you of being a French spy. And when someone asked if there was proof, he said yes!' She paused, her brows drawing together in a frown. 'Is Sir Joseph the man you suspected of spreading the rumours?'

'What? Oh, yes.'

'And are you going to stop him?'

'I shall deal with this matter in my own way. For the moment I am more concerned in getting you out of here without causing a scandal.'

'There will be no scandal. Apart from my maid no one knows I am here and it is still very early. We shall be back in Brook Street in plenty of time for breakfast.'

'Then the sooner you leave the better,' he retorted.

'My travelling carriage is due at any moment, and you must go before anyone else sees you.'

She stared at him. 'You are still leaving town?'

'Yes. Put up your hood. My man will show you out.'

Pru did not move. 'Surely you are not going to let Sir Joseph get away with this?'

Garrick gave a growl of impatience. 'My dear Miss Clifford, what I choose to do is no concern of yours.'

She bridled at that. He saw how she drew herself up, that determined little chin rising defiantly. 'My dear duke, it became my concern the moment you confided in me!'

Garrick admired her spirit. He thought idly how tall she was, her eyes level with his chin. Her lips not so very far beneath his own. Two steps closer and he could pull her into his arms. He fought back the sudden jolt of desire, replacing it with anger. How could she be so careless of her good name, of her own safety?

'No! Blast it, woman, this is *not your business*.' She regarded him defiantly and he drew a deep breath. 'Miss Clifford, I am grateful for your help in Bath, but believe me, there is nothing more for you to do. You may safely ignore any rumours you hear. Trust me, they will not last and if you interfere you will regret it.'

Her brows went up, but her clear gaze never wavered from his.

'Are you threatening me, Your Grace?'

'Of course not, but I would not have you drawn unnecessarily into dealings with these unpleasant characters.' He took her arm and led her towards the door. 'Go back to Brook Street and forget all about me. Enjoy the rest of your visit to town.'

He reached over to lift her hood and arrange it over

her soft brown hair. Then he rested his hands on her shoulders.

'Well, madam, will you give me your word not to interfere further?'

'If that is what you want, sir.'

'It is.'

She was looking up at him, those clear grey eyes searching his face. Then her chin tilted up a little more, as if in invitation and he could not resist. He lowered his head and kissed her.

Garrick felt the little tremor of surprise run through her, but she did not pull away. Instead, her hand came up to rest on his shoulder and she returned his kiss. It was a shy, hesitant response. Inexperienced, but that only inflamed him more. His arms ached to hold her. He wanted to deepen the kiss, to enjoy the honeyed taste of her lips beneath his. She smelled of summer flowers, sweet and innocent. Everything he was not.

It took every ounce of willpower to break off and lift his head, his hands tightening on her shoulders as he held her away from him.

'There,' he said roughly. 'If anything should convince you to stay away from me it is that!' He released her, averting his eyes from her startled gaze. He turned to open the door.

'Now go!'

She hurried away down the stairs and Garrick closed the door behind her. He leaned against it, his eyes closed.

'Hell and damnation!'

He had done his best. He had tried to put her off, told her to ignore the rumours but he knew she would not. Prudence Clifford was not a woman to stay quiet in the face of injustice. Left to her own devices she would refute the rumours. She would openly challenge anyone who accused him. And he knew only too well that the perpetrator of these lies was not a man to be crossed.

From the open window came the sounds of a carriage drawing up in the street below. He heard his driver's voice and moments later Stow's feet hurrying up the stairs.

He sighed. One thing was certain, he could not leave town now.

Chapter Nine

The early morning streets were beginning to fill up with carriages, street vendors and tradesmen going about their business, but Prudence saw and heard nothing as she hurried back to Brook Street. Her thoughts remained in Dover Street, with Garrick Chauntry.

He kissed me!

Her lips still tingled. She remembered the soft wool of his coat beneath her hand. The scent of him, that mix of fresh soap and sandalwood, far more enticing than the cloying perfumes that had assailed her senses at Fauls House last night. She should be outraged, shocked at his behaviour, but in truth she had wanted him to kiss her. If he had not stopped she had no idea what might have happened, for she did not think she would have been strong enough to break away.

A little shudder ran through her which should have been shame, but she knew it was not. What she felt was elation. Excitement. And a very strong desire to kiss him again.

'This way, madam.'

Meg's touch on her arm brought her wanton thoughts to an end. She followed the maid into a side turning and through a series of lanes until they reached the back entrance to Lady Borcaster's residence. Thankfully there was no one to see two red-cloaked maids hurrying up the servants' stairs and once they reached Pru's room, she handed her cloak over to Meg to return it to the servants' hall. She also gave the maid another silver coin for her silence, salving her conscience with the fact that she fully intended to employ the maid as her personal dresser when she returned to Bath at the end of the summer.

Prudence sat through breakfast in near silence. The duke would have left town by now and he had told her not to interfere further in his concerns. She had agreed, even though it would be very hard not to speak up when she heard people repeating the gossip about him. She had the distinct feeling there was something he had not disclosed, but why should he tell her anything? Perhaps it was something too shameful to be repeated. She cast about in her mind for possible answers, but her conjectures proved so lurid and outrageous that she scolded herself.

It is unlikely that I shall ever know the truth, she thought as she buttered another bread roll. *His Grace the Duke of Hartland has left town and there's an end to it. I have nothing to do now but forget him and enjoy myself.*

Having made her resolution, Prudence was determined to enter fully into Lady Borcaster's plans for her guests' entertainment, consoling herself with the thought that there was so much interest in the royal visitors there was unlikely to be much gossip about anything else for the next few weeks. Hopefully she would not need to defend the duke.

There was no shortage of diversions during the following week. The crowds were such that Lady Borcaster abandoned plans to see the Tsar riding out in Hyde Park in the early morning or to follow him on his various outings to Woolwich Arsenal or the London docks. Instead they enjoyed a series of carriage outings and card parties with the lady's friends. There was also a delivery of new clothes from the modiste, Mrs Bell, to divert them, and it was in no little excitement that Prudence donned for the first time the evening gown Lady Borcaster had given her.

It was far grander than anything she had owned before, but the apricot crepe enhanced the creamy tones of her skin and highlighted the golden tints in her hair. She had only a simple string of pearls and matching ear drops to wear with it, but when she came down to the drawing room to join the others Lady Borcaster declared that she looked very well indeed.

'Very elegant. There will be so many grand ladies in all their finery at Tarleton House tonight that there is no point trying to compete, my dear Prudence. Simplicity will serve you best.'

Pru was thankful for her advice although when they arrived at Tarleton House, she could not help feeling a little envious of the gorgeously attired creatures who filled the ballroom. Many were even more flamboyant than Lady Borcaster's frock of scarlet gauze heavily trimmed with gold lace. Pru had not been in town very long, but she knew some of the gowns on display cost a great deal more than the year's allowance Aunt Minerva paid her.

Lady Borcaster took great pains to find a partner for her young friend and Prudence was grateful not to be one of the young ladies languishing at the side of the room. After the first dances of the evening she returned to her party in high spirits after her exertions. Aunt Minerva and Lady Borcaster were in conversation with a fashionably dressed couple and as she approached, Lady Borcaster put out her hand to draw her forward.

'Ah, Prudence, my dear. We were just talking of you!'

It was only when the gentleman turned towards her that Pru recognised Sir Joseph Conyers. She schooled her face to a smile and gave a small curtsy.

'My dear Miss Clifford, we meet again.' He made her an elegant bow. 'And now I have the pleasure of introducing you to my wife. Helene, my dear!'

Pru turned her attention to the woman at his side and she was momentarily dazzled. The lady's golden hair was piled high and twinkled with crystals nestled amongst the curls while diamonds glittered at her neck and her ears. Lady Conyers might be on the shady side of thirty but she was undoubtedly beautiful.

She had a straight little nose, delicate brows that arched over a pair of deep blue eyes and rosy lips that were now uttering warm words of greeting. And yet, as she looked into the lady's smiling face, Prudence thought there was something rather cold and calculating about her.

Sir Joseph and Lady Conyers stayed to talk for a few moments and then moved on, leaving Mrs Clifford in raptures.

'Such an obliging gentleman! And his wife, so kind. How generous to invite us to their little party on Monday next.'

'Pity we already have our invitation for the White's Club Ball that evening,' replied Lady Borcaster.

'You are not so enamoured of them, ma'am?' asked Pru, quick to hear the note of reserve in the lady's tone.

'I think his interest is more that I am mama-in-law to Sir Timothy Flowers. I imagine he thinks I can give him entrée into diplomatic circles. He is quite wrong, you know. I have no influence at all.'

'But you have invitations to some of the most prestigious events taking place this summer,' exclaimed Mrs Clifford.

'Yes, the White's Club Ball, for example. Anyone who *is* anyone will be attending Burlington House on Monday night.'

'But not the Conyers,' murmured Prudence, 'if they are holding a party of their own.'

'They would like to be, but clearly did not receive an invitation,' replied Lady Borcaster, her tone dry. She smiled and touched Mrs Clifford's arm. 'My years in London have made me a little sceptical, Minerva. Believe me, I have nothing against the man or his wife. I am sure they are indeed pleasant company, but it is best to have the measure of one's acquaintances, and then you cannot be disappointed in them.'

Prudence was in complete agreement with this worldly-wise view. She was already wary of Sir Joseph, misliking his propensity for mischievous gossip, but she realised now that he had only sought her out to gain favour with Lady Borcaster. It was a lowering thought, but it did not unduly worry her. In fact, she was quite distracted by something else nagging at the back of her mind. At that first meeting with Garrick Chauntry, she recalled him telling her about the duel he had fought over a woman. A beautiful seductress called Helene.

Sir Joseph and Lady Conyers did not speak with Lady Borcaster or her party again that evening, but they were hard to ignore. Lady Borcaster remarked that the lady's dance partners were the most influential persons present, while Pru watched Sir Joseph circling the room, being charming to everyone. She also noticed that Lady Conyers had a herd of young bucks vying for her attention and wondered if she still enjoyed enslaving naive young men with her beauty. Pru tried to dismiss the thought as uncharitable, but could not quite do it.

After Tarleton House, there were only a few days for the Brook Street ladies to recover before the much-vaunted White's Club Ball at Burlington House. Pru was a little dismayed when she heard that upwards of two thousand guests had been invited but Lady Borcaster assured her she would enjoy herself.

'I have enlisted an old friend of mine, General Lechlade, to be our escort, so you may be easy.'

Prudence found it hard to believe that an elderly soldier's presence would add to her comfort, but she said nothing and, shortly after nine o'clock on the appointed evening, their little party joined the crowd slowly making their way into the grand ballroom. She was wearing the apricot crepe again and although part of her would have liked to be showing off a new gown, her sensible side argued that it did not matter what she wore. No one would be looking at plain Miss Clifford when there were so many exalted persons in attendance.

The Allied Sovereigns arrived at midnight, the Tsar delighting the guests by waltzing the night away at the upper end of the ballroom. Pru, who had not yet waltzed in public, preferred to join in the country dances taking place elsewhere.

She had no shortage of dance partners but the rooms were hot, crowded and noisy and Pru was very glad when the signal was given for supper at two o'clock. She dismissed her latest partner with a graceful word of thanks and was about to go off to find her aunt when she heard a deep voice at her shoulder.

'I thought I'd find you here.'

Pru's heart leapt. She turned quickly and found herself facing the powerful figure of Garrick Chauntry, Duke of Hartland. He looked quite magnificent in his evening coat of corbeau-coloured wool. A snowy cravat contrasted strongly with the dark coat and knee breeches and his hair had been brushed back, gleaming like a raven's wing in the candlelight. She thought he could not be called handsome, but those green eyes were certainly arresting.

'What are *you* doing here?' The shock of seeing him threw her quite off balance and she blushed at her own incivility. 'What I mean is, Your Grace, I thought you had left town.'

'And miss all this excitement?' he drawled.

She narrowed her eyes at him. 'I believe you dislike this crush as much as I.'

He grinned. 'I do, but being a duke I received an invitation and thought I might as well use it.' He held out his arm. 'Allow me to take you in to supper.' She hesitated and his brows went up a little. 'Unless you prefer not to acknowledge me...'

'You know that is not the case! I was going to look for my aunt, and Lady Borcaster.'

'You have little chance of finding them in these crowds. Come along.'

She rested her fingers on his sleeve, accepting that it would indeed be difficult to find anyone amongst the thousands crammed into the halls and marquees. The duke guided her unerringly to the supper rooms but made no attempt to follow all those who wanted to dine as close as possible to the royal guests. Instead he carried on until they came to a far less crowded marquee. It was set out more informally than the main rooms and had no musicians secreted in the walls.

'I think we will be more comfortable here,' he said, leading her to an empty table that was positively groaning with food.

'Should I be insulted?' she murmured, teasing him, 'This area is clearly for the lowlier guests.'

'I thought you would prefer this to being deafened.'

She relented and smiled at him. 'You are quite correct. But we must not be ungenerous. White's Club has gone to a great deal of trouble over this fête.'

'Indeed, they have. People will be talking about it for months to come.'

The supper was delicious and the duke proved an entertaining companion. Pru thought he looked very well in the full evening dress. It was a credit to the tailor that his broad shoulders and deep chest did not strain at the seams of his dark coat. He carried himself well and had a natural grace, but he was no courtier, she decided, pushing aside her empty plate. She was a little surprised that he showed no interest in mixing with his peers, but perhaps ten years in exile had embittered him.

'Well?' he demanded, interrupting her thoughts. 'What is your opinion?'

'I beg your pardon?'

'You have been studying me for the duration of the meal.'

He waved to a passing servant to refill their glasses, but his gaze never left her. Those strange holly-green eyes bored into her, challenging her to tell the truth.

'I think you prefer action to doing the pretty at occasions like this,' she said, selecting a sweetmeat from a small dish on the table. 'You would be happier out of doors. Riding or hunting perhaps.'

'Very true. Would not you?'

'I have not ridden since I joined my aunt in Bath.'

'Do I detect a note of regret, there?'

She hesitated. 'A little, perhaps. I used to enjoy riding when I was at home. And country walks. But my life is very full, so I do not repine.'

She remembered the restlessness that had come upon her those last months in Bath and quickly turned the conversation back to the duke.

'But if you would prefer to be elsewhere, why did you come tonight?'

His lip curled in self-derision. 'Can you not guess? Dukes are invited everywhere, whatever the ton might think of them!'

'But that does not answer my question,' she replied. 'You were not obliged to attend. When I last saw you, you were about to set out for Hartland. Why did you change your mind?'

She watched him sip at his wine while he considered his answer.

'I thought…someone might be here.'

'Who?' Pru leaned a little closer, even though there was no one sitting close enough to overhear. 'If you mean Sir Joseph Conyers, he was unable to obtain an invitation.'

'How the devil do you know that?'

'The Conyerses are holding their own little party tonight. He would not have done so if he could have been here instead. He sought my acquaintance in order to get closer to Lady Borcaster, but she is not deceived by him.'

'Ah, yes.' He nodded. 'Her late husband was a dip-lomat, was he not? And her daughter is married to Sir Timothy Flowers. I see how Conyers might well want to befriend her.'

She looked surprised. 'You are very knowledgeable… how do you know so much about Lady Borcaster?'

He smiled but did not explain.

'You could be wrong about Sir Joseph,' he said. 'Per-haps you piqued his interest.'

'Do you mean he was smitten by my beauty?' She laughed at that. 'How could anyone think so!'

Garrick frowned. 'Do not disparage yourself, Pru-dence Clifford. You are a very unusual woman.'

He liked the blush that painted her cheeks. He thought it very becoming and said so, but she only laughed again and shook her head.

'Pray do not tease me. I have seen Lady Conyers— Oh!' Her hand flew to her mouth. 'I beg your pardon. Is she the one who…?'

Garrick froze.

The one who used me. The one who took advantage of a naive young fool and almost made him a murderer.

'…the one you spoke of?'

She was watching him closely. The chicken that had tasted so delicious earlier was now like ashes in his mouth. He swallowed it and managed a single word.

'Yes.'

'And Sir Joseph. He was your adversary in the duel.' She nodded, not requiring him to answer. 'I see just how it is. You were the victor and that is why he is spread-ing such lies.' He heard the note of anxiety in her voice when she continued. 'He said there is proof. Evidence that you are a French agent.'

'He is wrong. Although he might try to fabricate something.'

'What a villain!'

'Do you see now why you should let well alone?'

'No. I am even more convinced that Sir Joseph should be shown for what he is. And for what he has been in the past.' She added vehemently, 'He and his wife should never have been allowed to get away with their wrong-doings.'

'There are many rogues like him in town.'

'That does not make it right.'

He saw the martial light in her eye and leaned forward.

'Miss Clifford. Prudence. Please, be true to your name and ignore any further rumours you hear about me.'

'I cannot. I cannot allow them to spread lies about you. It is *unjust*.'

He shrugged. 'They hurt no one but me.'

'And your family name.'

'My family name has borne much greater slurs in its time. Once I have left town the rumours will die down and soon be forgotten.'

She took another sip of wine, but her mind was clearly still on the injustice.

'So, you intend to walk away.' Two spots of angry colour were flying in her cheeks now. 'I did not think you such a coward.'

She was trying to goad him, and she was succeeding.

'I am no coward,' he ground out, holding on to his temper by a thread.

'Then why will you allow them to get away with this?'

'They won't. The truth will out, eventually. Why are *you* so intent upon me denying the claims?'

Pru sat back. Why *was* she so eager to see him vindicated? What was he to her, after all? Nothing more than a stranger whose story had evoked her sympathy.

'Well?' he demanded, his green eyes hard as granite. 'What is it to you if my name is dragged through the gutter?'

She was silent. She believed he had been treated unjustly in the past. She could understand that he might be able to shrug off Annabelle's rejection. That had been an arranged marriage, with little attraction on either side, but perhaps—something twisted inside her—perhaps he was still in love with the beautiful Helene and did not want her to be punished.

Garrick watched the play of emotion in Pru's countenance. He saw a shadow of reserve cloud those clear grey eyes. A small spark of hope flared that she actually cared for him but he squashed it firmly. He was nothing more than another of her charitable causes, something to amuse her while she was in town until another distraction came along. Women were fickle. No one knew that better than he.

But for all that he liked this woman. He did not want to quarrel with her. He smiled.

'No, no, do not frown at me so, Prudence Clifford. Here we are, at one of the most prestigious balls of the year and we should be enjoying ourselves.' He rose and held out his hand to her. 'What say you, shall we dance the night away?'

When they returned to the main ballroom couples were already waltzing again, including the Emperor of Russia. Such was the crowd gathered about to watch the Tsar that when the Garrick suggested they should go off and join in with the country dances, Pru readily agreed. She discovered he was an accomplished dancer and excellent partner, as she told him when the second dance came to an end.

'I enjoyed it, too,' he replied. 'Shall we dance again?'

'I really should go and find my aunt…'

Pru was enjoying herself far too much to want this to end and even to her own ears she sounded unsure. Garrick's green eyes rested on her, warm and smiling.

He said, 'You would not leave me just yet.'

There was only a heartbeat's pause before she capitulated. After all, she reasoned, Lady Borcaster's coachman had been ordered not to return before six and it would be far easier to find her party then, when the crowds would be much diminished.

She accompanied Garrick to one of the other marquees and enjoyed a glass of wine while they waited for the next dance to begin. It was a risk, dancing with Garrick again, but she salved her conscience with the knowledge that they had moved to another ballroom and amongst so many dancers, it was unlikely that anyone would recognise them.

'Heavens, that was exhausting,' she exclaimed when the duke led her off the floor after two lively reels. She laughed up at him, exhilarated and not a little light-headed. 'I do not think I can dance again without a rest!'

'Let us step outside to cool down a little.'

She made no demur as he guided her out of the crowded room and they slipped outside through a side door. A grey, cloudy dawn was breaking and Pru closed her eyes as she took in a deep breath.

'How blessedly cool it is out here. I cannot recall ever dancing so much before.'

'Never?'

'Not since I was a child.' She chuckled. 'We keep early hours in Bath, you know. Balls conclude promptly at eleven, even if a dance is in progress.'

'But surely there are private parties?'

'Perhaps, but not the ones I attend with my aunt, where one rarely dances. You must think my life was sadly flat.'

'Do *you* think that?'

She hesitated, then said carefully, 'It is the life I have chosen.'

She was glad to hold on to his arm as they strolled along shadowy paths. She could hear the muted strains of the orchestra coming from the buildings. It sounded magical, unearthly. Glancing up, she could even see the morning star twinkling from a gap in the clouds.

'And have you ever lived anywhere but Bath?' he asked her.

'Why, yes. My parents have a house in Melksham.'

'And you lived there until you became companion to your aunt.'

'Yes, although I am very fortunate. Aunt Minerva treats me more as a daughter than a servant.'

'And yet you are still unmarried.'

She stopped and turned to face him. 'I have had admirers,' she said, with careful dignity. After all, it was not a lie; before Walter's death there had been several of his friends who had shown an interest in her. 'None I wished to marry, however.'

'Really? What dullards they must be, the gentlemen of Bath!'

She laughed. 'No, it is rather that I am too particular in my tastes.' She waved a hand. 'But this is a very dreary subject.'

'I do not think so.' He tucked a wayward curl behind her ear. 'No one could ever call you dreary, Prudence Clifford.'

'How kind of you to say so.'

His own hair was tousled from the dancing, one wayward lock falling over his brow. Without thinking she reached up to brush it aside.

'There.' She smiled up at him. 'That is better.'

He caught her hand and pressed his lips into the palm. Without thinking Pru leaned closer, turning her face up to him, and when he lowered his head she closed her eyes, giving a little sigh as his mouth closed on hers. Then his arms were around her, crushing her close and he was kissing her with such fervour that her senses reeled.

Pru surrendered to her instincts, her lips parting as she responded to his kiss. Her heart was racing, the blood pounding through her body, and she was tingling, every nerve alive. There was an unfamiliar ache deep inside. Something was unfurling, growing. Possessing her. When at last Garrick lifted his head she leaned against his shoulder and gazed up at him. She felt at peace, languid, and very content.

He cleared his throat. 'We should go and find your friends.'

'Yes.' But she spoke without conviction and when he did not move she whispered, 'Garrick, will you kiss me again?'

His eyes darkened and he captured her lips again. She felt the pull of desire grow even stronger and slipped her arms about his neck, holding him close. She pressed her body against his and kissed him back, eagerly. Their tongues danced and excitement leapt inside Pru, leaving her breathless. Her bones had turned to water and she clung tighter, knowing her limbs would not support her if he released her now.

'Do you really want to dance until dawn?' he murmured, leaving a trail of burning kisses down her neck.

She sighed. 'What else is there?'

'My house. It is only a few minutes' walk from here.'

His house! She wanted to be alone with him, to give in to the urgings of her body. Pru was not ignorant of what went on in the marriage bed and at five-and-twenty she knew she was unlikely ever to find a husband. She had no illusions about her future. After this short season in London she would return to her dull, quiet life.

Suddenly, Pru was consumed by desire and a conviction stronger than anything she had known before. She wanted Garrick. She wanted to feel his body against hers, flesh against flesh. Why not allow herself this one experience of passion? No one had ever made her feel this way before, so full of such happiness and excitement and longing that she thought she might burst into flames.

'Then take me there,' she begged him.

Garrick tried to calm the tumult that raged through his body. It was madness, but this whole night had been folly. As if sensing his hesitation she sought his lips and kissed him.

'Take me, Garrick.'

She was smiling, in the dim morning light he could see her eyes were shining. They held no guile, no fear. Only trust.

Garrick released her and stepped away. 'Go and fetch your wrap. If you are still of the same mind then, come back here. I will be waiting for you.'

She stared at him for another moment then turned and ran off. Garrick drove his fingers through his hair as he paced up and down the path. He thought a few quiet moments of reflection would convince her that it would be folly to run off with him. It would leave her with a lifetime of regret. She would see sense. He hoped, prayed she would see sense.

'Curse it, man, you want nothing of the kind!' he growled to himself. 'You want her to come back and damn the consequences!'

He was still wrestling with his conscience when she returned. He watched her hurrying towards him, looking for some sign of doubt in her face.

There was none. Without hesitation she threw herself into his arms and he kissed her, hard, then he took her wrap and arranged it over her head and shoulders, some small protection against prying eyes. He led her to a wicket gate where a few coins persuaded the lackey standing guard to let them out.

They hurried to Dover Street, half walking, half running, caught up in a fever of excitement such as Garrick had never known. When they reached his door, he ushered her inside, growling to the sleepy lackey as they went in.

'You haven't seen us. Is that understood?'

The house was silent. Pru knew she should be afraid, or at least nervous, but with her hand firmly in Garrick's warm grip she felt perfectly safe. She was strangely light-headed, her body singing with joy. She knew this could not last, but she did not care. She wanted this one night of pleasure.

Garrick ushered her into a chamber where the unshuttered windows allowed in sufficient light for her to see the magnificent bed with elaborate carvings on the bedposts and the sumptuous red and gold hangings.

'Pru.' She felt Garrick's hands on her shoulders. 'Pru, you do not need to do this. In fact, I am damned sure we should not. Say the word and I will take you back.'

'No.' She turned to him, grasping his coat. 'I want this, Garrick, truly. I am no simpering miss. I know what the consequences may be and I am prepared for that.' She stepped closer, smiling up at him. 'I shall make no demands upon you after this. I have no thoughts of marriage, but I should like to know the pleasures of the marriage state, just once.'

'Pru—'

'No,' she said, resting her fingers on his mouth. 'Make me no promises tonight, Garrick.'

She stretched up and kissed him. He gave a little growl, deep in his throat, and she clung tighter as he teased her lips apart, deepening the kiss. Garrick's arms came around her, pulling her closer and she pressed against him, returning his embrace as fervently as she knew how.

He was a skilful lover, undressing her swiftly and with an ease that suggested he was well-practised, and all the while he teased her with kisses and caresses that kept her on the edge of swooning. Pru's fingers scrabbled with his clothes, impatient to feel his naked flesh against her own and it was not long before he was tumbling her onto the bed.

The kisses grew more fevered. Garrick wanted to go slower, but she was already trembling at his touch, her body receptive, back arching. He kissed her breasts and fastened his mouth over one hardened peak, his tongue circling it while his fingers teased the other. He delighted in her soft moans of pleasure that sent the blood pounding through his body. He smoothed one hand down over her flat stomach until he was exploring the heat between her thighs.

She gasped, pushed against him before she grabbed his wrist.

'Show me what to do,' she begged, her voice low but not quite steady. 'Show me how to pleasure you, too.'

'Oh, sweeting, just having you here is pleasure enough.'

But all the same he drew back, steadied himself then took her hand and guided it over his aroused body, holding out as long as he could against the demands of desire, then he shifted his weight and covered her. Pru was ready for him. Her hips lifted invitingly and the heat of her almost overpowered him as he entered her. She cried out, a sharp inward gasp quickly followed by a mewl of sheer pleasure as she moved with him, against him.

Pru's body was out of control. Waves had been rippling through her, building like a spring tide and now they crashed, flooding her body and her mind and then she was falling, falling. It was only later, when silence had descended on them and Garrick was lying with his back to her that she realised he had withdrawn from her before the end.

'Garrick?' She rolled towards him and put a hand on his shoulder. 'What is it? Are you well?'

'More than well,' he murmured turning back and kissing her nose. 'I did not wish to risk giving you a child.'

It was too dark to read his face and she felt a slight chill run over her skin. Was this consideration for her, or himself? Desire sated, she felt less sure of anything now, but her doubts faded when he pulled her into his arms again.

'I wish we could stay here longer, but I must get you back to your aunt.'

His kiss warmed her, she felt another kick of excitement deep inside as she ran one hand over his muscled back. She was hungry for his touch again and snuggled closer.

'Must we go just yet?'

Her hand travelled downwards, cupping his buttock and caressing his hip before slipping between their bodies. The effect upon him was immediate, and very satisfying.

He rolled on top of her. 'I think we can delay a few more minutes!'

It was gone six o'clock when they slipped back into the grounds of Burlington House. They made their way between the marquees, where the music was still playing, little more than a soft beat on the morning air.

'The last dance is not yet finished,' he said. 'Shall we go back inside?'

'I would prefer to remain out here, with you.'

Pru was still fizzing from all that had happened and wanted to cling onto the memory, cling onto *him*, for just a little longer. She had thrown herself at Garrick, as abandoned as any strumpet. She had asked him to make her no false promises and she was glad she had done that. She would not trap him into marriage, even if she was compromised now beyond redemption.

She knew herself too well to think she would ever be happy as his mistress. She could never live with the distress that would cause her family. Nor could she bear to think that at some point he must take a wife.

No. One night was all she could expect. She wanted to savour their time together, knowing it could never again be like this.

As the last strains of the music died away, he pulled her into his arms and kissed her again. Tenderly, a farewell embrace. People were leaving the ballrooms. Voices were coming closer, there were sounds of laughter and reluctantly they moved apart. Garrick slid his hands down Pru's shoulders and caught her hands.

'Well.' She tried to make light of it. 'What an interesting night this has been!'

'I beg your pardon,' he said. 'I should not have imposed on you.'

'No, no, I should beg *yours*,' she told him, squeezing his hands. 'I was lost as soon as you took me in your arms tonight. No one has ever kissed me like that before.'

'I should hope not!' He dragged in a breath. 'There is no time to talk now. I must take you back to your party.'

'Yes.'

He pulled her hand onto his arm and they made their way in silence back towards the house. As they approached the hall where guests were assembling to wait for their carriages, Prudence halted. It was time to live up to her name.

'It would be best if I went on alone. It might be awkward, if we are seen together.' She blushed a little. 'I do not want anyone to, to speculate.'

'Very well. But you will tell me, if there are any… *consequences* of what we have just done?'

She did not pretend to misunderstand him. 'Yes of course. I will inform you if I am with child. You have my word on that. Now, I must go.'

He released her arm and she took a step away, then stopped.

'What has happened, tonight,' she said. 'I want it to be very clear that I do not hold you at all to blame. It was nothing more than an, an aberration, caused by the excitement of the occasion. You need not call upon me. In fact, it is better if you do not. Please do not think I expect anything more from you. Good night, Your Grace.'

Without another word she hurried away.

Chapter Ten

Hell-fire, man, you have compromised a perfectly re-spectable lady!

Garrick berated himself as he made his way back to Dover Street. Pru had bewitched him, but that was no excuse. How could he have let himself be carried away like that? And if Pru thought he would allow the matter to end there she was very much mistaken. He was not such a rogue.

Prudence Clifford. He felt light-headed, euphoric just thinking of her. He could not stop smiling. She danced like an angel, made him laugh with her quick wit and having her in his bed had been a revelation. The last few hours were some of the happiest he had spent for years. The touch of her hand set his pulse racing, and when he kissed her—! Even now the thought of it sent desire spiking through his body.

He had believed himself immune to female charms but no, a woman he had met only a couple of times in his life had proved him wrong. Confound it, he had only just left her and already he missed her so badly it was a physical ache. But it should not be, she was not his sort at all. Too tall for one thing and her mouth, by her own admission, was too wide. True, she was intelligent, but she was also stubborn, which was the reason he had remained in town. To prevent her from ruining her reputation in a bid to save his.

And what a mull you have made of that! You have ruined more than her reputation now, you damned scoundrel. You will have to marry her.

It might not be what either of them wanted, but he would do his duty by the lady. It would have been better for everyone if he had retired to Hartland and let the ton say what it liked about him. But how could he leave Pru Clifford to stand up for him? If she publicly defended him, she would be ridiculed, perhaps even shunned. It might even be said she had set her cap at him. Or worse, that she was hopelessly in love!

His frown deepened. That was clearly not the case. What had her last words to him been? *'Please do not think I expect anything more from you.'* Did she mean that—would she refuse an offer of marriage from him? He was a duke. Her family would fall on his neck.

But would Pru?

Garrick knew she was angry about the rumours against him. He had told her the truth about Annabelle Speke and he thought she would live with that, if it meant protecting the lady. But he understood Pru now, and he was sure she would never tolerate the slur that he was a traitor.

His sole purpose in coming to the ball tonight had been to reason with her, and possibly to protect her, if Conyers was present. Instead he had made things a hundred times more complicated. But how could he resist, when she had been so close, looking up at him with her eyes shining like stars? He had lost his head like any greenhorn.

Confound it, he knew how fragile a lady's reputation could be and yet his actions this night had compromised her. There was no turning back the clock. Surely that was enough to make her accept an offer.

But the doubt persisted. Garrick decided that if Pru would not accept the protection of his name then he would keep his distance, but he needed to be sure she had no reason to publicly defend him. If she had been a wealthy eccentric she might have been able to set the town on its ears and walk away unscathed, but she was not. If his name was besmirched then hers would be, too. Lady Borcaster might even turn her out. Garrick could not have that on his conscience. He must put a stop to the rumours and if he was going to do that, then he would have to face his nemesis.

He passed a narrow house that he remembered from his time in London, when he had been a young buck with an allowance scorching his pocket. The brass plaque on the wall announced it was still a gentleman's club and, after a slight hesitation, he turned and retraced his steps. He rapped on the door. All those years ago he had needed someone to introduce him. Now his title ensured that he was admitted immediately.

He ran lightly up the stairs and strolled into one of the elegantly appointed salons. Morning light filtered through the muslin drapes at the windows, but candles still burned in the glittering chandeliers, lighting the small green baize tables that were dotted around the room, where gentlemen hunched over their cards in hushed concentration. For a moment he was nineteen again, a boy in a man's world.

A liveried servant approached with a tray and he took a glass of wine and sipped at it as his eyes swept over the players. He was in luck. His quarry was present and playing piquet at a small table on the far side of the room. The man was a little older, a little greyer at the temples but instantly recognisable. He was concentrating on his cards and Garrick moved away. He was in no hurry. He would to wait until the game was concluded.

When the man's opponent threw down his cards and quit the table, Garrick slipped into the vacant seat.

'To the victor the spoils, eh?' he murmured.

Sir Joseph Conyers looked up, his brows lifting in surprise.

'The Duke of Hartland.' There was the hint of a sneer in his greeting. 'How long has it been, ten years?'

'Not long enough,' Garrick retorted.

'What is your pleasure, cards or dice?'

'Cards. Piquet, I think, don't you?' He watched Sir Joseph open a fresh pack and shuffle it. 'I have heard your luck with the bones is, er, extraordinary.'

The sculpted eyebrows snapped together. 'That was never proven.'

Garrick allowed himself a little smile and the older man scowled. 'Be very careful, Duke. I will tolerate no slights against my name.'

'Nor I, Sir Joseph. Which is why I am come to see you.' He smiled. 'Shall we play?'

Garrick cut the lower card and dealt first. The two men played in silence, save for announcing their scores. They were both cautious at first, Garrick taking care over his discards.

'My game,' declared Sir Joseph at the end of the first *partie*. 'But you have improved, Duke. Since we last played.'

'I should hope so.'

His opponent smirked and his tone became a little patronising. 'I am sure you can do better.'

The second game was closer, with scores evenly matched until the sixth deal when Garrick scored a Pique.

'Your victory,' muttered Sir Joseph, clearly rattled. 'I made a foolish discard.' He nodded to the waiter to refill his empty wineglass. 'A beginner's mistake. Shall we play again or are you for your bed, Duke?'

Garrick said, casually, 'One more game, then, if you wish.'

'If *I* wish it? Are you not a gamester, Your Grace?'

'I am not. Cards hold little interest for me.'

Garrick noted with satisfaction the gleam of triumph in Sir Joseph's hooded eyes. Then he closed his mind to everything but the game.

'My dear Prudence, General Lechlade was just about to go looking for you,' exclaimed Lady Borcaster when she saw Pru hurrying towards her.

'I beg your pardon, ma'am,' she said.

'Well, well, I am not at all surprised,' replied my lady, chuckling. 'You young people always like to remain until the very end. And at least the crowd has thinned a little now.'

Mrs Clifford nodded. 'Indeed, we were jostled most unpleasantly on the way down to supper. Thankfully, the dear general was on hand to prevent too much inconvenience.'

'I hope you were not too worried for me, Aunt?' Pru ventured.

Remembering all that had happened to her this evening, she felt sure there must be some evidence of it in her appearance. Garrick had done his best with the buttons and fastenings of her gown, and thankfully her wrap covered up any deficiencies in her dress. As for her hair, several tendrils had escaped but she had seen a number of ladies looking far more dishevelled after just one dance this evening. She could only pray there was nothing in her countenance to give her away.

'Not a bit of it, my love. With the waltzing and country dances all going on at the same time, and the crowds so thick, it would have been impossible to remain together for the whole time. We looked for you at supper, of course, but there was no hope of finding anyone in that crush.'

'I said to Minerva, it was only natural that you should want to be with your young friends,' remarked Lady Borcaster, giving Pru an indulgent smile. 'But I told her you are a sensible puss and would come to no harm.' She broke off, listening to the stentorian tones of a footman announcing the carriages. 'Ah, that is ours now. Are you ready to escort us, General?'

Relieved to have escaped with so little explanation of her absence, Pru settled herself into a corner of the carriage for the short journey back to Brook Street. She felt quite dazed. Her hand crept to her lips and excitement sizzled through her again. How forward of her to ask him to kiss her. How wrong of him to comply! If only it had stopped there. If only she was as sensible as Lady Borcaster thought her.

Pru pulled her cloak a little closer. She had told Garrick she expected nothing more from him, but she had gone willingly to his bed and she might now be carrying his child. If that was the case then they must marry. They were both agreed on that. But what if she had been recognised as she danced half the night away with the duke? That would be scandalous, of course, but not a disaster. Her reputation might be harmed, but she hoped her aunt would not turn her off. If she could return to Bath and her charity work, life would continue as before.

The only problem was, Prudence was no longer sure if that was enough for her.

'Damn you, Hartland. The luck was with you tonight!'

'Not all luck,' Garrick replied, piling up the counters before him. 'I had the advantage of a clear head.'

His opponent gave him a malevolent look. The duke met it steadily.

He said, 'I have learned a great deal in the past ten years, Conyers. Some skill at cards is only one small part of it.'

'Why are you telling me this?'

Garrick sat back, his fingers playing with the stem of his wineglass. 'You have been spreading rumours about me.'

'The devil I have!'

'Do not attempt to deny it. Your bluster is wasted on me and the nearest tables are empty. There is no one to impress with your lies.'

Sir Joseph glowered. 'You cannot prove anything.'

'No, but I am sure in my own mind. I am minded to call you out.'

'You would not dare.'

'Would I not?' Garrick's lip curled. 'I am no callow youth now, Conyers. The first time I bested you it was pure chance. This time, you may be sure I will finish the task.' He scooped the rouleaux at his elbow and rose. 'Take heed of my warning, sir. I am willing to forget what has gone before, but only if it stops now. If you continue to spread your lies, be sure I will destroy you.'

Garrick turned on his heel and walked to the door. He could feel Sir Joseph's eyes boring into him all the way across the room. Garrick knew there was no foundation in the rumours. Conyers had been acting out of spite. He stepped out onto the street and stopped for a moment to take in the fresh morning air.

Hopefully he had done enough to put an end to the rogue's malicious meddling, but it did not fully resolve the situation with Prudence. Now he must steel himself to make everything right with her.

A full week passed and Prudence heard nothing from Garrick. There had been no repercussions from the night of the Burlington House ball. No one mentioned her dancing with the duke, but when her body gave her proof that she was not pregnant, the disappointment was so severe it shocked Pru to the core. Only then did she realise how much she would have welcomed a reason to marry him.

She was still coming to terms with this revelation when Aunt Minerva came into her bedroom, clearly great with news.

'Oh, my dear Pru, are you not dressed yet?'

She stretched her lips into a smile. 'As you see, Aunt. I thought I might rest another hour and I sent Meg away.'

'Well fetch her back this instant,' cried Mrs Clifford, coming further into the room. 'The Duke of Hartland is downstairs and desirous to speak with you.'

Prudence stared at her. 'W-with me?'

'Yes, yes! It was very fortunate that dear Jane is gone out, because I am sure she would not have admitted him, but when the servant told me the duke was wishful to speak with me, I could not bring myself to refuse.' Aunt Minerva came across to the bed and took her hands. She beamed down at Prudence and said in hushed tones, 'He is going to ask you to marry him.'

'No!'

'It is true, my love. He came in very nervous, and quite properly asked my permission to pay his addresses to you.'

'But he cannot!'

'My dear, why not?' Mrs Clifford blinked at her. 'You were the one who defended him against those vicious rumours.'

'I told you then that I did not wish to marry him!' Pru dragged the sheet up to her chin. 'You must go down and send him away. Tell him. Tell him there is *no reason* for him to marry me.'

'La, my love, I can do nothing of the sort. He is a duke, for heaven's sake. Why would you refuse him?'

'Because...because of his reputation,' said Pru, grasping at straws. 'Lady Borcaster's friends are right, no respectable female would countenance his acquaintance.'

'Have you lost your wits, Prudence love? We are not talking of being *friends*, this is very different. Marriage! You would be a duchess. Think of it. Think how proud your dear father would be.'

'No, he would not,' cried Pru. 'Papa cares more for, for goodness and honesty than titles. Besides, everyone knows Hartland has no fortune.'

'He is hardly a pauper,' retorted her aunt. 'You would be far richer than you are now, that is certain. And a dukedom, too! Do you not realise what an honour he is doing you?'

But it was not honour that Pru was thinking of, it

was marrying a man who did not love her. One who was marrying her because he thought it was his duty to do so. He would make her his duchess, but then the long years would stretch ahead of them. Years of polite indifference. Or possibly he would be kind to her, and she thought that would be even more unbearable.

'Please, Aunt, go down and tell him I do not *want* to marry him. Make him understand that our stations are too far removed.'

'My dear, that will not weigh with him if his affections are engaged.'

They aren't. He feels obliged to wed me.

But Pru could not say that to her aunt without disclosing the reason for it. She clutched at the sheet and spoke as calmly as she could.

'Aunt Minerva, I cannot marry a man with such a past,' she said. 'Then there are the accusations against him. It is one thing to defend such a man out of, of Christian charity, it is quite another to marry him.'

'Well, I never did!' Mrs Clifford plumped down on the edge of the bed, staring at her niece. 'Are you quite, quite sure, Prudence, my love? It is a flattering offer, and, at five-and-twenty...'

'I am unlikely to get another. I know that, Aunt, and I am resigned to it. I have enjoyed our holiday, but all I really want is to go back to Bath and return to my charity work at the infirmary.'

Mrs Clifford looked at her in disbelief.

'My dear girl, that is no reason to reject the duke. You could help the poor far more if you were richer.'

'My reason for helping the doctors goes beyond money.'

'Oh, I know, my love. It is guilt that takes you to that

wretched place week after week. Regret that you could not save your poor brother—'

'Ah, don't, Aunt!' Her voice cracking, Pru closed her eyes and took a few deep, steadying breaths. She said, quite slowly, 'I pray you will go back to His Grace and give him my answer.'

Chapter Eleven

London at the end of June was white-hot. The crowds that had thronged the capital for the visit of the Allied Sovereigns had left, but the streets were still busy with traffic, although Garrick barely noticed as he strode along Piccadilly. He had spent the morning with his man of business, signing the papers to dispose of several properties that he did not want and could no longer afford. It was a relief to be free of some of his burden and he planned to drive to Hartland soon and concentrate on improving what was left of his estates. Perhaps that would help him forget Prudence Clifford.

He had not seen her since that fateful night at Burlington House. Nine days ago. Nine long days in which he had thought of her almost constantly, remembering the taste of her, the feel of her in his arms. He had always known he must marry one day. Annabelle's brutal rejection had been a relief but he knew it was his duty to take a wife, so why not Prudence? He could not deny the attraction between them. Besides, he liked her and he had thought she liked him. Which was why he had decided to put it to the touch on Monday. He had called in Brook Street to ask Pru to marry him, but he had been turned away by her aunt. She had not even had the courtesy to tell him in person!

Even now he could not believe she had refused him. He had been convinced she would say yes, but she would not even see him. It was her aunt who had broken the news, laying out gently but with awful clarity the fact that Pru did not consider him respectable enough to accept his offer of marriage. He had argued, explaining to Mrs Clifford that her niece knew all about his protracted betrothal, now at an end, and the scandalous duel that had resulted in his fleeing the country. Her reply was like a blow to the gut:

'Yes, Your Grace, Prudence told me she is very honoured by your confidences. However, while Christian charity obliges her to defend you to your critics, she says she cannot accept such a man as a husband.'

Even two days on, those words brought him to a stand. He came to an abrupt halt just at the entrance to Albany, his hand tightening on his ebony stick as he tried to suppress the red mist of anger and remorse that enveloped him. Pru did not care for him. She had used him, as Helene Conyers had done. He meant less to her than her damned charities!

'Well, by my stars. Garrick Chauntry! I have been looking for you.'

The familiar voice snapped Garrick out of his trance. He looked around to see a fair-haired man striding towards him, immaculately attired in a blue coat, snow-white linen, with pale pantaloons disappearing into highly polished and tasselled Hessians.

'Jack! I thought you were in Sussex. What the devil brings you here?'

'You.' Lord John Callater gripped the outstretched

hand. 'I told you, I have been looking for you. Where the devil have you been hiding?'

'Nowhere. I have been in London for some months. Since leaving Bath, in fact.'

'When I called at Grosvenor Square all they would tell me was that you no longer lived there.' He glanced back through the entrance to the Albany courtyard. 'Will you come in and take wine with me? I want to know what you have been doing.'

'I am on my way to Dover Street.' Garrick waved his cane roughly in that direction. 'My new house.'

'Then I shall come with you.' Jack tucked his arm in Garrick's and they set off along the street. 'You will not escape me again.'

Garrick smiled. 'I have no wish to escape you,' he said mildly.

'But you have proved mighty elusive. You have not been to any of the usual haunts!'

'I did not come to town to be sociable.'

Jack scoffed at that. 'You were sociable enough when I met you in Vienna! *Here* you are doing your best to be invisible. And you are selling the Grosvenor Square house?'

'It is sold,' Garrick corrected him. 'I have just signed the final papers.'

'Congratulations. Damned barrack of a place, as I remember, and sadly in need of renovation.'

'Aye, like so much of the Hartland estate.'

'Is that why you have been keeping your head down?' asked Jack bluntly. 'Are you in dun territory?'

'No, no, not as bad as all that. Although if my father had not died when he did, I fear it would be.'

He had seen all the ledgers now. He had pored over the accounts with his man of business and they showed the old duke had not been too ill to travel, or to keep his mistress in luxury. In the years before his death his father had lived extravagantly and run up expenses to throw the estates into even greater debt.

He needed to go to Hartland, to see his mother and discover just how much she knew. Perhaps she was in ignorance of what had been going on. Mayhap she had put her husband on a pedestal. If so, Garrick had no wish to cut him down. It would break her heart, and he had already caused her enough pain.

He felt Jack's grip on his arm tighten for a moment in a gesture of sympathy. They had known one another since their schooldays. Jack Callater knew as much as anyone about his affairs. Almost. Garrick quickly stifled all thoughts of Prudence Clifford and walked on to Dover Street, where he took his friend up the stairs, calling for Stow to bring wine.

'I have not seen you since you quit Bath so precipitously,' said Jack, when they were comfortably seated in the drawing room. 'What happened?'

'I'd prefer not to answer that.'

'Damnation, Garr, we've never had any secrets from one another.'

Garrick waited until Stow had left them with wine and a tray of small fancy cakes before he replied.

'This isn't my secret to share. Suffice it to say I did not offer for Miss Speke.'

'Aye, I have heard the rumours about that, but I don't believe 'em,' said Jack bluntly. 'For God's sake, man, you can tell me the truth. I do not for one moment believe you jilted the girl.'

'I applaud your faith in me.'

'It ain't in your nature,' Jack replied. 'When you

didn't turn up at Sally Triscombe's that night some of the others thought you'd got cold feet, but you will remember that I was staying at the Pelican as well as you. When I knocked on your door the following morning your man told me you had gone to Royal Crescent.'

Garrick frowned. 'Stow doesn't know the whole truth.'

'No, I doubt anyone does,' retorted Jack. 'But I am certain that you did not desert the lady, despite the scurrilous talk.'

'I pray you, leave it there, Jack!' Garrick jumped up and strode over to the window. 'My reputation will survive being labelled a jilt. Miss Speke's would not.'

'Too chivalrous by half, Duke! And if there is no truth to the rumours, why have I not seen you in your usual haunts? Not because some fool has put it about you are a French spy...'

Garrick swung round, frowning. 'I thought I had put paid to that rumour.'

'Oh, I only heard a whisper of it, a couple of weeks since, and I was at pains to knock that back, I can tell you.'

'I suppose I should be grateful to you!'

'Aye, you should, since I have been in an agony of apprehension over you since you left Bath without a word.'

'Your concern was wasted. I have been in London all the time.'

'Playing least in sight and not answering my letters! I knew you hadn't gone to Hartland, so I came posting up to town. And now I am here,' Jack went on, fixing his friend with a determined eye, 'I don't mean to allow you to carry on skulking in the shadows, as if you have something to hide. Time to redeem yourself, Duke.'

'And if I don't want to be, er, redeemed?'

'Well, if you won't defend your good name then I shall be obliged to do so!'

A wry smile tugged at Garrick's mouth.

'Another one,' he murmured.

'What?'

'Nothing.' He shook his head. 'Very well, what do you propose?'

Jack grinned. He carried both their glasses back to the side table to refill them.

'I intend to restore you to your rightful place in society,' he said, handing Garrick his recharged glass. 'Starting tonight, we are going to attend every society event imaginable!'

The ballroom at Shrivenham House was the most magnificent chamber Prudence had ever seen. The ornate plasterwork around the ceiling had been gilded and the walls were covered with green and gold silk which glowed in the light of the chandeliers glittering overhead. Even more sparkling were the jewels bedecking the guests. The room echoed with voices and laughter, but Pru was finding it hard to feel any excitement about the forthcoming evening.

There had been so many parties since she arrived in London and she feared she was growing tired of the constant social whirl. Her spirits had been very low since she had rejected Garrick's offer. Aunt Minerva told her the duke had accepted her decision courteously and even sent her his compliments before leaving the house, but that was little consolation to Pru. His graciousness made her feel even more wretched.

Dancing was already in progress. Lady Borcaster led her little party around the edge of the room, introducing Prudence and her aunt to those she considered would be *useful acquaintances*. She quickly found Pru a dance partner, but immediately sent the gentleman on his way.

'These two dances have a good half hour to run yet,' she told him. 'Come and find Miss Clifford when the next set is forming. There are more people I wish her to meet!'

Pru found it a struggle, constantly smiling and making conversation, and at the first opportunity, she slipped away into the crowd. She made her way across to the long windows that filled one side of the room. She knew they overlooked Green Park, but since Lady Borcaster had declared they should arrive fashionably late, it was quite dark and impossible to see anything save the reflections of the twinkling lights from the ballroom.

How soon could she leave? she wondered. Could she say she was ill, perhaps, and take to her bed for a week? Lady Borcaster had invited them to stay until the end of August and the thought of spending another two months in London weighed heavily upon her spirits.

'You are not dancing, Miss Clifford.'

She gave a little start when she heard Garrick's deep voice and turned quickly.

'Your Grace!'

'You seem surprised.'

'I am.' She gripped her fan, determined to be honest. 'Surprised and embarrassed. I should apologise. For refusing to see you when you called. It was cowardly.'

'Let us not talk of it,' he interrupted her. 'It is forgotten.'

She peeped up at him. He looked quite at his ease, which meant he must be relieved she had refused him. Somehow that thought did not cheer her at all.

She said, 'I thought you had left London.'

'I had business that was not yet concluded. I thought I might as well stay to sign the papers rather than have them sent on to me.'

She nodded. How foolish to think for a moment that he had remained in town for her sake.

'Will you dance with me, later?' Now she was more than surprised. She was astonished. He continued. 'Can you waltz? Since the Tsar's visit it has become quite the rage.'

'Yes.' She felt quite dazed, conversing with Garrick like this, but with so many people around them she could hardly run away. She said, 'It is danced everywhere now, is it not? I *have* learned to waltz, but I have only ever danced it at private parties.'

'Which this is, albeit a very grand affair! So, you will stand up with me?'

Pru looked down at her hands, clasped tightly about her fan. She should not. She *must* not. It would only prolong her agony, since nothing could ever come of it.

Be sensible, Pru!

'I am sure there are other ladies you should ask first.'

'I have already danced with my hostess and her daughter. Now I want to stand up with you.' He added, 'We did not waltz together at Burlington House. An omission I now want to repair.'

His green eyes were fixed on her, causing her heart to beat a little faster, and when she finally met his gaze, she knew she was lost.

Why not? It is only a dance.

A tremulous smiled hovered. 'I would like that.'

She searched his face, alert for any signs of triumph, but she saw only a faint relaxing in his features. Relief.

'Until the waltz, then,' he said, and with a little bow he was gone.

Pru watched him walk away. She was like a moth, unable to escape the candle's flame. But what of it? It would be another memory to store against the long, lonely nights head of her. But she could not quite think of it like that. Her spirits were rising at the idea of another half hour in his company. With a gasp she suddenly remembered the young man who had claimed her hand for the next dance and she hurried off to find him. Her earlier weariness had evaporated, replaced by a sizzle of anticipation for what the evening might bring.

Garrick studiously avoided the matrons who were trying to catch his eye. He knew his hostess would think it his duty to choose a partner for every dance, but he was in no humour to do so. He moved to the side of the room and leaned against one of the marbled pillars. His height gave him the distinct advantage of having a clear view of the dancers who were forming a new set. He watched Pru taking her place on the dance floor. She was smiling and chatting as the dancers waited for the music to start, as if she had not a care in the world. She might be taller than her partner and not conventionally pretty, but Garrick could tell the fellow was captivated. Damn him. She might not have fallen in love yet, but it would happen, she was too attractive to remain single. One day she would meet a man who captured her heart. He was surprised to find how much he wished it could have been him.

When he had first seen Pru this evening Garrick had determined to avoid her. It was what his head told him to do, although his body objected strongly. He could not forget how good it was to hold her, to kiss her. To have her in his bed. How *right* that had felt. Although, clearly, she had not thought the same or she would not have refused to become his duchess.

He scowled. Another salutary lesson from a woman. When would he learn? He had agreed to come here tonight, but he was determined not to stay. Perhaps he could leave now, slip away before the waltz. Pru might be angry, even upset, but it would be best for them both. He should go off to Hartland and forget all about Pru Clifford. Leave her to live her own life. Give her the chance to find a better man.

His dark thoughts were interrupted by a hand on his shoulder.

'Don't think you can get away with this, Garrick,' drawled an amused voice. 'Since when have you taken to standing around at parties, glowering like a love-lorn hero?'

He shook off the hand.

'You insisted I come with you, Jack, but you cannot force me to make a cake of myself on the dance floor.'

His friend laughed. 'True, but you could make an effort to be sociable.' He threw up his hands. 'I know, you dislike society with a vengeance—and with good cause!—but refusing to dance will only give people more reason to think ill of you. That is not why I dragged you here.'

It sounded so much like something Pru would say that Garrick smiled, in spite himself.

'I haven't refused. You have seen me dancing.'

'With just two partners!'

'I have a partner for the waltz, too.'

'Ah?' Jack cocked a knowing eyebrow. 'The young lady I saw you talking with earlier? Well, that is something. Any more?'

'Is that not enough?'

'No! By heaven, man, I am beginning to wish I had left you brooding in Dover Street.'

'I wish you had, too!' Garrick glanced over Jack's shoulder. 'I see our hostess is bearing down upon us, her daughters in tow and looking very determined! I am off to enjoy a few moments' peace on the terrace.'

Jack grinned. 'Leaving me to their tender mercies?'

'It's no more than you deserve!' And with that parting shot, Garrick lounged away.

When the music finished, Pru's partner begged he might escort her back to her party.

'Yes of course.'

She accompanied him off the floor, directing his attention to her aunt and Lady Borcaster standing at the side of the room with Sir Joseph Conyers. Her partner slowed.

'Ah, Miss Clifford, pray forgive me, I have just remembered...'

Looking up, Pru saw that his chubby countenance had paled.

'Is anything wrong, Mr Trenchard?'

'No, no, not at all.' His eyes were darting around, anywhere but at her or the little group ahead of them. 'I need to go and talk to...'

By now Pru's mind was seething with conjecture.

'Is it perhaps Sir Joseph that you do not wish to meet?'

His sudden start and the dull flush that mounted his cheeks confirmed her suspicions, although he was quick to deny it.

'How, how absurd, ma'am. No, it's not that at all! A matter of, of urgent business...'

She pulled him to one side, into a space where they could speak without being overheard.

'Forgive me, sir, but are you...' How could she broach such a delicate business? 'Are you *enamoured* of Lady Conyers?' She fixed him with a steady gaze. The look of alarm in his face gave her the answer and she screwed up her courage to continue. 'Mr Trenchard, pray do not ask me how I know this, but you would be wise to avoid the lady. She has ensnared more than one young man.'

'I beg your pardon, ma'am, I have no idea what you mean!'

His bluster did nothing but convince Pru that her suspicions were correct.

She continued. 'I know it is not usual for single ladies to talk of these matters, sir, but in this case, I believe I must. I know something of the lady and I know that, in the past, she has engineered a compromising situation with her young admirer, where he is discovered by her husband.'

'No, no she wouldn't, I mean…' He broke off, looking alarmed.

Pru put a hand on his arm. 'It is not too late, sir. Give up the lady now. She is not going to leave her husband, whatever she might tell you.'

'You are q-quite wrong, ma'am. It is nothing like that, I assure you.'

He floundered on a little longer then excused himself and hurried away. Pru watched him go. She had done her best, spoken far more plainly than a single lady should and had no idea if her warning would do any good. She abhorred gossips, but in this case she could not stand by and see another young man hurt as Garrick had been.

Sir Joseph was still conversing with Lady Borcaster when Pru came up to the little group. Mrs Clifford saw her approaching and alerted Lady Borcaster, who turned and said in a lively voice, 'Ah, here is dear Prudence now! Not too tired from all your dancing, I hope?'

'Not at all, ma'am.'

'Miss Clifford dances very well,' purred Sir Joseph, giving her a little bow. 'It is a pleasure to watch her.'

Pru kept smiling although she really did not like being discussed as if she was not present. But Sir Joseph had not finished.

'I hope, Mrs Clifford, that you will allow your niece to stand up with me for the next, which is the waltz?'

'Oh, of course, Sir Joseph. I am sure—'

'Alas I regret I cannot,' Pru said quickly. 'I am already engaged. For the waltz.'

'Ah.' She detected a slight annoyance in those hooded eyes. 'A pity. Another time, then, perhaps?'

'Perhaps,' she agreed with cool politeness.

He stepped back, gave a little bow and sauntered off. All three ladies watched him disappear into the card room, then Mrs Clifford turned to her niece, her face alive with curiosity.

'I did not know you had a partner for the waltz, Prudence. Was this Lady Shrivenham's doing?'

'No, ma'am. The gentleman asked me himself.'

'Heavens, how forward of him,' exclaimed Lady Borcaster, mildly reproving. 'He should have requested an introduction from your aunt or your hostess, at the very least.'

'Neither were on hand,' explained Pru. 'But we are already acquainted and as I am not a young debutante, I thought it safe to accept.'

'Yes of course,' agreed Lady Borcaster. 'No lady wants to be sitting out if she can help it. Who is your partner?'

She looked around and Pru saw her stiffen, the smile frozen to her lips when her eyes fixed upon the man approaching them.

'Yes,' murmured Pru, trying hard not to giggle. 'It is His Grace the Duke of Hartland.'

Chapter Twelve

Garrick observed the older ladies as he approached to claim his dance partner. Mrs Clifford looked stunned and a little discomfited, as well she might after their last meeting, while Lady Borcaster's greeting was positively glacial. Prudence, by contrast was smiling widely, her eyes shining with mischief. Little witch, he thought, his own mouth twitching, she is enjoying this moment. It pleased him. There was nothing like shared amusement to banish constraint.

He said, as Pru took his arm and walked with him to the dance floor, 'I fear we have discomposed your companions.'

'I am very sorry they could not conceal their disapproval.'

'Do they disapprove of the dance, or your partner?'

'A little of both, but you, mostly.' They took their places, ready to begin, and she peeped up at him. 'They disapprove of me, too, for accepting you.'

The music started and Garrick escorted his partner around the room in a slow promenade.

'Then why did you?'

The dancers moved into the *pirouette*. Garrick held

Pru's hand in an arch above their heads as they slowly turned.

'Well?' he prompted her.

'I could hardly refuse to dance with a duke.'

'You refused to marry one.' Her eyes flew to his face and Garrick cursed himself silently when he saw the twinkle had faded. He said, 'I beg your pardon, I did not mean to remind you.'

'I need no reminding, Your Grace. The honour you conveyed upon me will last for ever.'

Her words ignited a small spark of hope, but this was no place to discuss such a delicate matter.

'You have not told me why you decided to dance with me,' he prompted her.

'Lady Borcaster was at such pains to find a dancing master for me, that I might perfect the steps. It seems a pity not to put the training into practice.'

She smiled at him and Garrick felt a sudden constriction in his chest. She was entrancing, every touch, every glance inflamed him. He never wanted to let her go.

The tempo changed, became quicker and Pru turned to skip beside him as the circle of dancers progressed around the room in the final movements of the dance. He was hardly aware of the other couples, he had eyes only for his partner as she skipped and twirled beside him in a flurry of silk skirts.

Prudence could not stop smiling. Her feet flew over the floor as the duke guided her expertly around the room. For someone used to looking over her partners' heads, it was a pleasure to dance with a tall man. The duke made her feel dainty, cherished. She would squirrel away these happy memories for the future.

They took their bows and she looked up at him, out of breath but exquisitely happy.

'Thank you, Your Grace,' she said, fanning herself. 'I enjoyed that, very much!'

'But it was warm work. Shall we sit out the next?'

'If we can find somewhere cooler.'

Pru took his arm and they walked across to the wall of long windows. The two doors in the centre had been thrown open to the summer night and she made no demur when he led her out onto the wide iron-railed balcony that ran along the back of the house.

The moon was rising, and once her eyes had adjusted from the glare of the ballroom Pru could see Green Park spreading out into the distance. They were not alone, other couples were on the balcony, taking advantage of the night air, but it still felt very daring to be here with Garrick, in the moonlight.

'I shall be in disgrace,' she murmured.

'Because you have come outside with me?'

He was standing at her shoulder, his voice dark and smooth as velvet.

'Perhaps. Or because I dared to dance with you. Not that I regret it,' she said quickly. 'Where did you learn to dance so well?'

'On the Continent.'

'Vienna?'

'Yes, and in Rome and Paris.'

'But surely those last two were in French hands until recently.'

'They were.'

Pru glanced around quickly. There were only two other couples on the balcony now and they were too far away to overhear the conversation. She turned to Garrick, trying to read his expression in the moonlight. He smiled at her and shook his head slightly.

'You have my word I am no spy,' he murmured.

It took all her willpower not to reach up and put her palm against his rugged cheek. Instead she gazed out over the park again. There was a dreamlike quality to the night and Pru breathed in deeply, content to be standing here with Garrick beside her.

'I am glad,' she said. 'Although I never really doubted your innocence on that matter.'

'I believe it is my reputation as a jilt, a breaker of hearts, that worries you more.'

She smiled into the darkness. 'But I know that is not true.'

'And yet you cannot have *such a man* as a husband.' Pru turned quickly and her eyes flew to his face. She saw the scornful twist to his mouth. 'Your aunt told me those were your very words.'

'I needed to persuade her that I could not marry you.'

She rubbed her arms, suddenly chilled.

'And yet you do not doubt my innocence! That makes no sense. Tell me the true reason you will not marry me.' He said roughly, 'Is it because I killed my father?'

'No! You did *not* kill him. I do not believe that.'

'My mother does.'

'But you said your father was in ill health.'

'He was. For years, but my youthful follies were too much for him.'

'Your father sent you away,' she persisted. 'He banished you, when it was you who was the victim. The duel was forced upon you.'

'Yes. But my actions hastened his demise.'

'No. He lived for years after you left England. Whatever else you have done, you did not kill him.'

'But his death still haunts me.' He fixed his eyes on the moon and sucked in a breath. 'You cannot know what that is like.'

Pru reached out and took his hands. 'Yes, I can. I do.'

She said slowly, 'My brother, Walter, had a riding accident five years ago. He fell and hit his head. He never regained consciousness, although he lived on for more than a week. My father was distraught and Mama had to look after him as well as the house and Home Farm. My younger sisters, too, depended upon her, so I took on the task of nursing Walter. We tried everything suggested by the doctors and the apothecary. I even consulted the local midwife. I could not save him.'

'Oh, Pru, I am so very sorry.' Garrick squeezed her fingers, his gentle touch warm and comforting. 'But if the doctors could not cure him, it was not your fault.'

'No, I know that, but it does not stop me feeling guilty. If I had only known more, acted sooner! Since moving to Bath I been working at the infirmary, helping the doctors to look after such injuries. Somehow, that helps with the pain of losing Walter.'

Garrick heard the wistful note in her voice and his heart lurched. He wanted to take her in his arms and kiss away her pain, but even if she wanted his attentions, even if she had not rejected his offer of marriage, there were too many people around them.

'Thank you for telling me,' he said gently. 'It could not have been easy, sharing your confidences.'

'You honoured me with yours, that night in Bath.' She smiled up at him. 'We are friends, are we not?'

Friends! Her trust in him was humbling. He was suddenly aware of how much that meant to him. It did not matter if she would not be his duchess. After all, what had he to offer, save a tarnished reputation and a lifetime of debt?

He said abruptly, 'We should go in.'

'What?' she teased him. 'Are you tired of my company already?'

'You must go back to your aunt before you are missed.'

Pru was surprised by this sudden change. One moment Garrick was smiling at her, kind, compassionate. Now he had withdrawn and he was scowling as if his thoughts were very dark. He must be impatient to be rid of her. He did not offer his arm so she slipped her hand onto his sleeve. Whatever demons he was fighting she did not believe his anger was directed against her.

They stepped back into the noisy glare of the ballroom. Little had changed, the candles still burned brightly and the dancing continued, but suddenly Pru felt exhausted. Desolate, too. Garrick was tired of her company, that much was clear. If she could not remain with him then she would rather go back to Brook Street immediately.

She was wondering if she could broach the subject to Lady Borcaster when a cold, disdainful voice cut through her thoughts.

'Well, well, it is the Duke of Hartland.'

She looked up quickly to see Sir Joseph Conyers and his beautiful wife blocking their way.

Chapter Thirteen

Garrick tensed. Pru felt his muscled arm harden beneath the sleeve of his coat.

'Sir Joseph.' He nodded, his voice cool. 'Lady Conyers.'

'Have you been enjoying the moonlight?' Helene glanced past them towards the open doors. 'How romantic.'

Her knowing smile brought the blood rushing to Pru's cheeks, but the duke replied calmly enough.

'After the exertions of the waltz we needed a little fresh air.'

'And the lady caught herself a duke for her partner.' Sir Joseph's cold smile turned into a sneer. 'I trust he did not disappoint you, Miss Clifford.'

'Not at all.' She lifted her chin. 'His Grace is a most accomplished dancer.'

She noted that Lady Conyers was studying her, as if she scented a rival.

'Something perfected during your years abroad, perhaps, Your Grace,' murmured Sir Joseph. 'I believe the waltz is very popular in France.'

'That I wouldn't know,' retorted Garrick.

A soft laugh came from Lady Conyers. 'I believe I

am considered to be moderately accomplished at the waltz myself,' she purred. 'I should very much like to dance with you, Duke, and have your opinion on the matter.'

The duke inclined his head. 'One day, madam, perhaps you shall. But not tonight.'

They moved on, but not before Pru saw the look Lady Conyers threw at Garrick as she passed. It was blatantly inviting. It angered Pru to think any lady would flirt with another man when she was with her husband.

She was even more unnerved by the jealous rage that ripped through her.

Garrick escorted Prudence back to her friends and went in search of Jack Callater. He had had enough of society for one night. What ill luck to bump into Conyers while he had Prudence on his arm. He wouldn't put it past the rogue to try and do her a mischief, if he thought Garrick might suffer for it.

He found Jack in the card room, but when it was clear that he would be engaged for some time yet, Garrick went away again. He rarely played at cards these days, although he knew he had a talent for it. In his darker moments he considered playing deep as a way to restore the family fortunes, but the idea of fleecing some fool and leaving him destitute did not appeal.

He returned to the ballroom where the cotillion had just commenced. He spotted Sir Joseph dancing with the eldest Miss Shrivenham. Worming his way into respectable society, he thought sourly. But to what end?

A light touch on his arm put an end to his musings. He looked down to find Helene Conyers beside him.

'Escaped from your Long Meg at last, Your Grace?' She was so close he could smell her perfume, a

heavy, cloying scent. It had once turned his head, but
not now.

'Miss Clifford honoured me with a dance,' he replied,
keeping his tone indifferent.

'I think she would like to honour you with much more
than that,' she purred. 'I saw the way she looked at you.'

Garrick was in no mood to play games. 'What do
you want, Lady Conyers?'

'Lady?' she moved closer still. 'You used to call me
Helene.' When he did not reply she went on. 'I wanted
to warn you that Joseph is planning mischief.'

'What is there new in that?'

'Mischief against *you*, Garrick.' She put a hand on
his arm, the jewels winking on her thin fingers. 'I could
help you.'

His lip curled. 'No thank you. I have some experience of your help.'

'Ah, Garrick, surely you feel *something* for me, for
old times' sake?'

Her red lips pouted and she peeped up at him from
beneath her lashes. He remembered that look. Allur-
ing, sensual. Full of promise. Once it had driven him
wild, now he was surprised that he felt nothing, not
even anger for her betrayal.

'You are wasting your time, Helene, your tricks will
not work with me now.'

She raised her finely pencilled brows, as if to imply
she did not believe him. Relieved that he was no longer in thrall to the woman, Garrick plucked her hand
from his sleeve and carried it to his lips. A brief, final
salute, for old times' sake.

'Go back to your husband, madam. You deserve one
another.'

He saw the flash of anger in her eyes and thought

for a moment that perhaps it was not wise to snub her. But he could not regret it. She had hurt him too much as a boy. It was good to know she no longer held any power over him.

Pru was standing with her aunt, watching the dancing when Garrick emerged from the card room. Not that she had been looking out for him. Of course not. It was merely that his tall, impressive figure was hard to miss. Her eyes followed him, admiring his lithe movements and remembering how well he danced. He was a large man but he had the natural grace of a sportsman.

The crowd had thinned a little and there was no one obscuring Pru's view. She saw Lady Conyers approach the duke, precious stones glistening from her golden curls. They were talking, the lady standing very close, her hand on the duke's arm. Every movement was designed to attract, thought Pru, unable to drag her eyes away. Garrick kissed the lady's hand and she noted how his eyes followed Lady Conyers as she moved off. A shiver ran down her spine. He was still in love with the beautiful Helene.

Garrick was hoping to find Jack and make his escape when he was waylaid by Lady Shrivenham. She was not about to allow a duke to slip away when there were ladies in need of dance partners. Resigning himself to his fate, Garrick gave in to the blandishments of his hostess. He fulfilled his obligations for the rest of the evening, smiling, dancing and saying all that was necessary to his partners. An exemplary guest, as he told Jack Callater when they finally made their way down the grand staircase at the end of the night.

'I hope you are satisfied!'

'It's a start, Garr.' Jack laughed as they stepped into the hall, where the guests were milling around, waiting for their carriages. 'Admit it, man, you enjoyed yourself! You always liked dancing.'

'I wish now I had spent the last few hours in the card room, as you did.'

'But *I* had already done my duty and danced with all the prettiest young ladies.'

Not all of them, thought Garrick, his eyes resting on a willowy lady in a rose silk cloak. She was standing at the foot of the stairs and, as if aware of his gaze, she turned and looked up, her grey eyes widening and a faint blush staining her cheeks. They were so close there was no avoiding her, even if he had wished to.

'Miss Clifford.'

'Your Grace. I am waiting for my aunt and Lady Borcaster...'

Garrick felt Jack's sharp nudge in his ribs and said, 'Will you allow me to present to you my good friend, Lord John Callater?'

He watched as Jack made an elegant bow and exchanged a few words with Prudence, drawing a shy smile from her with something he said. Curse it, the fellow was always so charming! Handsome, too. And the eldest son of a marquess. Was it any wonder he had ladies throwing themselves at his feet?

Not that Jack ever did more than indulge in a little flirtation with any lady, but that was enough to have some of them sinking into a decline once his interest had waned. Garrick did not want that to happen to Pru.

At last they moved on. Jack took his arm as they strolled in the direction of Dover Street, making their way past the string of carriages waiting at the side of the road.

'So that is Miss Prudence Clifford.'

'What of it?' Garrick was on the defensive.

'She was your waltz partner. I hope she appreciates the honour you have done her.'

'She is far too sensible for that!'

'But you like her, I think. Have you known her long?'

'We met in Bath.'

The moment the words were out, Garrick knew he had made an error.

'Really? When you went there to propose to Miss Speke? Or have you made another visit since?'

'Damn you, Jack, you know I have only been to the cursed place once! We met there by chance.'

'And you met again in town. How, may I ask, when you did not come here *to be sociable*?'

'She accosted me in Green Park,' Garrick admitted. 'She is a most resourceful lady.'

The memory evoked a smile, but it disappeared at Jack's next words.

'She has set her cap at you, then?'

'No! The truth is, she is an interfering wench who wants to help me.'

'Is that so?' Jack's brows rose. 'There is something you are not telling me, my friend.'

Garrick realised he was going to have to explain at least some of the story.

'Miss Clifford knows about Miss Speke. When I was in Bath I was obliged to tell her what had occurred. Her sense of justice objected to Lady Tirrill's version of events, which has been circulating in town.'

'What!' Jack stopped and because of their linked arms, Garrick was obliged to halt, too. 'Do you mean she knows everything you have refused to share with me? Just how close a friend is she, Garr?'

'For heaven's sake let us walk on,' Garrick urged him. 'We cannot talk here!'

'Very well, we are nearly at Dover Street. I shall come in with you. Be sure, Garr, I shall not leave until I have had the truth of this matter!'

An hour and several glasses of brandy later, Garrick has given his friend the whole story.

Jack shook his head. 'I find it hard to believe you divulged everything to a complete stranger. And a female, at that!'

'I was very drunk and feeling incredibly sorry for myself.'

'I daresay, but even so, that is unlike you, Garr.' Jack grinned. 'And the sensible Miss Clifford wants to be your champion.'

'She *did*. Hopefully I have nipped that in the bud now.'

'Sounds like a case to me. I saw the way you looked at her, my friend. By heaven, I think you are in love!'

'Don't be so damned foolish.'

'I knew it!' Jack cried, triumphant. 'And from what you have told me of the lady, I suspect she must return your regard. So, are you going to offer for her?'

Garrick pushed himself out of the chair and took both glasses to the side table to recharge them while he considered how best to answer.

'That is out of the question.'

Jack accepted his full glass and stretched his long legs out in front of him.

'Why? Do you intend to marry an heiress?'

'You know I don't.'

'Then why not put it to the touch?'

Garrick sat down and sipped at his brandy. Jack was his oldest friend; he could not lie to him.

'I can offer her a title, but there is no fortune to go with it.'

'Would that worry the lady?'

'It would worry *me*.' He realised he meant it. 'I want to give her all the pomp and ceremony that should go with the title.'

'By heaven, Garr, you really do love her!'

Garrick threw him a fulminating glance but did not deny it. Jack sat forward.

'Make Miss Clifford an offer and let her decide. You said yourself she is a sensible lady.'

'She is. Too sensible to marry a man with my reputation, however she may defend me in public. Then there is my mother. It is impossible to take any bride to Hartland until I have made my peace with her. She could turn the whole county against us. And I need to live at Hartland if I am going to turn our fortunes around,' he added, anticipating his friend's next suggestion. 'I have neglected my duties there for too long.'

'And you prefer to do so as a lonely bachelor.'

'Hell and damnation, Jack, do you think I enjoy being pointed out to everyone as the man who drove his father to the grave?'

'No, that I will not allow,' exclaimed Jack. 'We both know that is not true. The old duke had a weak heart, caused by a life of excess. Everyone who knew him is aware of it. The duchess too, only she prefers not to acknowledge it.' He emptied his glass and rose. 'I must go—no don't get up, old friend. I will see myself out.' He put a hand on Garrick's shoulder. 'You have done ten years of penance, Garr. Time now to live your own life.

Propose to Miss Clifford, if you think she is the one for you. What's the worst she can do?'

He went out then and Garrick was left alone to consider his words. The worst? His hands closed tighter around his brandy glass.

She had not laughed him as Helene had done, when he had been a mere stripling in the throes of his first love affair. Neither had she run away like Annabelle Speke, who preferred to leave her home and everything she had known rather than be his wife.

Pru's rejection had been kindly meant, he knew that, but it had hurt him far more than the others.

Chapter Fourteen

Following the Shrivenham Ball, Lady Borcaster developed a slight chill and did not leave her house for several days. Mrs Clifford and Pru kept her company, not wishing to attend any of the various entertainments without their hostess. Pru was grateful for a quiet period of reflection, because the attentions of the Duke of Hartland at the ball had left her confused and perplexed.

She had thought her rejection of his proposal had put an end to their friendship, but the interlude on the balcony proved that was not the case. The bond between them seemed as strong as ever. Yet the feelings that had raged through Pru when she saw him with Helene Conyers proved that friendship was not enough for her. She concluded it would be better to avoid his company altogether.

She hoped that being confined to Brook Street would help her to forget about Garrick Chauntry, but alas, a week after the ball, the duke was once more thrust into her thoughts. She was quietly engaged with the other ladies in the morning room when the butler came in, asking if Her Ladyship was at home to visitors.

'Lady Applecross is here to see you, ma'am.'

'Yes, yes, Cotton. I am quite recovered now,' said Lady Borcaster. 'Send her up. I am sure we could all do with a little amusement after being cooped up for so long.'

But then Lady Applecross hurried in and her news was not in the least amusing. She barely waited for the butler to withdraw before bursting into speech.

'My dear Lady Borcaster, have you heard the news? I had it from my sister Mrs Johnby this very morning and came directly to see you. And to warn Miss Clifford.'

Lady Borcaster stared at her visitor. 'News? Warn Prudence? My dear ma'am, pray sit down and tell us what on earth is the matter.'

'I can hardly credit it myself,' said Lady Applecross, sinking onto a chair. 'I know there have been rumours, but nothing prepares one for it…'

'For what, ma'am?' Lady Borcaster pressed her.

'The Duke of Hartland. Spying for the French! A witness has come forward.'

Pru clutched the arms of her chair. 'I do not believe it.'

'Alas, there can be no doubt now, Miss Clifford.' Lady Applecross gave her a pitying look. 'I know you want to think well of His Grace, but I understand there can be no doubting the evidence. Letters, papers, a sworn statement…his accuser was a junior official in Bonaparte's cabinet. He saw Hartland in Paris, and in the company of the monster's most loyal ministers.'

'And where did you learn this, ma'am?' enquired Aunt Minerva.

'Applecross himself heard it at his club. Everyone is talking of it.'

'But has anyone spoken to the duke?' asked Pru.

Lady Applecross fluttered one hand. 'Oh, he has denied it, of course, although one sees very little of him these days. What else can he do? And he has his supporters, but this does appear to confirm all the rumours that have been flying about concerning him.'

'Good heavens, a spy!' exclaimed Lady Borcaster, 'Surely the man should be locked up.'

Another pitying look, but not this time at Pru.

'He is a *duke*, ma'am,' Lady Applecross replied. 'He cannot be clapped in gaol without very good reason.'

'And the evidence might yet prove to be false,' put in Mrs Clifford, with an anxious look at her niece.

Lady Applecross gave a little shrug. 'That is unlikely. My lord tells me the witness is in hiding, fearing for his safety. Which is why I came directly to see you all this morning, and to caution Miss Clifford.'

Lady Borcaster fell back in her chair and closed her eyes in dismay. 'I *knew* she should not have danced with him at the Shrivenhams. The waltz, too! Oh, my dear Prudence, I am sorry now I insisted you take lessons.'

'Quite.' Lady Applecross nodded. 'It will do her no good at all to be too closely associated with the Duke of Hartland at the present time.' She hesitated again. 'It would also reflect badly upon her relatives and friends.'

While the three older ladies continued to speculate over the matter, Prudence was silent. Indeed, what could she say? The duke had told her he was no spy and she believed him, but how could she defend him, when the evidence was so strong, and Lady Applecross had pointed out that her actions might rebound upon her aunt and Lady Borcaster. Galling as it was for her to sit idly by, Pru would have to wait until she knew more.

Lady Borcaster's recovery meant the resumption of a busy social round of balls, routs and breakfasts, to say nothing of visiting the most fashionable shops and silk warehouses. Prudence saw nothing of Garrick and she did not know whether to be reassured or worried that he had withdrawn from society again.

Then came the news Pru was dreading. She was engaged in mending a flounce on her walking dress when her aunt came in, clutching a folded newspaper.

'Oh, my dear Prudence, the accusations against the Duke of Hartland,' she cried. 'They are all too true!'

'Indeed they are,' added Lady Borcaster, following her friend into the room. 'Lady Applecross sent word early this morning, telling me to look out for it in today's *Morning Post*. It is all there, reports of the letters, the accusations, even details from the witness's statement.'

Prudence took the folded newspaper and scanned the page. She wanted to argue that they did not accuse Garrick by name, but that would be foolish. Who else could they mean by *the D— of H—*?

'I thought he had been in Vienna,' was all she could think to say.

'He was abroad for some years and it is very likely he visited many places,' replied Aunt Minerva. 'But you will see, there is evidence he was in Paris on the dates his accuser mentions.' She sighed. 'It looks very bad for the poor man, I have to say.'

Pru ran her tongue over her dry lips. 'Has he been arrested?'

'Not yet,' said Lady Borcaster. 'Lady Applecross says he has been questioned, but nothing more. If Sir Timothy were in England, I would ask him to look into it. As it is, we must rely upon my friends and the newspapers for information. I am only thankful we have kept a proper distance.'

A proper distance! Pru fought down a slightly hysterical laugh at that.

Lady Borcaster went on, 'He only called here the once, when I was out, and you sent him away, did you not, Minerva?'

'Why, yes,' replied Mrs Clifford, with a quick, guilty look of apology towards her niece. 'Yes, I did.'

Prudence was well aware her aunt had not disclosed the reason for the duke's visit to their hostess and guessed she must now be profoundly thankful for it. She sat down beside Pru and laid a hand on her arm.

'I am so very sorry for this, my love.'

'If he is cleared, of course, then I should be happy to welcome him here to Brook Street,' declared Lady Borcaster. 'Until then, I would advise that you have nothing more to do with the man, Prudence.'

'No, of course. I understand.'

My lady smiled, clearly relieved at Pru's quiet acquiescence, but after a moment she threw up her hands, exclaiming, 'Goodness, what a to-do! I have no doubt it will be the main subject of conversation at Carlton House tonight.'

The idea of listening to everyone gossiping and gloating over the subject made Pru feel slightly sick.

'Must I go, ma'am?'

Aunt Minerva stared at her. 'Of course you must go, my dear. The Prince Regent's ball! We shall never have such an opportunity again.'

'Yes, yes, you must go, Prudence,' declared her hostess. 'Why, it will be the grandest event of the season and it would be a great shame for you to cry off now, especially when Sir Timothy went to such lengths to procure the invitation. Heaven knows whom he had to impress to add my name to the list! My dear, Field Marshall the Duke of Wellington himself will be present. Think of how much you will have to tell your friends, when you return to Bath.'

Pru realised she was in danger of offending her hostess and she quickly tried to repair the damage.

'Then of course I shall go. It was very thoughtful of Sir Timothy to ask his friends to arrange this for you while he was away and I do not want to see his efforts wasted.'

'Indeed, it was. My Susan was very lucky to find such a husband.'

She stopped, looking a little guiltily at Prudence, as if regretting her young friend's misfortune in not being similarly blessed. There was an awkward silence and Aunt Minerva stepped into the breach.

'Well, well, I am sure it is a very great honour, Jane, and we are very grateful you wish us to go with you. We must make sure we are all looking our best this evening. Prudence, my love, I shall lend you my diamonds!'

And that, thought Prudence ruefully, was all that appeared to matter. The Duke of Hartland was forgotten as the two older ladies decided upon what jewels they would wear for the ball.

Myriad lamps were already twinkling at Carlton House when Lady Borcaster's party arrived. They moved slowly forward with the crowd and for once the colourful gowns of the ladies were overshadowed by the magnificence of the uniforms on display. Even Lady Borcaster was impressed.

'My dears, the assembly bears a strong resemblance to a military fête,' she remarked, her bright eyes sweeping over the crowd. 'And I see several old friends here, including General Lechlade!'

She sailed off to accost her elderly admirer, leaving Pru and her aunt to follow in her wake.

'Well, this is such a crush I am sure there will be no room for dancing,' declared Aunt Minerva as they moved into yet another lavish reception room. 'I—' She broke off suddenly and gripped Pru's arm. 'My dear, look who is here! I suppose, given his rank, I should have expected it, but how he has the nerve to show his face I do not know.'

But Pru had already seen the Duke of Hartland walking towards them.

Garrick had come early to Carlton House. He might curse Castlereagh for insisting he be included in these events, but for once the invitation was useful, since it allowed him to meet with several persons he needed to see, rather than going through the official channels, where it could take weeks to grant an appointment. However, it would be best not to stay. With the current accusations about him flying around, his presence might prove embarrassing to the royal family.

As soon as his business was concluded, Garrick made his way back through the rooms to the entrance. He was halfway across the chamber celebrating the country's military triumphs when he saw Pru. She was wearing a gown of kingfisher blue trimmed with cream lace and a diaphanous spangled scarf draped over her arms. Diamonds winked at her throat and ears, and her hair was piled up on her head with only a few soft curls framing her face. Garrick's breath caught in his chest. He had seen many beautiful ladies this evening, most of them far more lavishly dressed than Prudence Clifford, but she was the one who held his attention.

He thought she looked glorious.

Even if he had wished to avoid a meeting, he could not do it without turning back. Mrs Clifford and her niece were standing just inside the double doors that marked his exit. A few more steps and he was standing before them. He bowed and received the smallest of curtsies in return. One look at Pru's face told him she had heard the rumours.

'Come, my dear,' said Mrs Clifford, clutching her niece's arm. 'We dare not lose sight of Lady Borcaster. Your Grace, if you will excuse us?'

'Of course.'

He stepped aside, keeping his eyes on Prudence and willing her to look at him, but she stared resolutely ahead. Nothing could be clearer. She believed those damning stories about him. The sudden pain he felt took his breath away and at that moment he realised just how much he cared for her good opinion.

Garrick turned and continued on his way until he was out of the building and on his way back to Dover Street. As soon as he had learned of the accusations, he had fired off several letters and his efforts tonight had resulted in promises of support, but those who could help him most were out of the country, and their replies could take weeks. In the meantime, details of the accusations were appearing everywhere. Garrick knew he would be exonerated eventually, but for now there was nothing he could do to prove his innocence or prevent a scandal bigger than any other clouding the Hartland name.

Chapter Fifteen

Pru accompanied her aunt through the crowded rooms, seeing nothing of the elegant decorations or the military trophies on display. Garrick's rugged countenance was imprinted on her mind. Their brief meeting had only increased her confusion.

He had looked grim and drawn, the eyes shuttered against expression, but he had none of the swagger of a man attempting to cover his guilt. She wondered if she was merely trying to convince herself of his innocence, but the conviction remained stubbornly in place, even when they reached the tented ballroom.

Lady Borcaster was in her element. As the widow of a prominent diplomat, she was well acquainted with many of the guests and able to recognise most of the important figures present. She performed numerous introductions and Pru could only nod when her aunt whispered that they would never remember the half of them.

There was no shortage of dance partners for Prudence, who obligingly stood up for several dances without pause. It was as she was leaving the dance floor after a particularly energetic reel that she glimpsed a familiar face. It was Lord John Callater, the man Garrick had introduced to her as they were leaving the Shrivenham Ball.

Pru quickly dismissed her escort and slipped through the crowd to follow her quarry.

'Good evening, Lord John.'

'Miss Clifford.' He gave a smile of recognition. 'Quite a crush is it not?'

'Yes.' She clasped her hands together. 'I saw Sir Garrick here earlier.'

'Why yes, but he did not stay.'

The smile remained in place but she saw the wary look in his eyes. She must take her chance.

'Is he quite well, my lord?'

'As well as one can expect.'

It was a cautious reply and Pru hesitated. This was really none of her business. Garrick would not thank her for it, yet she could not turn back now.

'You are his friend, I believe,' she said, keeping her eyes on his face. 'His *good* friend, he called you. I have heard. That is…'

She was floundering and Lord John held out his arm. 'Let us go to one of the supper tents. There will be only the servants there at this hour, and they will not disturb us. We shall tell them you were feeling faint and then we will be able to talk privately.'

Amazed at her own temerity, Prudence accompanied him. She was very sorry for the gentleman who would look in vain for his next dance partner, but it could not be helped.

A short time later she was sitting at one end of a long supper table with Lord John beside her.

'You should make use of your fan,' he suggested, smiling. 'Swiftly, as if you are overcome with the heat.'

'Yes, of course.'

'Now.' He swung his quizzing glass idly but his gaze remained watchful. 'How much do you know?'

'Only gossip, and what I have read in the newspapers.'

'Well, there is some truth to the allegations.'

She raised her eyes to his in alarm and after a moment he gave a little nod.

'Garrick trusts you, so I will, too, and tell you what the duke has discovered so far. His accuser, Albert Vence, had some minor role in Bonaparte's government. His statement is in most respects correct. Garrick was in Paris at that time and he did have meetings with some of Bonaparte's ministers, but not the ones mentioned by Vence. The duke is not, nor ever was, a *French* spy.'

Relief flood through her. Lord John leaned closer.

'I tell you this in confidence, Miss Clifford, because I believe you have the duke's interests at heart.'

'I do. He thinks me interfering but...'

'You care for him.'

She felt the tell-tale blush warming her face. 'As I would for anyone wrongly accused!'

'Of course.' He spoke gravely, but Pru wondered if he believed her. How much had Garrick told him about her? He went on, 'The thing is, Miss Clifford, Lord Castlereagh is the only one who can vouch for Garrick. But he is out of the country and it will be some time before we can expect a response from him.'

Pru plied the fan more quickly, trying to hide the sudden fear that gripped her, but Lord John was not fooled. He smiled slightly.

'It is not quite so bad. Two witnesses would be required to testify in order to gain a conviction, but whoever is doing this either has no idea of the law, or has merely set this particular hare running to cast more slurs upon Garrick's good name.'

'And the longer it goes on, the more damage it will do,' she added bitterly. 'I observed for myself how society gloated over the earlier rumours. It made me so angry!'

'Aye, Garr told me you had tried to be his champion.'

'Champion!' She flushed at that. 'I doubt that was the word he used for me.'

He grinned. 'Well, no. The duke has never been one to accept help easily, but he needs it now. If you are willing.'

'Me?' she looked at him in surprise. 'No, no, Lord John. You are far better placed to help him than I.'

'Alas, ma'am, I have the reputation of being a frippery fellow, whose only interest is fashion. I should be looked upon with suspicion if I begin asking questions. Also, everyone knows Hartland and I have been friends since childhood.'

Pru looked at him. 'Why should that be a hindrance? Surely everyone will understand your wish to discover the truth?'

'Not everyone, Miss Clifford. The person who instigated this mischief will not wish for it to be concluded too soon.'

'And you know who that is?'

'No. My first thought was that Lady Tirrill had started it, out of spite, but Garrick says not.' He gave a sigh of exasperation. 'The duke can be damned tight-lipped when he chooses! I will be frank with you, Miss Clifford. He wants me to leave well alone. He insists the truth will out in due course.'

'He is trying to protect you.'

'From what?' Lord John frowned at her. 'What is it that you are not telling me, ma'am?'

Pru hesitated. What did she know of this man, after all?

She said at last, 'If you are indeed the duke's close friend, you will know about the, the duel that caused him to leave England?'

'Aye, it was a dashed hum! Garr was bamboozled by a woman. It hit him very hard…but never mind that. Go on, ma'am.'

'The duke's opponent in that duel is in town now. Earlier this summer I overheard him spreading rumours about the duke being a French agent. I told His Grace, but he refused to act. He said the gossip would die down of its own accord and that I should leave well alone, which I did. Then, a week ago, the allegations appeared in the *Morning Post*…'

'And you think it is the sneaking husband that Garrick wounded in the duel? Damnation, if only I could remember the doxy's name…'

Prudence swallowed, unable to speak the lady's name. Then she gave herself a mental shake. This was no time for missish hysterics.

'Conyers,' she said. 'He is now Sir Joseph Conyers, and the last time I saw him was at the Shrivenham Ball, three weeks since. It was very clear there is no love lost between him and the duke.'

'I can imagine, after the dastardly trick he and his lady played upon Garrick.' Lord John frowned. 'It is possible he is involved, I suppose, although after all this time—'

Pru felt the knot of anxiety tighten inside. Perhaps Sir Joseph was merely passing on tittle-tattle he had heard, and if that were the case then how were they ever to discover the culprit?

'Very well,' declared Lord John, 'I will make enquiries, and I would be grateful for anything you can discover, Miss Clifford. Lady Borcaster has acquaintances in government circles—I hope they might be able to tell you more about this Frenchman.'

'I believe there is a charitable society set up to support the émigrés,' said Pru, frowning a little. 'I have read reports of it. A scandal like this will certainly be of interest to them. They may even know who the man may be.'

'Good. How does one find them, talk to them?'

This was familiar territory for Pru. She said, 'I have some knowledge of charitable work, Lord John. Leave that to me.'

'Thank you, I shall. Let us agree to meet again. Shall we say Wednesday next, in Green Park?'

Pru recalled her meeting there with Garrick. How long ago that seemed now. How much had happened since.

'What is it, Miss Clifford?' Lord John interrupted her thoughts. 'Do you not think the park a suitable place for a rendezvous?'

'I think the circulating library would be better,' she suggested. 'My aunt and I are regular subscribers to Hatchards, in Piccadilly.'

'Then we shall meet there. If you need to contact me in the meantime, you can send a message to Albany, where I have rooms.'

'Pray do not be too hopeful of my helping, sir. I am not sure I can be of any use at all.'

'Garr confided in you, Miss Clifford. He also told me you are a very resourceful lady. That is a high compliment coming from the duke, I assure you. His experience of your sex has not been the happiest.' He rose. 'I had best get you back to the ballroom before we are missed.'

'Yes, indeed.' She smiled, trying to be as resourceful as Garrick thought her. 'Let me go in first. It will not do to have anyone think we are plotting.'

The rest of the evening was a trial for Pru. She was on the alert now for any whisper regarding the duke. Not that there was any lack of gossip, but it was the sort of tittle-tattle she had heard many times and from people who could have little knowledge of the facts. The more she considered the matter, the more she was convinced that Sir Joseph Conyers was behind this latest scurrilous attack.

When the ladies finally climbed into their carriage, Pru sat quietly in her corner, going over her conversation with Lord John Callater. They were almost at Brook Street when her attention was caught. Lady Borcaster was discussing with Aunt Minerva the evening party she was planning for early the following week.

'I shall be delighted to help with the arrangements, Jane,' declared Minerva. 'It is very kind of you to put on this little party for us. Do you not agree, Pru?'

'I do indeed, Aunt. Who is invited, ma'am?'

'Oh, it will be a quiet affair, my dear. A dozen or so close friends whose company I think you might enjoy. And perhaps we may have a few country dances for the younger ones, if we remove some of the furniture.'

Pru brushed a speck of dust from her skirts, saying casually, 'Are Sir Joseph and Lady Conyers invited?'

'They are not,' replied my lady. 'I did not take to the

man, although I hear he is quite the favourite now, and invited everywhere.'

'I have heard that, too,' replied Pru. 'I wonder, then if perhaps you should include him?'

Lady Borcaster chuckled. 'Oh, that is a relief! I was very much afraid you were going to suggest I should invite the Duke of Hartland! Given his present circumstances, I should have had to refuse you, my dear.'

'I understand that,' said Pru. 'But going back to Sir Joseph, I think perhaps it would not do to be backwards in any attention.'

'Goodness, Prudence, you are becoming quite at home in town, these days,' declared her aunt, impressed.

'But she is quite right, Minerva. If the man is a rising star, then Sir Timothy would wish me to further the acquaintance. Although, my dear Prudence, I was under the opinion that *you* did not care for him.'

'No, ma'am, my first impression was not favourable, but I think that was because I am not accustomed to society manners.'

Her explanation appeared to satisfy Lady Borcaster. Nothing more was said, and when Prudence climbed into bed that night, she realised the die was cast. She would do what she could to discover if Sir Joseph was behind the accusations against the Duke of Hartland.

Chapter Sixteen

Lady Borcaster's reception rooms were transformed. Furniture had been rearranged or removed to make space and the hostess had the satisfaction of knowing that apart from one elderly dowager, who was indisposed, not one of her invitations had been refused.

Pru was already acquainted with most of the guests, but there were a number of government ministers whom she did not know. She did her best to be polite and charming to all of them; if the duke was arrested, it might be useful to have such contacts. When Sir Joseph arrived with his beautiful wife, Pru was in no hurry to approach them. She was not sure what she would say, or even what she expected from the evening.

In the event it was Sir Joseph who made the first move. Lady Conyers was on the far side of the room, flirting with one of the government ministers, when her husband came up to Pru. They exchanged civilities and a passing waiter afforded Sir Joseph the opportunity to procure two glasses of wine.

He handed one to Prudence, remarking, 'I see your favourite is not here tonight, Miss Clifford.'

'Oh, who had you in mind, sir?' Her look was all innocent enquiry.

'Hartland.'

She frowned, as if having difficulty placing the name. 'Ah, the Duke of Hartland. I remember him now. I have not seen him since the Shrivenham Ball.'

'You danced the waltz with him.' Sir Joseph was smiling, but his hooded eyes were watching her closely. 'Some might think that dance a bold choice for a single lady.'

Pru's eyes widened. 'But since the Tsar's visit *everyone* is dancing the waltz.'

'You refused to waltz with *me*, if my memory serves.'

'Because I was already engaged.' She added, hoping to stop him asking her to dance again, 'To be honest, Sir Joseph, I did not really enjoy the experience.'

'Perhaps it was the choice of partner that was at fault,' he purred. There was a lascivious glint in those hooded eyes and she was obliged to suppress a shudder.

'Perhaps it was.'

He laughed softly. 'And His Grace is quite out of favour now, is he not? I suppose that is why he is not present.'

'This is Lady Borcaster's party, sir. She and my aunt wrote the invitations. But I am quite content with the company, I assure you.'

Pru could not replicate his lady's flirtatious glances, but she gave him her sunniest smile, and there was no mistaking Sir Joseph's satisfaction with her response. He remained at her side, conversing on unexceptional topics until Lady Conyers came up to them.

'There you are, Joseph. I should have known I would find you with a pretty young lady.'

Her friendly smile should have robbed the words of any offence, but Prudence felt a chill of apprehension. She knew her opinion was coloured by what Garrick had told her of the beautiful Helene, but she could not like the woman. She sincerely hoped the duke was no longer in thrall to her.

'Miss Clifford and I have been having the most interesting coze, my sweet.'

'Indeed?' She turned those limpid blue eyes back to Pru, who wondered if she was being assessed as useful, or a rival.

'Yes, most interesting. Have you invited Lady Borcaster to join us tomorrow, Helene? I hope you made it clear that her guests are invited, too.'

'Why, of course, although I am not sure our little party will be quite to Miss Clifford's taste. There will be no music, no entertainment.' She pursed her mouth into a comical moue. 'I fear the conversation will be all politics.'

'I should be delighted to attend,' cried Prudence. 'This is my first, possibly my only visit to London, and I am anxious to enjoy everything I can!'

Her enthusiastic response appeared to please Sir Joseph, if not his wife, although Helene did her best to appear gracious when she replied.

'Then we look forward to welcoming you tomorrow evening, Miss Clifford. Your aunt, too.' She slipped her hand onto her husband's arm. 'Come, my love. Let us seek out Lady Borcaster now and make sure there is no misunderstanding.'

They moved away and Prudence felt the tension easing in her shoulders. Dissimulation was abhorrent to her but she had an invitation into the Conyerses' inner circle, and she must make the most of it. For Garrick's sake.

Sir Joseph had rented a house for the season, not far from Brook Street, and Lady Borcaster decided they should take chairs, rather than call out her carriage for such a short journey. They arrived to find the house glittering with light and the reception rooms already full.

'There is no denying he has done very well for himself,' muttered Lady Borcaster, casting an approving glance around the assembly. 'Two government ministers, a former treasury minister, as well as Lord and Lady Fauls. Sir Joseph has ambitions in a political direction, I suspect.'

'Is that a bad thing?' Pru asked her.

'No, no, although I suspect his politics will shift with the prevailing wind.'

On this cryptic statement Lady Borcaster carried off Mrs Clifford to greet a bejewelled matron, leaving Prudence to her own devices. She did not object; she had several acquaintances amongst the guests and went off to sit down with a little cluster of ladies who welcomed her in a very friendly way.

The wine flowed freely and the conversation became much more relaxed as the evening wore on. Prudence tried to circulate, never stopping too long with any one group. As she expected, she soon heard mention of the Duke of Hartland. Some people were shocked by the revelations concerning him, others gloated over his misfortunes. One matron was particularly scathing in her comments and Prudence was surprised when Sir Joseph, who was passing, stopped and wagged a playful finger at the speaker.

'Now, now, Lady Slocombe, we must not be hasty in our judgements.'

'Hasty!' scoffed the lady. 'The man's a rogue. I have heard nothing but scandal attached to his name this season. *And* I am old enough to remember the grief he caused his sainted father when he first came to town all those years ago. What *I* say, Sir Joseph, is that a leopard does not change his spots!'

Her host laughed gently. 'Perhaps not, but one should not judge a fellow on his youthful peccadillos. We must be charitable and believe the best of a man until it is proven otherwise.'

Listening to this interchange, Pru felt a slight quiver of uncertainty at his words. Perhaps she was wrong about the man. Then he turned away from the group and she saw the smirk of satisfaction on his face as he walked off. Her doubts vanished like smoke.

By midnight, Pru had seen and heard enough. She was ready to leave, but Lady Borcaster and her aunt were enjoying themselves and she resigned herself to staying for another hour at least. She moved away from the chattering groups and amused herself by looking at the various paintings that adorned the walls. Most were copies of famous landscapes or scenes from the classical world, but on one wall she found a pleasant little watercolour. It was so different from everything else that she stepped closer to examine it.

'Had enough of politics, Miss Clifford?'

She turned to find the Earl of Fauls at her shoulder, smiling at her in his good-natured way.

'I am very ignorant of such matters, my lord, and fear I have little to offer,' she said, ruefully. 'Is it very bad of me not to join in?'

'No, no, not a bit of it! But if you are hoping to improve your knowledge of art you won't do so here.' He stepped a little closer to the wall, raising his quizzing glass to inspect a gaudy landscape. 'Copies, all of 'em, and not the best, either.'

She acknowledged this with a smile. 'I thought as much. But this is not a copy, surely?'

She indicated the watercolour.

'No, that is a depiction of Alder Grove. Somewhere near Dartford, I believe. It used to be the Conyerses' family seat, although Sir Joseph has recently vacated it and bought himself a new property in Buckinghamshire. Much more in keeping with his ambition.'

She detected the slight disapproval in the Earl's tone and ventured to comment.

'That is the second time I have heard the word *ambition* used in connection with our host,' she remarked. 'Is he planning on entering politics?'

'If he was offered a sinecure, perhaps. Something to advance his own fortunes.'

The Earl stopped. He looked a little uncomfortable, as if he had been caught out in an indiscretion and changed the subject. Pru made no attempt to question him further but when she finally climbed into her chair for the journey back to Brook Street she felt sadly deflated. She had learned nothing that might help Garrick. Nothing at all.

Wednesday dawned wet, and the rain had barely ceased when Prudence set off with her maid for her meeting with Lord John Callater. She decided to wear the walking dress of flax-blue muslin with the sarsnet pelisse that she had purchased from Mrs Bell. The pelisse was trimmed *à la Russe*, and had a matching bonnet *à la militaire* and, regarding herself in the long glass, Pru was quite pleased with the result. She thought that at last she might be acquiring what Lady Borcaster termed *town bronze*.

Hatchards bookshop and circulating library in Piccadilly was Pru's destination, a reasonable walk but Pru enjoyed the exercise. When they reached the door, she handed her umbrella to Meg and left the maid to wait outside the bow windows while she stepped into the shop. She politely waved aside the assistant who hurried towards her and made her way over to the bookshelves, where she had spotted Lord John Callater.

It was only when he turned to greet her that Pru noticed Garrick Chauntry standing in the alcove behind him.

Lord John touched his hat to her. 'Miss Clifford, good morning to you.'

She heard the note of warning in his voice and schooled her face to one of surprise.

'Why, Lord John, good day to you. And to you, Your Grace.'

The duke was glaring at her but not by the flicker of an eyelid would she betray any agitation at seeing him.

'My aunt asked me to collect a book for her,' she explained, adding with a twinkle, 'However, I can never enter a bookshop without taking a moment to browse their stock.'

'Exactly, ma'am,' replied Lord John. 'That was just my intention this morning, then Hartland arrived and decided to accompany me.'

Garrick uttered a small growl of annoyance.

'There is no need to carry on with this charade, Jack,' he said bluntly. 'I knew from the outset that you were up to something.'

'Now, Garr…'

'Don't *now Garr* me! What is going on?'

Pru interrupted them, aware of the helpful assistant hovering nearby.

'I thought I might look at those books over there, on the next counter.'

She moved across to a more deserted area of the shop and the two gentlemen followed her.

'Have you read this one, Your Grace?' She picked up a book and glanced through it. 'I thought it might interest my aunt.'

'Byron's *Corsair*. A courageous choice.' His eyes glinted at her. 'I do believe you are heading into dangerous waters, Miss Clifford.'

She did not pretend to misunderstand him, but before she could reply Lord John cut in, keeping his voice low.

'Enough, Garr. Miss Clifford and I want to help you!'

Garrick was doing his best to keep his temper. To discover that the two people he trusted most were conspiring against him was almost too much! He selected a book at random and inspected the cover.

'I have told you,' he ground out. 'I neither want nor need help.'

'You really have no choice in the matter,' retorted Prudence. 'If you insist on being obstinate then I suggest you go away and leave Lord John and I to handle the whole.'

'And allow you both to put yourselves in peril?'

His friend pounced on that. 'Aha, you admit your situation is dangerous!'

'No, Jack. My situation will resolve itself, in time.'

'And meanwhile your good name is sullied. Dash it, Garr, what sort of friend would I be if I allowed that?'

'Quite right, my lord,' Prudence agreed, smiling her approval.

Garrick scowled. He recognised that stubborn tilt to Pru's chin and Jack was staring at him, challenging him to argue. Damned fools, both of them!

He sighed, his anger fading. He did not deserve friends like this.

'Very well,' he muttered. 'Tell me what you have discovered.'

Jack's frown was telling.

'To be truthful, nothing that can advance our cause. The Frenchman is in London, but I could not find out where, nor who brought him here. Perhaps Miss Clifford has had more luck?'

'Alas, no. I attended the Conyerses' soirée last night and, from what I learned, Sir Joseph is clearly intent upon gaining favour at Whitehall.'

Garrick met her eyes. She was expecting him to say I told you so, but he refrained. He had no wish to tease her. He wanted to drag her into his arms and cover her face with kisses. Or carry her back to Dover Street and take her to his bed. What he would give to hear her moan with pleasure again…

Damnation he must stop thinking about that!

'I see.' Quickly, he turned away. 'And is that all, ma'am?'

'Well, I am taking tea with Lady Elsdon later today,' she said. 'She has established the Philanthropic Society for the Relief of French Émigrés and is raising funds for them. I am hoping I might learn something there.'

Garrick nodded, forcing himself to think about charitable causes rather than the delights of the flesh. It worked, for now, and he was able to concentrate on what she was proposing. He could not see how visiting Lady Elsdon would help his cause and a glance at Jack's face told him his friend thought very much the same. However, he did not wish to dampen Pru's spirits and it seemed an innocent enough activity for her. He nodded.

'Good idea, that might be useful.'

The pleasure in her face caught at his heart. He reached out towards her, only to snatch his hand back again immediately. But he was not quick enough, she had seen the gesture and understood it. He knew that from the way her grey eyes softened and warmed. She believed in him, which made his spirits rise. If only she did not think of him as an object of pity!

Garrick fixed his eyes on the book in his hands and said gruffly, 'You should go, Miss Clifford. The less time we spend together the better for you.'

'Of course.'

He was surprised that she did not argue with him. Disappointed, too, because he could not deny he wanted her to stay. Grasping her copy of Byron's latest tale, she walked away. He pretended to flick through the book he was holding, but all the time he was watching her, the proud tilt of her head and straight back, the way she seemed to glide across the floor.

Beside him, Jack gave a low whistle. 'Damn my eyes, Duke, if ever I saw two people more in—!'

'Enough!' barked Garrick. 'I wish to heaven you had not involved her in this damned tangle.'

Jack shrugged. 'She is unlikely to come to any harm at a tea party.' He took out his watch. 'What do you do now? I have an appointment with my tailor shortly, do you want to come with me?'

'Thank you, but no. I have another engagement.'

'Then dine with me later.'

'I do not know when I shall be back.'

Jack's eyes narrowed. 'And may one enquire where you are going?'

'No, one may not!' Aware of heads turning towards them, Garrick lowered his voice. 'I wish you would leave me to my own business.'

'Let me come with you.'

'And miss your appointment with your tailor?' he grinned. 'I assure you, Jack, it is not worth that sacrifice. Now, we have been here long enough. Let us be gone.'

'We can hardly leave without purchasing something.'

'If you recall, this was your suggestion, so you must pay. Here, take these.' He thrust a pile of books into Jack's hands.

'What is it? Oh, a novel in three volumes.'

'Aye,' said Garrick. '*Pride and Prejudice.* High time you read something other than the *Gentleman's Magazine*!'

Chapter Seventeen

Garrick and Jack parted ways at the bookshop door. Jack making his way to Jermyn Street to visit the fashionable tailor who enjoyed his patronage while Garrick raised his ebony cane to hail a passing cab. He gave the driver an address in Somers Town and settled himself back against the squabs. Then he reached into his pocket and pulled out the note he had received that morning.

It was very short, the language formal.

If His Grace wishes to present himself at the sign of the Golden Cockerel, Somers Town, today at two o'clock in the afternoon, he will find his Accuser in residence and enjoying the benefits of the Private Parlour. Alone.

A Well-Wisher

'But *is* it someone who wishes me well?' Garrick mused.

He did not recognise the hand, although the neat, precise writing suggested a man of letters. A clerk perhaps. It might well be a trap, but he was prepared for that. His grip tightened on the handle of his cane. The trusty sword stick had helped him escape far more dangerous situations during his time abroad.

It was not long before the carriage was making its way through a semi-rural area with several streets of shabby-genteel houses leading off the main highway. There were signs of recent development, but the building work appeared to have ceased, leaving unfinished shells of houses lining the road. The cab lumbered on and eventually stopped outside a small inn where a sign with a gaudily painted cockerel swung above the door.

Garrick jumped out of the cab. Everything was peaceful. The sky had cleared and a skylark trilled joyously over a nearby field. He threw a coin up to the driver, ordered him to wait and walked into the inn.

There was no sign of the landlord, but a tap boy directed Garrick to the private parlour and received sixpence for his pains. Garrick hesitated for a heartbeat in the passage before going in. There was only one occupant in the room, a small man in the plain black coat and knee breeches of a clerk. As he heard the door open, the man jumped up. He looked frightened, but not startled. As if he had been expecting a visitor, which put Garrick on his guard.

'Good day to you,' he said pleasantly, closing the door behind him. 'Monsieur Albert Vence, is it not?'

'*Oui, Excellence.*' The man had backed away a little, towards a door at the side of the room.

'You know who I am?'

'*Oui.* The Duke of 'artland.'

Garrick studied the man, taking in the slightly shabby clothes and thin face. He could not remember seeing him before.

He said, 'Forgive me, monsieur, but have we met?'

'I know you, Your Grace. I saw you in Paris.'

'Did you indeed?' drawled Garrick, leaning on his cane. 'Do remind me, when was that?'

'Three years ago. I was a clerk in the office of the Comte de Montalivet.'

'The French minister of the interior?'

'*Oui, Excellence.* You came to see him.' Vence licked his lips, nervously. '*Mais*, you were not the Duc then.'

'We both know you are lying. I never met with Montalivet. Who is paying you?'

'I—I do not know what you mean.' The man was visibly shaking now.

'I think you do,' said Garrick. 'Tell me—'

Vence turned and hammered on the door beside him. '*M'aidez! Viens!*'

Almost immediately two men appeared and stepped in front of Vence.

'This is a private parlour,' barked one, a tall spare man with a balding head. 'What is your business here?'

'He is the Duke of 'artland,' shrieked Vence, cowering against the wall. 'He is come t-to k-kill me.'

Garrick frowned. 'Nonsense.'

The men looked uneasily at one another.

'Is it true?' asked the tall man.

'It is true I am Hartland,' said Garrick, 'but I only came here to talk—'

'He attacked me!' cried Vence.

The second man stepped forward and cleared his throat. 'If it please, Your Grace, you should not be here. We have been instructed that Monsieur Vence is to see no one.'

'Instructed by whom?' Garrick demanded.

'The home secretary, Lord Sidmouth.'

Garrick considered this. Both men were dressed

neatly in dark tailcoats and cream trousers. Not servants, he thought, but quite possibly Whitehall aides.

The balding one edged over to the door and opened it. 'Please leave, Your Grace. We cannot allow you to stay here.'

Garrick knew he would get nothing more from the Frenchman now and he nodded.

'Very well, I'll go. But you will have to answer my questions in court, Monsieur Vence, under oath!'

On that parting shot he went out. The door closed behind him and he heard the key scrape in the lock. Aye, let them keep the fellow safe. Vence would not hold out long under questioning.

Garrick climbed into the waiting cab and set off back to town. Whoever had found the Frenchman was playing a dirty game. Garrick could not remember Vence, but it was possible the fellow had seen him in Paris, although not with Bonaparte's loyal ministers. Far from it. But why would the fellow perjure himself, unless someone was paying him well for his false testimony?

He pondered the idea as the carriage rumbled back towards town, slowing down to pick its way through the derelict area at the edge of Swallow Street. Garrick thought nothing of it until the cab came to a stand and the door was wrenched open. He found himself looking down the barrel of a pistol.

'Now, what have we here?' cried a rough voice. 'Step out, good sir, and let's have a look at ye.'

The owner of the pistol had a muffler wound around the lower part of his face, and his hat was so low over his eyes it was impossible to see his face. Glancing past him Garrick saw several burly individuals standing close by. One of them was levelling a pistol at the cab driver.

'No need for that,' he said, calmly. 'I have little of value, save my purse.'

'I said get out, and hurry up about it.'

Shrugging, Garrick picked up his cane and jumped out of the cab. Although he looked at ease, every nerve was on the alert. A quick glance showed that the houses here were empty ruins, the only people around would be beggars or scavengers. No help to be had there. The man with the pistol took a few steps back.

'Come along, sir, over here and give us your purse.'

As Garrick stepped away from the coach he heard someone bark an order to the driver, who whipped up his horses and clattered off. Surprised, Garrick swung around, but before he could shout out, he was stunned by a blow to the head.

The ground was still damp from the earlier rain but the dust and dirt cushioned his fall. As he tried to get up a boot smashed into his body and he fell back, winded. Another blow, this time to his head, left his senses reeling and he lost consciousness.

When Prudence left Lady Elsdon's elegant townhouse she was tempted to walk the two miles back to Brook Street. There was plenty of time to change for dinner and she wanted to think over all she had learned. However, Lady Borcaster had insisted she should go by cab and, remembering the rather dilapidated areas she had passed through on her way to Russell Square, she allowed her hostess to summon a hackney carriage for her return journey.

Pru had much to occupy her mind and she stared, unseeing, out of the window as the hired vehicle rumbled through the unfamiliar streets, until the sight of a figure clinging to the railings of an empty house caused her to rap sharply on the roof and order the driver to stop.

Even before the carriage came to a halt, she opened the door and jumped out with no thought for decorum.

'Garrick! What has happened to you?' She ran up to him, shocked by his bloodied face and dirty clothes.

'Footpads,' he muttered, before collapsing to the ground.

Chapter Eighteen

Garrick was regaining consciousness. He had a splitting headache and it was difficult to think. Carefully opening his eyes, he stared at the yellow-stained ceiling and the walls with their dark wainscotting. He was propped up against a bank of pillows but this was not his bedchamber, nor was the lumpy mattress beneath him anything like his own featherbed. And apart from his coat and boots, he was fully clothed. He heard a movement in the room and shifted his gaze.

'Prudence.'

She was busy placing a bowl on a table beside the bed but when he spoke her name she looked up.

'You are awake, thank heaven!' Her face lit up with relief. For a moment she looked as if she might cry, but the shadow passed and she smiled at him. 'How are you?'

He really wasn't sure, and some instinct told him he did not want to move and find out.

'What happened?' Just speaking was painful; his lip was swollen.

'You told me footpads attacked you.'

'Ah, yes.' Some memory was returning, but so was the pain. His ribs in particular were on fire, hurting with every breath. His face, too felt odd. Stiff. He lifted a hand to his throbbing cheek but she caught it.

'No, don't touch. We have yet to clean you up.'

It was easier to comply than argue and he allowed her to push his hand back gently to his side.

'Where am I?' he mumbled. 'And what are you doing here?'

She dipped a cloth in the bowl of water and began to wipe his face, very gently.

'We are in a tavern called The Dun Cow,' she said.

'That does not explain your presence.' He winced at the initial sting of the water.

'I was on my way back from Lady Elsdon's house when I saw you. You have a cut on your head and from the marks on your clothes, you have taken blows to your ribs. Consistent with a beating,' she added, her face clouding again with anxiety. 'I did not want to risk further injury by bundling you into a cab and jolting you over the cobbles all the way to Dover Street.'

'Then how did you get me here?'

'I enlisted the help of the builders working nearby. They lifted you onto an old door and carried you.'

She continued to clean the dirt and blood from his face and Garrick concentrated on breathing, trying not to move his ribs more than necessary.

'There.' Finally, she stepped back, satisfied. 'You have a bump on your head and cuts on your face, but nothing too serious, I hope.' She pulled a fresh cloth from a jug and wrung it out. 'There is no ice to be had, but the water is cold and it might help with the swelling.'

She placed the cool rag gently against his temple then lifted his hand up to hold it in place.

'You are very sure of yourself,' he observed.

'I have some experience of caring for victims of attacks such as these. From my charity work with paupers and vagrants, in Bath.' A shadow of pain crossed her face. 'And you know I nursed my brother.'

'But you should not be nursing *me*.'

'There is no one else,' she said simply. 'Before you passed out, you were most insistent that I should not summon a doctor.' She began to unbutton his waistcoat. 'You took quite a beating and I need to ascertain what other injuries you may have.'

'Only my ribs, I think. I remember one of the rogues kicking me.'

Her brow darkened, she looked angry but said nothing as she continued loosening his clothes. When she began to unbutton the waist of his pantaloons his free hand shot up and closed over hers.

'Enough!'

'Why? I have seen your bare chest before.'

Her eyes widened when she realised what she had said. The faint blush colouring her cheek was telling and despite his pain, Garrick felt a rush of satisfaction. The attraction between them was as strong as ever. If only he was fit enough to take advantage of it! He kept a firm hold of her hand, reluctant to allow her to see his injuries. He hated feeling so helpless. He should be protecting *her*, not the other way around.

She said, 'I need to pull out your shirt in order to examine your ribs.'

'It is not fitting,' he told her. 'You are not married.'

'But neither am I a child. As you are well aware.' She met his eyes then, and something sparked between them. A flash of recognition that they were equals. Friends.

Gently, she pulled her hand out of his grasp. 'Trust me, it is not the first time I have examined a man,' she told him, calm, in control. 'Although, never a duke, I admit.'

Her riposte made him want to smile, but she was easing his shirt free and despite her care, he had to brace himself against the pain.

'You are a constant surprise to me, Miss Clifford,' he muttered, between clenched teeth.

'Thank you. Now, I am told one can sometimes hear broken ribs creaking on an inbreath, so I must listen. Just stay silent and relax, sir.'

But that was the one thing he could not do. It was not merely the agony of his cracked or broken ribs every time he breathed, nor the throbbing of the cut on his cheek. He closed his eyes but was still agonisingly aware of her gentle fingers on his skin and the faint citrus smell of her perfume as she leaned over his chest. Did she not realise how tantalising it was, to have her mouth so close to his bare skin?

In truth, he was glad of the pain, otherwise he was afraid his body would have given him away.

She filled his senses. He clenched his fists at his sides, but he could not prevent his mind racing off into highly inappropriate scenarios involving tangled sheets and moonlight…

'I am sorry, did I hurt you?' Her soft voice brought his thoughts back with a jolt. He opened his eyes and found her watching him anxiously.

'You groaned. I am afraid you might have sustained some injury to your internal organs.' When her fingers slid over his abdomen, he caught her hand again and she said crisply, 'I have no time for your stubborn male pride, Your Grace!'

'There is nothing wrong with my organs, internal or external, Miss Clifford.' She tried to free herself, but he tightened his grip. He said softly, 'I would prove it to you, if I were not in so much pain.'

She blushed furiously at that and he grinned, which turned to a wince as it stretched the cuts on his face. Immediately she was all concern.

'Hush now, you need to rest. I could not hear anything to indicate your ribs are broken, which may be good news, but you will need to be careful.'

'Aye, dash it. I feel as weak as a cat.'

She smoothed his hair back from his brow with her free hand. She was gazing at him so tenderly that his pain faded. Something shifted inside him.

'Pru, are you sure you cannot marry me, even though I am *such* a man?' He smiled as far as his split lip would allow. 'Will you not allow me to make an honest woman of you?'

She froze and stood, motionless, looking down at him. She had not recoiled and he thought he saw a wistfulness in her grey eyes. He was about to press home his advantage when the door burst open, shattering the silence and the moment.

'Here we are, ma'am, more hot water. And I have the laudanum you asked for, too.'

There was no mistaking Pru's relief. She freed her hand from his gasp and turned away from him to greet the newcomer.

'Ah, our landlady. Thank you, Mrs Hayes.'

'Is there anything else I can do?' asked the woman, putting the jug down on the table. 'P'raps I can help you undress your man and get him into bed.'

'Yes, thank you, that would be very helpful, but not until after I have administered the opium and it has taken effect. I fear it will cause him a deal of discomfort to be moved.'

'In that case, ma'am, I'll come back and help in a while. And shall I bring you up something to drink? I've put another kettle on to boil.' She added, with a hint of pride, 'I can offer you both tea and coffee.'

'Coffee would be very welcome, thank you,' said Pru.

'Very well, Mrs Garrick, and I'll bring a jug of ale for your husband, in case he's thirsty.'

With a curtsy she bustled out again but Garrick knew better than to return to the subject of marriage. Instead he risked the pain of raising his brows and teased Prudence.

'Well, *Mrs Garrick*?'

'I think you should take the laudanum now.'

'That is not what I meant.'

'She naturally assumed that you...that I.' She eyed him resentfully. 'I judged it best, in the circumstances, to allow her to think you were plain Mr Garrick. You were so dishevelled I doubted anyone would believe your true identity.'

'You are right about that,' he replied, becoming serious. 'However, you have done your duty and can leave me now. Go back to your aunt. You will be missed.'

She shook her head. 'I paid the driver to take a message to Brook Street, informing them I am dining in Russell Square with Lady Elsdon. Thankfully I was using a hackney, Lady Borcaster and my aunt having an engagement this evening and needing their carriage. If it had been my lady's coachman, I would have been in trouble.'

'You are in trouble in any event,' he retorted. 'You really should not be here, Pru.'

'And who else could look after you? Mrs Hayes and her daughter run this tavern alone, they do not have time to tend you as well.'

'You should send for Stow.'

'And so I will, later,' she replied, a stubborn look in her eye. 'My work at the infirmary has taught me that I cannot leave you until I have ascertained there are no lasting injuries.'

'Ah yes. I am one of your charitable causes.' He tried to laugh, but it ended in a grimace.

'Nothing of the sort.' She picked up a small phial and brought it across to him. 'And pray do not try to tell me you are not in pain. Take this.'

He tipped the medicine down his throat and handed her back the bottle. 'There, are you satisfied now?'

'Not quite.' She sat down beside the bed. 'I wish you would be honest with me.'

'When have I been otherwise?'

'You said you were set upon by footpads.'

'I was. Too many for me to defend myself. Which reminds me, did you pick up my cane?'

'No, although I looked for it. I concluded you did not have it with you.'

'I had it when they attacked me. The rogues must have stolen it.'

'Strange that they should take your cane but leave your purse. I found it in your pocket when I removed your coat.'

She looked around as the landlady returned.

'I brought you up your coffee and the ale, ma'am, and some of my plum cake, too, which I thought you and the master might like.'

When she had gone away again Prudence poured some of the small beer into a tankard.

'Can you hold it, or shall I?' she asked Garrick.

He took the tankard and sipped gingerly while Prudence sat beside the bed, watching him. The liquid stung his split lip, but it soothed his parched throat and was soon finished.

'Thank you.' He handed her the empty tankard, hoping he had distracted her from their discussion, but when she had returned it to the tray, she fetched a cup of coffee for herself and sat down again at his bedside.

'Now perhaps you will tell me truthfully how you came to be attacked, Your Grace.'

'I have told you. Footpads.' She narrowed her eyes at him and he knew that would not do. He sighed. 'My cab was stopped by a group of men armed with pistols. I was ordered to step out and the driver was sent on his way. Then one of the rogues clubbed me from behind.'

'And continued to beat you when you were on the floor.' Her grey eyes were dark with anger.

'Yes. Hence the sore ribs.'

The laudanum was having an effect. The pain in his chest was easing and he could watch Pru in more comfort. She was sipping her coffee and he thought how beautiful she was. He would very much like to kiss those ruby lips again. Not that she would allow it. She had made that very clear.

'It is very unusual for such an attack to take place in daylight,' she said slowly. 'Could they have been lying in wait for you?'

'I am almost certain of it.'

'Perhaps they were hired by the same person who wants to see you arrested.'

'That thought had occurred to me,' he said sleepily. 'The only question is, why did they not kill me?'

'Because whoever is behind this does not want you dead.' She added ominously, 'Yet.'

Garrick fought against the drowsiness. He had said too much. Pru should not be worrying about such matters.

'What a devious mind you have, Miss Clifford,' he murmured.

She smiled but was not distracted. 'It begins to make sense, I think.'

'What does?' Her silence made him suspicious. 'Pru?'

She looked up quickly, as if she had forgotten he was there, and shook her head.

'Nothing that cannot wait until you are feeling better,' she said briskly. She rose to her feet. 'Mrs Hayes and I will undress you and then you must rest.'

'Pru.' He reached out and took her hand. She gave him a tight little smile.

'You need not be anxious, sir. While you sleep I shall send a note to Dover Street and summon Stow to attend you.'

'No, no that's not it!' He gave her hand a little shake. 'You must not leave while I am sleeping. Promise me.'

His touch and the intense look in his green eyes sparked a sudden excitement in Pru, but it was outweighed by concern. Fear for Garrick was uppermost in her mind. Everything else must wait. If he was not lucid the next time he woke up then she would summon his doctor, despite his objections.

'Promise me!' he insisted.

She tried to speak calmly, as she would to any patient. 'No, I shall not leave just yet, you have my word.'

He gave a slight nod of satisfaction and closed his eyes as the laudanum began to take effect. Pru's fingers tingled in his grasp and she reluctantly eased her hand free. She was in danger of losing her heart to the duke but she must not lose her head. He needed her nursing skills now, nothing else.

Slowly Pru carried the empty coffee cup back to the tray, taking her time, not rushing back to the bedside.

She must not to fuss around him like a mother hen. The man had enough troubles without having a lovesick female fawning over him.

And yet.

Pru resumed her seat at his bedside. He had asked her again to marry him. He might be delirious, that would account for it, but she thought it far more likely that he was trying to protect her. Why would he do that if he did not like her?

A ragged, derisive laugh clogged her throat.

'There is a vast difference between liking and love,' she told herself sternly. 'What would the Duke of Hartland see in a lanky, plain Jane like me?'

But even this was not enough to kill the tiny seed of hope that had taken root inside her.

When Garrick woke again, night had fallen. A few lighted candles had been placed around the room and their dim light showed him he was alone. He was in the bed now, clad in a nightshirt and with a thin cotton sheet pulled up across his chest. His ears caught the sound of someone on the stairs. The next moment the door opened and Prudence came in. He glared at her.

'Who undressed me?'

She gave him a wicked look. 'Perhaps it is best that you do not ask that.'

An angry retort sprang to his lips, but before he could utter it she laughed and shook her head at him.

'No, no, I am teasing you,' she said, the candlelight dancing in her eyes. 'It was Stow, with the landlady's help. I was not even in the room.'

'Stow is here?'

'Yes. He has taken your clothes away to do what he can with them. Most are ruined but he hopes your coat may be saved.' She came closer and straightened the sheet. 'How do you feel now?'

'Sore.'

'That is to be expected.'

'The headache has eased,' he admitted. 'What time is it?'

'Gone midnight.'

'Confound it, you should not still be here! Why did you not wake me?'

'I was about to do so, had you still been sleeping,' she replied, laying a cool hand on his brow. 'I told you I wanted to ascertain there has been no damage to your brain. There is no fever, and you appear to be your usual curmudgeonly self, so I think I may safely leave you now.'

'Witch!'

She laughed. Garrick watched her put on her pelisse, thinking how much he liked having her with him.

'How will you get back to Brook Street at this late hour?'

'Stow came here in your carriage. Your driver is even now waiting for me. I shall be quite safe.'

'But how will you explain yourself?'

'They know I was visiting Lady Elsdon.' She smiled again. 'I shall say, quite truthfully, that I have been engaged upon charitable work.'

A black cloud descended on his spirits. There was that word again, he thought bitterly. She might as well say outright that she pitied him! His man came into the room and she turned to speak to him.

'I shall leave His Grace in your capable hands now, Mr Stow. I rely upon you to send me word at Brook Street of how he goes on.'

'You may be sure I will, ma'am, and thank you.'

She picked up her reticule and went out, pausing at the door to cast one final glance towards the bed before closing the door. Garrick listened to her footsteps on the stairs, then there was only silence and a strange hollow feeling inside him.

Chapter Nineteen

Pru arrived in Brook Street before the other ladies returned from their supper party and she slipped quickly up to her room. There would be time enough for evasions and explanations in the morning. There might be no need for her aunt or her hostess to know that she had not dined with Lady Elsdon. Neither was particularly interested in her charity work and she hoped that she might be able to deflect their questions without telling a direct lie.

The events of the past few hours had taken their toll and she felt exhausted, but when she finally blew out the candle, she found her mind would not be still. She went back over everything that had happened after finding Garrick, the sickening fear that had gripped her as he had been carried to the inn. She was haunted by the memory of Walter being brought home in just such a condition, from which he had never recovered.

Being able to nurse Garrick, albeit for such a short time, was a bittersweet comfort. She had been glad to be busy, tending his wounds and bathing his face, but sitting beside him as he slept was a trial, unable to do anything for his unseen injuries and afraid she might lose him. It did no good to tell herself he was not hers to lose.

* * *

Pru was confident Stow would look after his master equally well. He might even persuade Garrick to be examined by a doctor, although she doubted it. Proud, obstinate man! She resolutely turned her thoughts away from the duke to consider the other interesting event of the day: taking tea with Lady Elsdon.

It had started very much as expected; Pru had been introduced to Lady Elsdon's guests, all of whom were a little surprised to find a young and unmarried lady so intent upon helping the émigrés, but Pru's experience in Bath stood her in good stead.

After an hour of talking, Lady Elsdon declared Miss Clifford would be a very valuable member of the group. Not, perhaps, in financial terms, but full of useful suggestions for setting up a refuge and raising funds. However, as the afternoon wore on Pru began to think she had learned nothing of any use to Garrick. Then, just as she was about to make her excuses and leave, another guest hurried in, gushing apologies.

'My dear ma'am, I beg your pardon for arriving so late! I trust I have not missed anything of importance?'

'No, no, Lady Conyers. We have barely begun.'

Prudence was sitting with her back to the door when Lady Elsdon welcomed the latecomer, but that soft, melodious voice was unmistakable. Removing all trace of shock or surprise from her countenance, she fixed a smile in place and turned.

Pru smiled again now, in the darkness, but this time with genuine amusement as she recalled the astonishment on the beautiful Helene's face when she saw her. Lady Conyers had been suspicious at first, but Prudence greeted her calmly enough and gave such a good account of herself in the following discussions that there could be no doubting her extensive knowledge of charitable work. The meeting had given Pru much to think about, but when at last she drifted off to sleep, her thoughts returned to Garrick and her dreams were troubled by concern for him.

Garrick was back in Dover Street shortly after noon the following day. Ignoring his man's suggestion that he should go to bed, he insisted on taking a bath before changing into a fresh suit of clothes. He was standing before the mirror in the drawing room, tying his neckcloth, when Jack Callater burst in.

'So you *are* here, Garr! What the devil has been going on?'

'And a good day to you, Jack.' Garrick tried not to wince as he moved away from the looking glass. 'I'd be grateful if you could moderate your language. I have a shocking headache, you know.'

'From what I've heard you have a damned sight worse than that,' retorted Jack. 'I have just spoken with Miss Clifford—'

Garrick made no effort to moderate his own language and cursed roundly.

'Damned interfering woman.'

'She rescued you, confound it!'

'I did not need rescuing,' he said, lowering himself gently into an armchair.

'No?' Jack threw himself down onto the sofa and looked at him, his brows raised. 'God knows what would have happened to you if she had not come upon you when she did.'

'Someone else would have found me.'

'Aye, thieving rascals who would have stripped you clean!'

'Not everyone is a villain, Jack.'

'Perhaps not. In any event you could have lain in the dirt for hours.' He paused as Stow came in carrying a tray.

'I didn't order wine,' barked Garrick, glaring at his man.

'No, Your Grace, but Lord John is partial to a glass of claret in the afternoons,' Stow replied, unmoved by his master's anger. 'And I thought one glass would do you no harm, Your Grace, if you would care for it. Or would you prefer the laudanum the apothecary has sent round?'

Garrick's look left his man in no doubt of the answer to that.

Jack laughed and Garrick bade Stow put the tray down on a side table, saying, once the man had withdrawn, 'I take it your meeting with Miss Clifford was not by chance?'

'No, she sent me word and we met in Green Park this morning,' said Jack. 'After that, I went directly to The Dun Cow only to be told you had left. Against Miss Clifford's advice, I am sure.'

'Aye, if she had been nursing me I should be there still.' A smile tugged at Garrick's mouth. 'A most redoubtable woman. But her concern and yours is misplaced. I am perfectly well now.'

'Do not try to gammon me! Your face looks as if it's taken a battering from Gentleman Jackson.'

'It will heal.'

'And your ribs? Pru said they kicked you while you were down.'

'Pru?' Garrick's brows snapped together. 'Getting might friendly with the lady, ain't you, Jack?'

'Don't change the subject...or do I detect a hint of jealousy there, old friend?'

Garrick almost ground his teeth when he saw the amused glint in Jack's eye, but he was too wise to argue.

He said, 'It's possible the ribs are cracked. But it could have been much worse.'

'So, who do you think was behind it?'

'I am not sure yet, but I think it was connected to my appointment yesterday.' Garrick described his visit to Albert Vence, ending, 'It seems too much of a coincidence that I should be attacked on my way back from Somers Town.'

Jack frowned. 'Aye, damned suspicious, if you ask me.'

There was a knock at the door and Stow came in again.

He said woodenly, 'Viscount Sidmouth is downstairs and wishes to see Your Grace.'

Garrick met Jack's eyes. 'Is he, by Gad. I wonder what the home secretary wants with me?' With an effort he levered himself out of his chair. 'Send His Lordship up.'

'Good of him not to barge straight in,' muttered Jack, also rising.

There was no time for more. Stow ushered the visitor into the room and Garrick managed to incline his head in greeting without wincing with the pain.

'Lord Sidmouth. To what do I owe the pleasure of your call?'

'I did not know you had a visitor, Your Grace.' His Lordship bowed to Jack. 'Lord John.'

'Oh, Jack and I are old friends,' said Garrick cheerfully. 'We have no secrets from one another. Shall we sit down?'

Lord Sidmouth indicated he would rather stand.

'This concerns the charges that have been made

against you, Your Grace,' he said. 'You are aware of them?'

'Of course.'

The home secretary was looking a little uncomfortable and Garrick decided to help him out.

'I presume you know I called to see Monsieur Vence yesterday.'

'Yes.' Lord Sidmouth frowned. He said heavily, 'I was informed you attacked him.'

'I did not,' Garrick retorted. 'The fellow panicked and shouted for his guards. They will tell you that I left when they asked me to do so.'

'And you did not go back?'

'Of course not.' It was Garrick's turn to frown. 'What is this about?'

'Last night someone tried to murder Albert Vence.'

Chapter Twenty

Garrick stared in silence at the home secretary.

He said, slowly, 'It was not I.'

'Your Grace, can you prove you did not return to the Golden Cockerel, can anyone vouch for you?'

Jack shifted and Garrick threw him a warning glance.

'No.'

'And the bruises on your face?'

'Footpads. I was attacked on my way back to Dover Street.'

Lord Sidmouth's eyes narrowed suspiciously but Garrick did not look away.

'Perhaps, Lord Sidmouth, you should tell me what happened last night. That is, I should like to have the account of what your men saw or heard.'

'Monsieur Vence was distressed by your, ah, visit, Your Grace, and he retired early, as soon as it grew dark. Someone broke into his bedchamber shortly after and attacked him. Fortunately, my men were on guard in the next room, and heard the commotion.'

'The Frenchman seems particularly nervous,' observed Jack. 'Can you be sure he was not having a nightmare?'

Lord Sidmouth threw him a disdainful glance. 'It was no dream, sir. My men saw a figure climbing out of the window, but by the time they ran downstairs he had vanished.'

'Was Vence seriously hurt?' demanded Garrick.

'A blow to the head. He is convinced it was you, Your Grace.'

'It was not. You have my word for it.'

'Then why was your sword stick found in his room? The coat of arms on the silver handle is unmistakable.'

Jack stifled a curse.

'I lost in when *I* was attacked.' Garrick looked Lord Sidmouth in the eye. 'Are you here to arrest me?'

With an oath Jack took a step forward. 'On what grounds? Did anyone actually *recognise* the intruder as the duke?'

'Sit down man,' growled Lord Sidmouth, waving him away. 'This is a very delicate situation. If His Grace will give me his word that he will not leave town, I will accept that. For now.'

'Then you have it,' said Garrick promptly. 'What about Vence—has he been moved?'

'He has gone into hiding in the country. He has friends with whom he feels safe.'

Garrick nodded. 'Believe me, Lord Sidmouth, Vence poses no threat to me. I told you to ask Castlereagh about my actions in France. Once you have his testimony, and the reports from my fellow agents at the time, it will become clear that Vence is lying, and I am innocent of the charges brought against me.'

'As to that, we shall see,' replied His Lordship, unconvinced. 'But it will go ill with you, Your Grace, if people think you tried to murder your accuser.'

With a brisk nod to both men, Lord Sidmouth departed and Garrick sank thankfully, but carefully, back into his chair.

'So now we know why those rogues took your cane,' said Jack.

'Aye. Someone is trying to make me look guilty. I have my suspicions who it may be, but no proof, as yet.'

'I think I might be able to help you there,' said Jack. 'Pru told me about her visit to Russell Square yesterday. Lady Elsdon's charitable work for French émigrés,' he added, when Garrick looked blank. 'We both thought it a waste of time, but now I am not so sure. Lady Conyers was there.'

Garrick was suddenly alert. 'Go on.'

'She turned up shortly after Pru arrived.'

'Another coincidence? I cannot believe it.'

'Nor I,' Jack replied. 'The point is, she is one of the charity's most ardent supporters.'

'Is she, by Gad? That is the first I have heard of Helene doing anything for anyone other than herself.' Garrick shook his head. 'But Pru should not have gone there. I don't want her caught up in all this.'

Jack grinned. 'Not sure you could stop her, my friend. The lady knows her own mind.'

'She's damned obstinate.' Garrick glanced at his friend's face and he sighed. 'I know, I owe her a great deal, but you must keep her away from me, Jack. She is far too careless of her reputation.'

'You could change that. Marry her.'

Garrick's hands clenched into fists. He could not bring himself to admit she had rejected him, even to his friend.

He said, 'You know I cannot do it while this, this cloud is hanging over me.'

'She does not care for that.'

'But *I* do! Prudence Clifford is not of my world. Pray do not look at me like that—I am not saying she is beneath me. On the contrary, she is too good, too kind. She would be honouring *me* if she agreed to be my duchess.

'No. I mean the scandal that surrounds me would embarrass her family, her friends and the charities she cares so much for. That would cause her distress. Even if she can overlook my past demeanours, these current, unfounded accusations are far more serious and must be refuted. Only then can I ask a woman such as Pru Clifford to marry me.'

'I suppose you would not believe me if I said I thought you were wrong about that.'

'You may think what you like, Jack, but you must keep Pru from behaving rashly.'

'I will do my best, my friend, but she is her own mistress. And you have yet to hear what she learned about Lady Conyers. It appears that the beautiful Helene joined Lady Elsdon's committee in early March, working with the émigrés.'

'It is highly likely, then, that Helene knows Vence. Or at least knows *of* him.'

'Yes. I think she may have passed the information to her husband.'

'And out of spite, they persuaded the fellow to make the accusations against me.' Garrick waved a hand, suddenly too exhausted to talk. 'It matters not, Jack. Once Castlereagh sends word I shall be cleared.'

'But a reply could take weeks, months to come back. Until then do you want to stay in London, kicking your heels while your name is bandied about by everyone? If Conyers is trying to smear you then the longer it goes on, the more mud will stick.'

Garrick knew he was right. He wanted to be free of

this latest slur so he could set about courting Prudence in earnest. He wanted to prove himself worthy of her, and of his name.

He looked up as Stow came in.

'Miss Clifford to see you, Your Grace.'

Garrick muttered under his breath. What sorcery had conjured her? He closed his eyes and ordered his man to send her away.

'I knew you would say that,' replied Pru from the doorway. 'Just as I guessed you would return here as soon as my back was turned. I needed to know how you are recovering.'

She was again wearing the cherry-red cloak in the mistaken belief that it made her look like a servant. In Garrick's opinion nothing could disguise the lady's quality. His concern for her made his reply sound rough and ungrateful, even to his own ears.

'You did not need to do anything of the kind. Jack would have informed you.'

'But I wanted to see for myself. No, don't get up.'

He had tried to rise and was glad to slump back in the chair, but this sign of weakness did nothing for his temper.

'By God, woman, do you not understand?' he said irritably. 'The home secretary was just here. If he had seen you—'

'But he did not. I waited until his carriage had turned out of sight before I approached the house.'

Jack laughed. 'By Gad, ma'am, you're a cool one!'

Garrick ground his teeth, hating to agree. He had never known anyone like Pru Clifford. He watched her remove the cloak and drape it over a chair-back. Annabelle Speke had always been such a timid little creature and his sharp tongue would have had her in tears,

or going off in a dead faint. Helene would have raged
at him, possibly hurling anything that was to hand in
his direction.

No, this woman's calm, unflappable demeanour re-
minded him most closely of the duchess. The old duke
had been profligate and unfaithful, but Mama had loved
him deeply and without question. Yet she had not railed
at Garrick in her letters, even though she blamed him
for his father's death. Her missives were always cool,
considered. The language had been temperate but un-
yielding and when she told him she never wanted to see
him again he had known there was no arguing with her.

'You are as stubborn as my mother,' he muttered. 'I
pray to heaven the two of you never meet!'

Pru flinched at his words but she gave a little shrug.
'It is very unlikely we ever shall, so let us waste no
time on futile conjecture. Tell me instead what Lord
Sidmouth wanted.'

'Garrick's head,' Jack interjected.

She stared at him, the blood draining from her face.
'What has happened?'

'It's to do with the fellow Garr went to see yesterday.'

'What fellow?' Pru looked from one to the other.

'The Frenchman. Did Garr not tell you?'

'I was in no state to tell anyone anything,' snapped
Garrick. 'Besides, it is none of her business.'

'I believe it is, Your Grace.' She sat down and folded
her hands in her lap and addressed Jack. 'Pray tell me
everything.'

Pru listened in growing horror as Lord John explained about Garrick's meeting with Monsieur Vence
and the home secretary's visit. When he had finished,
she turned to Garrick.

'They think you tried to kill him.'

'But you know I did not. You were with me until midnight.'

'Did you tell Lord Sidmouth that?'

'How could I, without implicating you?'

Pru bit down her annoyance. 'You will have to tell him, if they decide to put you on trial.'

'It will not come to that. Castlereagh's evidence will prove Vence is lying.'

'Where is the Frenchman now?'

'Sidmouth said he is in hiding.'

'Where?'

'With a friend. Someone he trusts.'

'That could be the man who put him up to this in the first place,' she reasoned.

'Very likely. Now what is it that makes you frown?'

'I saw Lady Conyers yesterday.' She stopped, looking uncertain. Garrick nodded.

'Jack told me about that.'

'Yes, of course. I heard her say Sir Joseph was going out of town today.' She raised her eyes to his face again. 'What if *he* has taken the poor man away? What if he murders him and blames you for it?'

'Even he wouldn't be such a villain!' exclaimed Jack.

'Quite,' said Garrick, frowning. 'You are being fanciful, Pru.'

'Am I? Lord Sidmouth already thinks you are responsible for one attempt upon the man's life.'

'Only because I refused to give him your name as a witness.'

'But Sir Joseph could not have known I would find you,' she persisted. 'He may have hired the henchmen who beat you unconscious and stole your cane. You said yourself the attack took place in a deserted area. If I had not come across you, who knows how long you might have lain there? And you would have had no one to vouch for you at the time that Vence was killed.

'We know Sir Joseph hates you,' she went on. 'I have no doubt now that it is he who started the rumours about your loyalty to the Crown. Then there is Lady Conyers. I cannot believe it is pure chance that she is part of Lady Elsdon's charitable group.'

'No, neither can I,' Jack agreed. 'Doesn't it strike you as odd, Garr, that she began helping Lady Elsdon shortly after you returned to this country?'

'Perhaps, but what can we do?' said Garrick. 'If it is Sir Joseph who has hidden the fellow away, how are we to find him?'

'We could go to Lord Sidmouth, tell him what we suspect,' Jack suggested.

The duke shook his head. 'No, he would not act against one of his own on mere suspicion. On the other hand, he is not a man to take a risk. He must be very sure of Vence's protector.'

'Even if it is Conyers?' said Jack.

'The fellow is extremely plausible.'

'Which makes him particularly dangerous,' Pru insisted. 'What if he arranges for the poor man's death and then fabricates more evidence of your guilt? Lord Castlereagh cannot vouch for your actions here in England, can he?'

'She's right,' said Jack. 'It could be difficult for you if the fellow should die now. We need to find him.'

'Aye, but where do we start?'

'I think I know.' Pru found two pairs of eyes fixed upon her. She said, 'I attended a party at Sir Joseph's townhouse and saw a watercolour on the wall. A painting of Alder Grove, in Kent. Lord Fauls told me it is Sir Joseph's old home. He said the house was empty now,

Sir Joseph having bought a larger property, more fitted to his station.' She frowned trying to recall details of the little painting. 'The house looked to be in a very rural landscape. It is surrounded by woodland, but near Dartford which is not, I think, too far from town.'

'A perfect hideaway then,' declared Jack. 'Well, Duke, what do you think, could Vence be there?'

Garrick shrugged. 'It is worth a try. We have nothing else to work on. We could ride there tomorrow.'

'*You* cannot,' Pru declared. 'You are already under suspicion, besides being unwell. I could—'

'No!' exclaimed Garrick. 'I will not have you involved further in this!'

'No need for anyone to accompany me,' said Jack hurriedly. 'Sidmouth expressly forbade you to leave town, Garr, but I can go.' He pulled out his watch. 'I will ride to Dartford tonight and make enquiries as to the location of Alder Grove. If Vence is there I will try to persuade him to come with me and put himself back into Lord Sidmouth's protection.'

'*Can* you persuade him?'

Garrick heard the doubtful note in Pru's voice.

'I shall do my best. The first thing is to locate the fellow.' Jack grinned. 'Don't look so anxious, Pru, my dear. We will come through this.'

'Pray, my lord, be careful.'

'I shall, no need to fret.'

Pru received a reassuring smile from Jack—damned charming fellow that he was—who then picked up his hat and gloves and went out. His footsteps could be heard running down the stairs and Garrick shifted restlessly in his chair.

'Don't worry,' he said. 'Jack can take care of himself.'

'But he is a stranger to Monsieur Vence, why should the man trust him?'

'If he refuses to budge then I will take my suspicions to Lord Sidmouth and let him deal with it. At least he will have been warned.'

'I should go with you. I could tell him I was with you until midnight yesterday.'

'No.'

'Garrick—'

'No!' He drew a breath. 'Don't you see, you have already done enough. I cannot involve you further in this.' She was still looking stubborn and he raked one hand through his hair. 'Hell and damnation, Pru, I expect a visit from your aunt at any moment, *insisting* that I marry you!'

'And neither of us want that!' she retorted.

Garrick bit his tongue and glared at her. Why did she insist on putting words into his mouth?

'No one knows I am here,' she said, turning away from him. 'I kept the hood pulled up to disguise me from any inquisitive glances.'

'By God, madam, you are too reckless. I would like to pick you up and *shake* you!'

No, he admitted, but only to himself. He wanted to pick her up and carry her to his bed, only he was too damned weak to do so. His head was beginning to throb again. He sighed and rubbed a hand across his eyes.

'You must go now. There is nothing more you can do here.'

'Very well.'

She threw her cloak about her shoulders and fastened it.

'Prudence.' He reached out and caught her hand as she

passed him. 'For heaven's sake act up to your name for once. Go home and stay there until you hear from me.'

'As you wish.'

There was a note in her voice he had not heard before. She sounded weary, defeated. It flayed him.

'It is not that I am ungrateful, believe me. I owe you a great deal already, but you must not call here again.' His grip tightened and he said roughly, 'Do you understand? I shall give Stow instructions that you are not to be admitted.'

Pru felt suddenly close to tears.

'I thought we were friends,' she said, her voice low.

'Friends!' He gave a bark of laughter but it lacked any humour and merely grated on her nerves. 'How the devil can we be that, after all that has occurred?'

Feeling sick at heart, she nodded. 'You are quite right. I shall wait to hear from you, or Lord John. You will keep me informed, will you not?'

'Of course.' He released her. 'Now get you gone, madam. I need to rest.'

Chapter Twenty-One

Keeping her head high, Pru walked slowly down the stairs. Stow was waiting to let her out of the house.

'Thank you for calling, madam.' He gave her a little bow. 'A few days' rest and His Grace will be back to his old self, I am sure.'

There was no mistaking the sympathy in his eyes.

'Of course.' She answered him calmly enough and pulled her hood up as she stepped out of the building into the rain.

Garrick was afraid for her. That should have been a comfort, but his comments cut deep. She remembered the night they had met in Bath, when he had told her of Lady Speke's letter and that he was obliged to marry Annabelle. There had been a bleakness in his eyes that night and she had seen it again today. It was also in his voice, when he said he anticipated Aunt Minerva calling upon him. If he married her at all it would be from a sense of duty. Pru felt a hot tear slip down her cheek. And now he had said they could not even be friends.

Stow was right, of course. The duke was not himself, but his current malaise had merely stripped away prevarication. He had told her nothing but the truth, and it hurt.

What a fool she was to lose her heart to a man who did not want her help or her friendship.

Friday passed in Brook Street with no word from either Garrick or Lord John. Pru was not surprised. She knew it might take Jack some time to locate Alder Grove and even longer to discover if the Frenchman was in hiding there. She did not want to believe that Garrick was deliberately keeping her in the dark, but she could not quite suppress the suspicion. However, the next day an unexpected morning visit gave her thoughts quite another turn.

All three ladies were in the morning room when Lady Conyers was announced. She sailed in, resplendent in a powder blue promenade dress and a delightful French hat of blue and white satin. There was a flurry of activity as polite greetings were exchanged and refreshments brought in, but as soon as they were all settled Pru found herself the object of Lady Conyers's attention.

'My dear Prudence—I may call you that, I hope? I feel we are such good friends now! It was quite a surprise to see you in Russell Square the other day. I had no idea you were interested in our little cause.'

'Oh, my niece is a great one for charitable works,' declared Aunt Minerva. 'She is quite renowned for it in Bath. The Widows and Orphans, Relief of the Poor or nursing the sick at the infirmary! Prudence has such a kind heart.'

'Indeed?' Helene's beautiful smile never wavered but Pru detected a hint of contempt in those blue eyes. 'Miss Clifford is a veritable saint, then.'

'That is too kind of you, my lady, I am no saint,' replied Pru, giving the lady a smile every bit as false as her own. 'But I do find great satisfaction in helping those less fortunate. Which is why I was so pleased to support Lady Elsdon's efforts on behalf of the French émigrés.' She paused. 'You mentioned yesterday Sir Joseph had been obliged to go out of town. I hope he has returned safely?'

'No, he is still away.' Lady Conyers gave a little trill of laughter. 'He may be waiting for me when I get home but, in truth, I have no idea when he means to return.'

'Was he called away on business, ma'am?' asked Aunt Minerva. 'I do hope he will not miss the Grand Jubilee on Monday. It promises to be a great spectacle.'

'It does indeed, but my husband is not one for these celebrations, you know. Are you planning to attend, Lady Borcaster?'

'Why yes, it is not to be missed, if the reports are to be believed.'

'Oh, quite so, ma'am, quite so. It will be a very grand affair. I wonder—' She paused, as if hesitant to make her request. 'I wonder if I might steal away your young guest for the day?' Her charmingly diffident smile swept over all three ladies. 'That is the reason for my call today. I am come to invite Miss Clifford to join me on Monday. You see, I promised to help Lady Elsdon at the fair and would welcome a little company. She has hired a booth from which the committee will sell the little pieces of art that the poor émigrés have been making. You will know the sort of thing, ma'am, fancy boxes and reticules, purses and pincushions made from scraps of silk or velvet, painted notebooks, toys...' She laughed. 'French rags, we call it, but those sympathetic to their plight will buy them as gifts or keepsakes, I am sure.'

'What an admirable cause,' declared Lady Borcaster. 'Although, sadly, I do not intend to visit the fair booths. The crowds there will be fearsome.' She turned to Mrs Clifford. 'I thought we would take in Green Park, and perhaps even St James's Park, if it is not too busy.'

'That sounds delightful, and I am sure we will manage without Prudence, if she wishes to be elsewhere,' replied Aunt Minerva. 'I certainly have no objection to her joining you, Lady Conyers, but it really is up to Prudence.'

With the eyes of the three ladies upon her, Pru was obliged to think quickly. She had no idea what had prompted the invitation and was a little suspicious. Yet it was a perfectly reasonable request.

'I do remember Lady Elsdon mentioning the fair,' she said now. 'However, I thought all the arrangements were in place for the ladies of the committee to take their turn in the booth.'

'They are, but my lady expressed the hope that I might find someone to assist me for an hour or two. An extra pair of hands and eyes would be most helpful.' Lady Conyers leaned forward, saying earnestly, 'Oh, do say you will come, Prudence. Sir Joseph is very impatient of my good works, as he calls them, and is not minded to come with me, even if he is returned by then. And after we have performed our duties, as it were, we may go off and explore the rest of the entertainments.'

'I should like to see as much as possible of the celebrations,' Pru admitted.

'Excellent! Then it is settled.' Lady Conyers smiled broadly and clapped her hands. 'I shall send my carriage to call for you. Oh, we shall have such a splendid day, my dear!'

The conversation moved on and Pru sat back to drink

her tea. She had no idea what had prompted Lady Conyers to invite her, although it was possible Helene had no close female friends willing to go with her. In fact, she thought uncharitably, that was very likely. And spending a few hours with Lady Conyers might be advantageous.

Lord John might return with Vence today or tomorrow and if so, Pru could always cry off from joining Helene at the fair. However, if there was no sign of the Frenchman, she would be well placed to learn something more about Lady Conyers and her husband. And working in the booth would also be an ideal opportunity for her to discover if any of the committee knew where the Frenchman might be.

Whatever Garrick might say, thought Pru, rebelliously, she could still be useful.

Garrick slept most of Friday, which prevented him fretting too much over how Jack was faring in Kent. By Saturday, although his ribs still hurt, he felt physically much recovered. However, he could not settle to anything and raged inwardly against his enforced inactivity. It was not merely Jack's mission to Alder Grove that preyed upon his mind. He had been less than kind to Pru.

He knew his weakened state and anxiety for her had made him more irritable than usual. He was unable to shake off the black depression that clouded his thoughts, but that was no excuse. He wanted to go to Brook Street immediately and apologise, but Jack might return at any time and he needed to be here when he called. Garrick considered writing a note to Pru, begging her pardon for his boorish behaviour, but after several aborted attempts he gave up. What he wanted to say, what he *needed* to say, could not be written in a letter.

If she was angry with him so much the better, it might keep her from calling in Dover Street again. He wanted to see her so badly that it hurt quite as much as his bruised ribs, but he did not want her good name dragged through the mud. She did not deserve to be vilified for her association with him. However, when this damned business was over, he would find her. He would prove to her how much he loved her, even if it took him a lifetime.

Jack arrived in Dover Street at noon, still dressed for riding.

'Forgive me for coming in all my dirt,' he said, tossing his hat, gloves and riding crop on the table. 'I did not want to waste time changing my clothes.'

Garrick waved away his apology. 'What news?'

'Not good, I'm afraid. Vence is at Alder Grove—I saw him for myself—but he never leaves the grounds. He is as good as a prisoner there.' He took a brimming tankard of ale from Stow and drank deep before continuing. 'I did talk to him, though.'

'Oh, how did you manage that?'

'I, er, persuaded one of the maids to take a message to him.' Jack's wicked grin appeared, briefly, then he was serious again. 'The fellow came out to take the air this morning and we exchanged a few words, over the wall. I tried to convince him to come back to town with me, but to no avail.'

'Confound it!'

'I told him he has nothing to fear from you, Garr. I said we would both give him our protection and support him if he tells the truth, but he will not budge. I gained the impression he is more afraid of Conyers than anything you or the court can do to him.'

'Damned fool.' Garrick stared into his own tankard, frowning. 'Then our only hope is to lay the whole before the home secretary. Perhaps Vence will trust Sidmouth enough to put himself back under his protection before it is too late. I must speak to him.'

'Now?'

'If he is to be found. The longer we wait the more chance there is that something will happen to Vence.'

'Very well. Give me time to go to Albany and change my clothes and I will come with you. We'll try Whitehall first, then his house in Richmond Park.'

It was dark by the time the two friends arrived back in Dover Street, and Garrick's bruised ribs were making it plain they did not appreciate being bounced around in a travelling chaise, albeit a luxurious one. He let out another hiss of pain as he climbed out of the carriage.

'You should have let me go alone,' complained Jack.

'This is my problem and I must deal with it, although I admit your father being a friend of Lord Sidmouth is an advantage when talking to the man.'

'Very magnanimous of you!'

'Aye, and I shall repay your assistance by inviting you to dine with me tonight.'

'I would rather you took to your bed and rested. You have been in agony all day.'

'You are exaggerating. I have had a little discomfort, nothing more.' Garrick caught his friend's eye and exclaimed, 'Damn it, Jack, I ain't an invalid, and I need a good meal, even if you don't!'

'Very well, let us eat together, since it is pointless

arguing with you,' Jack retorted. 'How soon, do you think, before we hear from Lord Sidmouth?'

'Not before tomorrow night at the earliest.'

'You really believe he intends to travel to Alder Grove on a Sunday?'

'Aye, he said he would do so. Sidmouth's no fool. He knows better than to ignore our warning. I only hope he is not too late already.'

'And Prudence,' said Jack, following him up the stairs. 'Will you write and tell her about Vence?'

Garrick did not reply immediately. She was never far from his thoughts, but he was strangely loath to contact her. Everything might yet come to nought and, if that were the case, what was the point? She would be better off without him.

'She will want to know what is happening,' Jack persisted. 'I could send her a message—'

Garrick hissed out a curse. 'Let it be, Jack! I will write, once we are sure of Vence.'

It was in fact late Sunday night when Garrick received word from the home secretary. Jack had once again dined in Dover Street and was about to take his leave when Stow came in with a note. Garrick tore it open and quickly perused the contents.

'Well?' Jack demanded.

'All is well. Vence is now at White Lodge with Lord Sidmouth. He expects the fellow to make a full confession in the morning.' Garrick held out the letter. 'Once that is done, Sidmouth will be able to use his evidence to indict Conyers for perverting justice.'

'But Vence will still be guilty of making false accusations against you.'

'Aye, poor devil, but at least he will be alive. When

the truth finally comes out, that he was coerced into this, I hope he will be shown some mercy.'

'And you have promised to give the fellow your support, which should count for something.' Jack handed back the paper and rose from his chair. 'Well, a good day's work, my friend. It is time I was going.'

He took his leave, but at the door he stopped and turned back.

'And you will send word to Prudence?'

Garrick sighed, causing his ribs to protest again. He waved a hand.

'I will write in the morning. She will be sleeping now.'

He felt Jack's gaze upon him and glared across the room, daring him to argue, but there was only understanding in his friend's eyes.

Jack nodded and smiled. 'Aye, get some sleep, Garr. You look spent.'

Garrick slept late the next morning but woke up much refreshed. The black melancholy that had dulled his spirits since the attack had lifted and he was eager to get about his business. His ribs hurt a lot less as he climbed out of bed and he decided he would go and see Prudence. He would apologise for his boorish behaviour and tell her the news about Vence.

And perhaps, if the moment seemed propitious, he would tell her how much he loved her.

However, when he looked at his face in the mirror, the bruising on his cheek had spread to cover almost half his face in varying shades, from red to an ugly dark purple.

'Curse it, that is no sight to inflict upon a lady!'

'If I might say, Your Grace,' said Stow, pulling a clean shirt from the linen press, 'I do not think you need worry that your appearance will shock Miss Clifford. She has seen Your Grace in a far worse state.'

Garrick knew it and that grated on him, too. He knew it was mere vanity on his part. Stubborn male pride, as she had called it. Whatever it might be, he did not want her to see him like this.

'I shall write to her,' he decided. 'Fetch me pen and paper, Stow, and you can take a message to Brook Street for me.'

The morning was well advanced by the time Garrick was dressed and ready to sit down and write his letter. Then the words would not come. How did he explain his temper, or admit he did not feel worthy of her? After several false starts he penned a simple apology, vowing to explain everything when they next met. He followed this with the news about Monsieur Vence and ended with a promise to call in Brook Street as soon as he was fit to be seen.

Garrick put down his pen and read the letter through again before sealing it and addressing it to Miss Prudence Clifford. Then he summoned his man.

'There,' he said, handing it over. 'Not the most eloquent prose I have ever written, but it will have to do. I would be obliged if you would take it in person, Stow. I do not expect a reply, but if you should see Miss Clifford, if she should have a message for me...'

'I understand, Your Grace.'

With a bow, Stow took the letter and went out. Garrick sat back in his chair, knowing full well he would not rest until his man returned.

When he heard a hasty step on the stairs, Garrick threw aside the book he had not been reading.

'Well?' He frowned when he saw Stow's face and said urgently, 'What is it, what has occurred?'

'Miss Clifford was not at home, Your Grace,' he said, between panting breaths. 'She is gone to Hyde Park. To the Great Fair.'

'Ah yes. I had forgotten about the Jubilee celebrations today. That explains the unusual amount of noise coming in from the street.'

'Aye, Your Grace. There are so many people abroad that London has almost come to a stand. That is why I ran back rather than taking a cab.' He put a hand to his heaving chest and gasped out, 'She has gone with Lady Conyers!'

Chapter Twenty-Two

Garrick ignored the screaming pain of ribs as he hurried to Hyde Park, weaving through the crowds that thronged each street. Stow had learned at Brook Street that Lady Conyers had taken Pru off to help in Lady Elsdon's booth, raising money for the émigrés. He had no reason to believe Helene meant any mischief, but the doubts would not go away.

He remembered the speculative look she had given him at Shrivenham House, when he had come in from the terrace with Pru on his arm. If she thought his affections were engaged, that alone might be enough for her to wish Pru harm, but if she thought the lady was actively helping to thwart her husband's plans...

The doubt hardened into certainty. His fingers tightened on the Malacca cane, wishing it was his sword stick, but that was still in Lord Sidmouth's possession. He lengthened his stride, praying that his quarry was indeed in Hyde Park.

Lady Conyers's note arrived as Pru was drinking her morning hot chocolate. It informed her that my lady would call at ten o'clock, which meant Pru had to rush her breakfast and scramble into her walking dress. Once they reached the booth she made herself useful, helping to unpack the items made by the French men and women who needed support in a strange land.

Pru would have been happy to work with the other ladies for much longer, but after an hour Helene suggested they go off and look around the fair.

'It will be a sad crush, I fear, but we have Ronald in attendance,' Helene told her, glancing towards her liveried footman. 'We will be perfectly safe.'

Pru's kind heart suggested that the lady might be lonely and in need of a companion, so she readily agreed and they set off into the throng.

Several hundred tents and booths had been erected selling everything from trinkets and ribbons, small pots and fancywork to all manner of food and drink. Printing presses had been set up, offering engraved views of the Temple and Chinese Pagoda for a few pence.

Helene was going out of her way to be charming and Pru could not deny she was enjoying herself. After they had tried several of the little delicacies on offer in the food tents, Helene suggested they should walk to Green Park.

'There is to be a re-enactment of the Battle of the Nile here, but that does not start until six o'clock and we can easily come back later, if you wish to watch it.'

Prudence had seen enough of the stalls and hawkers and readily agreed to move on. They strolled away from the bustling fairground and Pru was glad of her straw bonnet with its wide brim to protect her face from the sun. Green Park was just as busy. Lady Conyers took Pru's arm and guided her towards the large wooden edifice that had been erected, chattering all the while.

'That is the Fortress,' she explained. 'It was fashioned by builders from the Theatre Royal, I believe, and is cleverly designed to transform into a Temple of Concord later this evening, which I think will be very exciting.' Helene's fingers tightened on Pru's sleeve and she gave a little cry of delight. 'Look, my *caro sposo* is come to join us. Over here, my dear!'

Pru's spirits sank when she saw Sir Joseph coming towards them. Not that there was anything to fear, she told herself. They were amongst so many people, she was perfectly safe. All the same she was suddenly on her guard and her greeting was civil, but not warm.

The gentleman laughed gently as he bowed to her.

'Oh, dear, I fear Miss Clifford is angry with me for interrupting your *tête-à-tête*, Helene. I must be on my best behaviour to regain her favour.'

Pru smiled politely but did not respond. She was relieved that Sir Joseph took his wife's arm and left her free to walk beside them. Gradually her tension eased. The gentleman's behaviour was polite enough, he made no attempt to flirt with Pru or to tease her and he was well enough informed on all the exhibits to keep the ladies well entertained. All the same, she wished now that she had not accepted Lady Conyers's invitation. She would have been much more comfortable with her aunt and Lady Borcaster.

Garrick had been searching for two hours and still he had not found Prudence. He sent word to Albany, asking Lord John to join him at Stanhope Gate and made his way there, waiting impatiently until he saw two familiar figures coming towards him.

'I fetched Stow along with me,' said Jack by way of greeting. 'I thought he might be useful.'

'I'd like to help, if I can, Your Grace.'

Garrick put his hand briefly on the man's shoulder to convey his gratitude. 'Thank you, Stow.'

'You say Pru is here somewhere with Lady Conyers?' asked Jack.

'Yes. They were both at Lady Elsdon's booth this morning, but then they went off and are not expected to return. I have no idea where they are heading, and the crowds are such I have not seen them yet.'

'Well, three of us will stand a better chance,' said Jack.

'Aye.' Garrick felt a little of his anxiety easing. He explained his plan for searching the three parks where the Jubilee celebrations were taking place and they agreed various points to meet throughout the day. As they prepared to move off Jack gripped the duke's arm.

'Don't worry, Garr. This could be nothing more than an innocent outing for two friends.'

'You do not believe that any more than I,' Garrick retorted.

Jack held his eyes for a moment, then he shook his head. 'No, sadly I don't. We had best get searching.'

Sir Joseph accompanied the ladies back to Hyde Park to watch the naval re-enactment and after that he announced that he had hired a supper booth for them all in St James's Park.

'How clever of you, my love. You think of everything,' sighed his wife, admiring. 'Is that not wonderful, Prudence dear?'

But Pru had had enough. She said, 'You are both very kind but you must forgive me if I do not stay. I have been out all day and I should be getting back to Brook Street.'

'Oh, but we have not seen the Chinese Pagoda!' exclaimed Helene. 'Surely you would like to see that. It has the new gas lighting, too, which will look splendid now it is growing dark.'

'And my carriage waits on the Mall, on the other side of St James's Park,' added Sir Joseph. 'We may see the Pagoda on the way.'

'I am happy to find a cab to take me back to Brook Street,' said Pru. 'I would by no means curtail your enjoyment.'

'I would not hear of it,' exclaimed Helene. 'You are my guest. What would your aunt say if I allowed you to go home unattended?' She sighed. 'What a pity we sent Ronald away when Sir Joseph arrived. He might have accompanied you. But I do not think it would be wise for you to go off alone, and in the dark, too.'

'I agree.' Sir Joseph nodded. 'I fear some of the spectators have been drinking too freely.'

A sudden roar of raucous laughter added weight to his words and Prudence bit her lip. Sir Joseph had done nothing so far to arouse her suspicion and she could not deny that the crowd was becoming unruly. Helene took her arm again.

'I am sure your aunt will not expect you to leave before you have seen the fireworks, my dear. We will take you home directly after that, if you wish to go.'

'An excellent idea, my dear,' purred Sir Joseph. 'Well, Miss Clifford, will that do for you?'

Prudence could not deny she had been looking forward to the firework display, which promised to be a magnificent spectacle. It had been a long day, but she had seen nothing in the behaviour of Helene or her husband to suggest they had any motive for this outing, other than to enjoy themselves.

'Very well,' she said last. 'I will leave directly after the fireworks.'

* * *

Garrick walked to the toll gate at the corner of Hyde Park for the next rendezvous. The area was well lighted with oil lamps and he looked at his watch. Ten o'clock. And there was Jack, coming towards him.

'Anything?' he asked, although one look at his friend's face told him no.

'It is hopeless, Garr. The crowds are constantly moving. We would need the devil's own luck to find anyone here tonight.'

His final words were drowned out by the sudden thunder of artillery.

'The fireworks in St James's Park,' said Garrick. 'We will go there. It is my last hope. After that we should go to Brook Street. Prudence might have returned there by now.'

Brave words, but he could not bring himself to believe them.

'Your Grace!'

Stow's voice made him spin around, his hopes rising once more. 'You have found her?'

'No, Your Grace, but I did notice Sir Joseph's carriage standing in the Mall. I got talking with the driver and he told me he had orders from his master to wait there for him.'

'That's better,' exclaimed Jack. 'News at last!

'It is, although you say the man mentioned his master. Does that mean Sir Joseph is here somewhere, too?'

'Aye, sir.' Stow nodded at him. 'The driver said he had brought his mistress and her friend to Hyde Park early this morning and had to make the same journey again, some hours later, with Sir Joseph.'

'It is likely they are all together in one of the parks, then,' said Garrick, his spirits reviving.

'And that ain't all, Your Grace,' Stow went on. 'Since we was none of us in a hurry to move on, I treated the driver and the footman to a pie from a passing hawker. After which we fell into quite a conversation. It seems the footman had been following the ladies around the parks all morning, until Sir Joseph turned up. Then he was sent back to wait at the carriage, but he did mention that his master had booked a supper booth for the evening. To watch the fireworks.'

'Excellent work, man. Remind me to increase your salary when we get to Hartland!'

Stow grinned. 'Thank you, Your Grace.'

'Come along, we'll get to the Mall.' Garrick put a hand to his aching ribs. 'If Sir Joseph's carriage is still there then Stow and I will keep a watch on it while you, Jack, take a look around the supper booths, to see if you can find the Conyerses.'

The plan agreed, they set off, accompanied by the noisy woosh and bang of the firework display, which lit up the night sky. When they reached the Mall, they soon spotted the Conyerses' carriage. Keeping to the shadows, Garrick and Stow strolled under the trees that divided St James's Park from the thoroughfare while Jack went off to search the hired booths.

'This is as far as we can go,' muttered Garrick, when they drew level with Sir Joseph's coach. He led Stow further into the shadows. 'All we can do now is wait.'

When they reached the supper booth Sir Joseph had reserved Lady Conyers insisted upon Pru having first choice of the dishes. The food looked delicious, but she merely picked at it. She was growing increasingly uneasy, although she could not say why.

'Lost your appetite, Miss Clifford?' remarked Sir Joseph.

He offered to top up her glass, which was still half full, but she refused politely.

She said, 'It has been a long day, sir. I fear I am too tired to be much company now. I really think it would be best if I left.'

Lady Conyers cried out immediately at that.

'Oh, my dear, but the fireworks have just started. Will you not stay until the end?'

'I think not,' said Pru, having made up her mind. 'In fact, I think it is just the time to go, for the display is lighting up the whole park as bright as day. Pray do not get up—it is but a short walk to the Mall, where I am sure I can find a cab to convey me back to Brook Street.'

'No, no I will not let you go alone,' exclaimed Lady Conyers, pushing aside her plate. 'Mrs Clifford would never forgive me! We shall come with you.'

Nothing Pru could say would dissuade them and as they stepped out of the booth Helene took her arm.

'I should hate us to be separated by the mob,' she said with a theatrical shudder.

'No indeed,' said Sir Joseph, walking close on the other side of Pru. 'We might never find each other again.'

Pru made no reply. Perhaps she was being over-anxious, even melodramatic, but it was clear that any attempt to escape would be instantly foiled.

The fireworks lighting the skies overhead had brought even more people into St James's Park and Prudence quite lost her bearings as they wove their way through the crowd. She felt very tired and a little light-headed when at last they emerged onto the Mall. The road was lined with stationary carriages including, Pru noticed, a number of vehicles for hire.

'There really is no need for you to accompany me further,' she said. She was so fatigued now that her words were slurring. 'I can easily find a cab here to take me home.'

'Nonsense, my dear.' Lady Helene's hold on her arm tightened. 'It is not far out of our way, and our carriage will be far more comfortable.'

Sir Joseph lifted his cane and pointed. 'Look, it is but a step away.' He caught Pru's free arm. 'You look very pale, Miss Clifford. Let me help you.'

She did indeed feel a little unwell now, but when Sir Joseph put his hand beneath her elbow, she was overcome by panic. She began to struggle against the hands holding her.

'No. No. Let me go! Let me *go*!

But Sir Joseph's arm came around her like a vice, squeezing her so tightly against him that she could scarce breathe, let alone scream for help. Her head felt very heavy and it was difficult to think clearly.

'There, there, ma'am, do not take on so.' Sir Joseph turned his head to address a concerned passer-by, saying ruefully. 'Wife's sister, having one of her turns. We should not have brought her out.'

'The wine,' she mumbled. 'You poisoned the wine!'

Pru struggled to cry for help but could not catch her breath and the straw bonnet, which had served her so well during the heat of the day, now cast a deep shadow over her countenance. Even if they should pass someone she knew, there was little chance of them recognising the struggling, confused woman as Miss Prudence Clifford.

'Nearly there,' declared Helene, holding Pru's arm

tightly. 'You will soon be at home, my dear, safe in your own room.'

They were approaching the carriage now and Sir Joseph shouted to the footman at the back.

'Ronald, open the door. Quickly now, the lady is not well!'

The driver was gathering up the reins and Pru forced her numbed limbs to struggle. She made a last feeble attempt to cry out, to no avail. She was lost.

Garrick and Stow were in the shadow of the trees, watching the crowds spilling out from the park. Men, women and children were strolling along the Mall, bumping into one another as they looked up and exclaimed at the spectacle in the sky above them.

'Where are they?' muttered Garrick, shifting his weight to relieve his aching body. Then his heart contracted. He saw Sir Joseph and Helene, half dragging, half carrying a drooping figure between them.

'There they are. Come on!'

He pushed his way through the press of spectators, shouting as he went.

'Stop! Abduction!'

But his words merely added to the noisy confusion of the crowd and he was obliged to barge past the last few people to reach his quarry.

'Conyers, stop!'

Sir Joseph had just reached the carriage. He released his hold of Pru and turned to face Garrick.

'Hartland.' He spat out the name; his face was contorted with rage. 'I have not finished with you yet!'

'Oh, I think you have. Sidmouth has the Frenchman safe. He knows of your plans.'

'No matter, I shall be in France by tomorrow, but

I shall still make you pay before I leave!' He swung around to address his wife and the footman, who were bundling Pru towards the coach. 'Get her away. I will follow you.'

With an oath Garrick made for the carriage but Sir Joseph barred his way, the gleaming point of a sharp blade between them.

'You may have lost your sword stick, Hartland, but I still have mine.'

'I'm with you, Your Grace!' declared Stow, stepping up, but Garrick threw out an arm to stop him.

'No, you are unarmed.'

'But I am not!' Jack appeared, a sword in his own hand. 'Leave this to me, Garr.'

Sensing a drama, the crowd had moved away, but only to form a circle at a safe distance. They were very ready to be entertained by the anticipated brawl. With a snarl Sir Joseph turned to face the new threat.

'Ronald, to me, to me!' He shouted over his shoulder to his footman, who was closing the carriage door upon the ladies.

Garrick ran towards the coach. The lackey was in his path but Stow charged forward, knocking the man out of the way.

'Go on, Your Grace, I'll deal with this!'

The driver was whipping up the horses, the wheels were turning. Garrick sprinted onto the road and made a desperate leap for the back of the coach.

Chapter Twenty-Three

Pru's head was spinning. She was thrust roughly into the carriage and had not gathered her wits before Helene was behind her, one arm around her neck in a choking hold. Despite her diminutive form, Lady Conyers was strong and Pru scrabbled to loosen the suffocating grip as the coach lurched into motion.

'Interfering jade!' Helene screamed at her. 'Do you think Garrick Chauntry could ever be yours?'

'I don't think that,' was all Pru could manage. She was gasping for air.

'But you have been spying for him! Well, you will regret it now, and so will he! You will both be ruined by the time we have finished with you.'

From the corner of her eye, Pru saw Helene raise her free hand and the sudden flare of a streetlamp glinted on the small glass phial she was holding. It smelled sweet, very like the laudanum Pru had given to Garrick, and she pressed her lips together, determined not to swallow it. The carriage was swaying wildly now and it was difficult to keep her balance as her hands clawed at the arm around her neck.

'But it's not only the duke, is it?' Helene hissed in

her ear. 'Remember young Trenchard? I saw you dancing with him at the Shrivenham Ball. He was ready to fall into my hands like a ripe plum before you warned him off. You must pay for that, too!'

A sudden lurch threw them onto the seat and Pru broke free from the stranglehold. She thrust Helene away and saw the phial fly from her hand, but Pru barely had chance to draw a breath. With a shriek of rage, Helene launched herself at Pru again, kicking, biting and spitting.

Garrick clung on to the back of the coach, fighting down a sudden bout of dizziness. He couldn't faint off now, he needed to help Pru. At last his head cleared. He climbed up and scrambled across the roof to the box. He wrestled the reins from the driver, but in the ensuing struggle the man lost his balance and fell. Garrick was still untangling the reins but he glanced back and was relieved to see the fellow climbing to his feet. He appeared to be unharmed, and Garrick turned his attention back to the task of controlling the horses. Now all he had to do was find somewhere to stop. And stop soon, judging by the noise from inside the coach. The screeches and thuds suggested that the two women were fighting like wildcats.

Garrick drove away from the parks, looking for a quiet street into which he might turn and stop the carriage. His ribs were sore from the exertion, which was also making his head swim, but finally he found what he was looking for. He drew up and called to a man walking towards him.

'You, fellow, would you like to earn yourself a shilling?'

'What, me? Earn a shilling?' The man stopped and

looked up. He did not sound quite sober, but he looked respectable enough, and Garrick had little choice. He could not leave the restive team unattended while he jumped down.

'Two shillings then, if you will hold the horses' heads for a while.'

'Aye, sir. Gladly.'

The man took up his position and Garrick scrambled down from the box. He snatched open the door, half afraid of what he might discover, but it was Pru's voice that came from the darkness.

'Thank goodness, it is you,' she exclaimed. 'I thought we would never stop.'

'Did you follow us, Your Grace?'

Pru sounded unhurt and Garrick felt some of the tension ease from his body.

'No. I, er, ejected the driver.'

His eyes were adjusting to the dark interior. He could see she had lost her bonnet and her hair was hanging loose about her shoulders. She seemed to be crouching on the floor, but a closer look showed that she was in fact sitting upon her adversary.

He glanced back towards the horses. They were standing quietly with their minder and he turned his attention back to the ladies.

'Perhaps you should let Lady Conyers get up now.'

Prudence moved back onto the seat and Helene climbed up from the floor. In the dim light she looked even more dishevelled than her opponent.

'Thank heaven you are here, Garrick,' she said, her voice shaking with rage. 'This, this *harpy* tried to kill me!'

'Indeed, I did not,' Pru retorted. 'You were going to

drug me! Laudanum,' she said, when Garrick smothered an oath. 'I think they had put some in the wine they served with supper. Thankfully I did not drink too much of it.'

'Thank God for that,' he muttered, climbing into the coach and sitting down. His head was hammering fearfully.

'What do we do now?' Pru asked him.

'Not too sure.' The pain had shifted to his eyes, his vision seemed to be narrowing. He tried to make his spinning brain concentrate. 'I think...'

The blackness closed over him.

'Garrick!' Pru flew across the small space between them. 'Garrick!'

He was slumped in the corner and she tapped his cheek. There was nothing, not even the slightest flicker of life. But he was breathing. That gave her some comfort.

Lady Conyers jumped up, but Pru turned on her, fierce as a lioness.

'Sit back down!'

Helene subsided, eyeing her warily. 'What do you propose to do now? You cannot keep me here and tend the duke at the same time.'

She was right, Pru acceded as she eased the unconscious duke down onto the bench seat. Garrick was far more important to her.

'Very well,' she said, 'Take yourself off. I am sure Lord Sidmouth will find you soon enough.'

For the first time Lady Conyers looked uneasy. 'You cannot steal my coach!'

'I will do whatever is necessary to save the duke!'

Prudence climbed out and went to have a word with

the young man holding the horses. He looked terrified when she suggested he should drive the carriage to Dover Street.

'I could run for a surgeon,' he suggested.

Pru shook her head. She had no idea what sort of man he might bring back with him and she knew that a bad doctor could do more harm than good. Biting her lip in frustration, she ran back to check on Garrick, who was still stretched out on the bench seat. She put her fingers gently on his neck. It was a relief to feel a faint pulse. It was erratic, but definitely there.

'What are you doing?' Helene demanded. 'What is happening?'

'We must get him back to Dover Street with all speed.'

'And what about me?'

Pru was very tempted to say she neither knew nor cared. Instead, she said, 'Can you drive this carriage?'

'Of course not!'

'Then you are no use to me.'

Spotting her reticule lying on the carriage floor, Pru snatched it up and jumped out, ordering Helene to follow her. Gently closing the carriage door upon Garrick's unconscious form, she went up to the young man at the horses' heads.

'Keep them steady while I gather up the reins.' She handed him her purse. 'Then I would be obliged if you would find a cab and escort this lady to her house.'

'Y-yes, ma'am.'

Ignoring Helene's continued protests Prudence walked back to the carriage. She glanced up at the box seat, high above her head. She was accustomed to driving a gig and had occasionally handled the reins of the waggon, when everyone was needed to help with the harvest on Home Farm, but she'd never driven such a vehicle as this. However, there was no one else to do it.

Swallowing hard, Pru hitched her skirts and climbed up. She gathered up the reins and, heart thudding, she called to the man to release the horses.

Somehow, Pru managed to drive the team to Dover Street without mishap. Lights shone from Garrick's house and Stow and Jack Callater rushed out as soon as she drew up. While Stow took care of his master, Jack helped Pru to descend from the perilously high box seat. He wanted to carry her off to the drawing room, but Pru would have none of it. The danger was not over yet and she knew she must remain in charge, at least for a while.

Once Stow and the servants had carefully undressed the duke and put him into his bed, Prudence insisted on staying beside him. Calmly, she gave orders to his servants and sat beside his bed, bathing his forehead with lavender water. Only when the duke's own doctor arrived did she join Jack in the drawing room.

'Ah, the sawbones is here, then,' said Lord John, pouring a glass of brandy for her.

'Yes. I have asked him to report to us once he has finished his examination.'

'Good. Now, sit down and drink this. You are looking alarmingly pale.'

He settled her into a chair, pressing the glass into her hand, and it was a measure of how frail she felt that Prudence did not refuse. She took a sip, trying not to gasp as the fiery liquid burned her throat.

'I was very glad you came out to meet me,' she told him. 'I was trembling so much I could not have climbed down to knock on the door.'

He said, 'We were keeping watch, although, frankly, we had little expectation of seeing either of you before morning.'

'How did you know what had happened?'

'Stow called at Brook Street with Garrick's note, telling you that Sidmouth had been to Alder Grove and taken Vence away to safety. He reported that you had gone to the fair with Lady Conyers and Garr set off immediately to look for you. Stow and I joined him later, and it was fortunate that Stow spotted the Conyerses' coach or we would never have found you.' He grinned. 'Garr was quite the hero, leaping onto the carriage as it drove off.'

'He did that, to rescue me?' She felt suddenly quite tearful.

'Yes. Stow and I saw Garr hanging on the back but there was nothing we could do until we had dealt with Conyers and his servant.'

'Oh, dear, I appear to have caused you a great deal of trouble.'

'Devil a bit,' declared Jack cheerfully. 'But how came you to be driving it back?'

'There was no one else,' she said simply. 'Garrick had overpowered the driver and pushed him off. When we stopped, he climbed into the carriage to see if I was safe and, and collapsed, unconscious. All I could think of was to bring him here to Dover Street, with all speed.'

'I see.' Lord John went over to the side table to refill his brandy glass. 'What happened to the belle Helene?'

'I was obliged to let her go.'

'Stow and I failed to apprehend Sir Joseph, too. He and his footman ran off. Ah well, it hardly matters. We sent word to Lord Sidmouth as soon as we got back.

With our testimony and Vence safe in his keeping, he will deal with the matter now.'

He went on to tell her that the Frenchman had withdrawn his accusations against Garrick. Pru was relieved, but even that seemed of little importance, compared to Garrick's present predicament. When the doctor came in she looked up hopefully, but he could give them little cheer. There was nothing he could do until the duke regained consciousness.

'*If* he does,' he concluded. 'You said he was attacked recently, Miss Clifford? Well, it is very likely that the exertion of this evening was too much too soon. Now all we can do is wait.'

It was then that Jack voiced the questions Pru was afraid to ask.

'But will he recover, Doctor, and will his brain be damaged?'

'As to that, only time will tell. Call me again once he shows signs of consciousness.'

The doctor departed, leaving behind him an atmosphere of gloom. Pru refused to give in to melancholy and turned her thoughts to practical matters.

'The duke will need someone at his bedside constantly, in case he becomes fractious. I suggest Mr Stow and I do that between us.'

'That is impossible,' declared Jack. 'You cannot stay unchaperoned in a bachelor's house.'

'I can and I will,' Pru retorted. 'I have more experience with head wounds than anyone else here.'

Lord John looked mutinous, but Pru found an ally in the duke's man, who had come in at that moment.

'Miss Clifford is right,' Stow concurred. 'She is by far the best person to care for His Grace.'

Jack continued to argue, but Pru would not be moved

and at last he went back to Albany, leaving Stow to keep watch over his master for the next four hours, while Prudence was shown to the guest room, where she soon fell into a deep sleep of sheer exhaustion.

The first flush of dawn was creeping into the bedroom when Pru opened her eyes. She stared up at the unfamiliar canopy for a moment as the events of the previous day flooded back, then she pushed back the covers and sprang out of bed, eager to be up and doing something. It had been agreed she would relieve Stow at six o'clock and she hoped Mrs Almond, the duke's housekeeper had not forgotten to send a maid up, for she judged it must be nearly that time now.

She had no wrap with her and was grateful for the shift she had borrowed from Mrs Almond. It was a little short, but roomy and warm enough for her to sit down at the little table and finish writing the letter for Aunt Minerva that she had started last night.

She had just added a carriage clock to the list of items she wanted sent over from Brook Street when a maid came bustling in.

'Good morning, ma'am, I'm Betty. Mrs Almond sent me up to wait on you.' She nodded towards the clothes over her arm. 'She says to tell you she's cleaned up your gown as best she can, and mended a torn flounce on the skirt, but there's nothing she can do for the stain on the sleeve of your pelisse.'

'No matter, Betty, I shall not need that today.'

She was dressed in a matter of minutes then asked Betty to wait while she finished her letter.

'It will only take me a moment and then you may go downstairs and ask Mrs Almond if she would kindly have someone carry it to Brook Street for me.'

'Very well, ma'am. And shall I show you to the break-fast room?'

But this offer Pru politely declined. In truth, she was too anxious to eat anything until she had seen Garrick for herself.

The duke's bedchamber was much as she had left it last night except for the tell-tale smoky haze hanging in the air where the candles had recently been snuffed out. Stow looked up as she came in and answered her unspoken question.

'He has not stirred, ma'am.'

Stifling her fears, Pru came across to the bed and laid a hand on Garrick's forehead.

'At least there is no fever. Thank you, Mr Stow. I will sit with him now while you get some sleep.'

'Aye, ma'am, thank you. Is there anything I can fetch you?'

'Thank you, no. Mrs Almond is sending up tea and bread and butter for me. And she has agreed to make some lemonade for the duke. She says he was very fond of it as a boy.'

'Aye, he was.'

Her brows rose. 'You knew him then?'

'I did, Miss Clifford. I was footman at Hartland in those days, and training up to serve as valet to the old duke when Sykes, his own man, was growing too old to do everything. Then Lord Garrick, as he was then, went off to France and asked me to go with him, as his valet. We've seen some hard times together, His Grace and me.' A shadow passed over his face and for a moment Pru was afraid he might break down, but he shook it off and gave her a cheerful look. 'But we came through them all and we shall do so again.'

With that he went out and Prudence turned back to the figure lying in the great bed. If it had not been for the steady rise and fall of his chest beneath the snowy nightshirt, she might have thought him lifeless. His face was still badly bruised, but this did not worry her so much as his immobility. She had no idea how deeply unconscious he might be. Despite that, she knew what she must do.

'Good morning, Garrick.' She bent and gently kissed his cheek, feeling the rasp of stubble against her skin.

He did not respond. There was no miraculous recovery, not even the flutter of an eyelid to show he was aware of her.

Perfectly natural. No need to lose heart yet.

'I hope you do not mind me making you a little tidier,' she said, gently straightening the bedcovers. 'When Stow returns I shall ask him to shave you, but for now all I can do is to wash your face. Tomorrow, I hope to have a book to read to you. Lord Byron. *The Bride of Abydos.* Do you know it? I believe it is very popular, although I did not come across it until I came to Town this year. I have asked my aunt to send it to me, since I have not had chance to open it. I thought we might read it together—how will that be?'

She chattered on, eliciting no response from Garrick. She expected none, but more than one doctor had told her that patients often reported they had heard what was being said around them when they were unconscious. In Walter's case, sadly, she would never know, but Prudence would not give up hope.

Chapter Twenty-Four

'Stow!' Prudence looked up in surprise when the bedroom door opened. 'Surely it is not yet time for you to relieve me?'

'No, ma'am, but Lady Borcaster and Mrs Clifford have come to see you. I have put them in the drawing room and asked for refreshments to be sent up.' He coughed. 'I thought you might like to go down immediately, ma'am.'

Pru nodded. She was not surprised to hear they had called, and could imagine their anxiety. She quickly made her way downstairs to the drawing room, pausing to take a deep breath before she opened the door.

She had barely uttered a greeting before Aunt Minerva fell upon her neck.

'Oh, my dear girl, we have been so worried about you!'

'I am very sorry, Aunt, but I thought it better to wait and write this morning, to tell you I was safe. The garbled words that were flowing from my pen in the early hours made no sense at all and would only have added to your fears.'

'But what happened?' demanded Lady Borcaster.

'And why are you now here, in the Duke of Hartland's residence?'

'Will you not sit down?' said Pru, conscious of her duty. 'Perhaps you would like to take a glass of wine?'

'I will do neither,' said Aunt Minerva, wiping her eyes.

'Nor I,' declared Lady Borcaster.

'I see,' said Pru. 'Have you brought the things I asked for in my letter, Aunt?'

'No, my love,' Mrs Clifford replied. 'We have come to take you back to Brook Street.'

'Ah.' Pru tried a smile. 'I'm afraid I cannot come back quite yet.'

Finding two pairs of eyes fixed on her with a mixture of horror and disbelief, she again suggested they should sit down.

'It will take some time to tell you everything,' she added.

Pru described all the events of the previous day, explaining that Sir Joseph and Lady Conyers's actions were the result of an ancient grievance. What that grievance might be she did not say and was grateful that the ladies were too stunned by her tale to enquire deeply.

'Well, well, it is all very shocking,' remarked Mrs Clifford, when Pru had finished. 'But now that His Grace is back in his own house, my love, there can be no need for you to stay.'

'But there is, Aunt. The duke needs me to nurse him.'

'Nonsense!' declared Lady Borcaster. 'Hartland will have the finest doctors at his disposal. It is quite unnecessary for you to stay. And highly improper, too. Bad enough that you have been here since the early hours, but if you come back with us now, we can—'

Pru interrupted her. 'I beg your pardon, ma'am, but

I will not leave the duke. He is unconscious, and I must look after him until I am sure he is recovered. Or…' Her clasped hands tightened until the knuckles glowed white. 'Or not.'

Her Ladyship looked outraged, but Mrs Clifford understood and said, by way of explanation, 'You know, Jane, that Pru's brother, Walter, died after falling from his horse. Pru tended him for several weeks. Until the end.'

'But that was her brother,' snapped my lady. 'Quite understandable that Prudence should nurse *him*. This however…' She began to fan herself vigorously. 'Why, every feeling is offended.'

'I will not leave him,' Pru repeated, stubbornly.

'I understand your concern, my dear,' said Aunt Minerva gently. 'But you must think of your reputation. Hartland has any number of scandals attached to him, to say nothing of this latest charge.'

'But that is now proved to be false, Aunt. The duke is no spy, as everyone will learn very soon.'

'Is that so? Well, well, I am relieved, but that is not all,' replied Mrs Clifford. 'It is common knowledge that he kept poor Miss Speke dangling for ten years and then abandoned her. And now someone has unearthed the rumour that he fought a duel with the husband of his mistress, and then ran off to France leaving his opponent for dead! What will people say when they know you are staying here in his house, unchaperoned?'

Pru shook her head. 'What they say of me is irrelevant. I have more knowledge of head wounds than anyone else in this house. I would never forgive myself if I did not do everything I can to aid the duke's recovery.'

Lady Borcaster gave an impatient huff. 'If you care nothing for your own reputation then pray consider your aunt! Do you not see how she too will be tarnished by this? She will be the object of ridicule and speculation. The best that people will say is she threw you at the duke's head. As for the worst...'

She broke off, spreading her hands in a gesture of despair. Mrs Clifford patted her friend's arm and turned again to Prudence.

'My dear, what do you expect to be the outcome of all this, if the duke recovers? Is there some understanding between you?'

'No, Aunt.'

'Perhaps you think he will offer for you out of gratitude?'

'I hope he will not,' replied Pru. 'I should never allow him to do that.'

'Then come away now, my dear, while it is possible for us to protect your good name.'

'I cannot.' Her fingers writhed together and she struggled to explain herself. 'I am not at liberty to explain everything to you, but the duke does not deserve his reputation. Any of it. The women he has known in his life have all betrayed or abandoned him when he needed them most. I cannot, will not do that. He is lying unconscious now because he was trying to help me and I will stay with him as long as I can be of some use.'

Lady Borcaster shook her head. 'Poor, deluded girl. You would be well served if your aunt disowned you.'

Pru ignored this and fixed her eyes on Mrs Clifford.

'I am aware I am flouting convention and I shall take the consequences. That is my choice, my decision and no blame should fall upon you, Aunt. We are only related by marriage, after all. If you feel you cannot support me in this, then I quite understand.'

'I will not abandon my late husband's niece, how can

you think it, Prudence?' Mrs Clifford gave a long sigh. 'Very well, stay here, my love. If Jane will have me, I will remain at Brook Street, but I shall quite understand if that is not possible. I shall find myself a hotel where I may stay until I can carry you away from town. I very much fear that you will not be able to take up your life with me in Bath again, but the least I can do is to see you safely restored to your parents.'

Lady Borcaster had listened closely to this interchange and now she surprised the others by declaring, 'Well, if you are going to show such Christian charity, Minerva, then it behoves me to show some compassion, too. There is no question but that you will remain as my guest. We may yet be able to hush up all this. We will put it about that Miss Clifford has been called away. That man Stow appeared to be a very sensible sort and assured us that the duke's household will not gossip. I believe my own servants can be trusted to stay silent on the matter, too.'

'Thank you, Lady Borcaster. And thank *you*, best of my aunts.'

She kissed her aunt's cheek and the two ladies went away, leaving Pru to consider all that had been said. Despite the brave words at the end, both her aunt and Lady Borcaster were convinced that by remaining in Dover Street to nurse Garrick, her reputation would be ruined. Sadly, she had to agree.

Prudence went up to her bedchamber. She needed to rest if she was to nurse Garrick again in the evening and she tried to put the ladies' visit firmly to the back of her mind. However, despite her exhaustion, when she lay down on her bed sleep would not come.

She knew that her actions would reflect badly upon

both her aunt and Lady Borcaster if they stood by her, which made her doubly grateful for their support. Yet with that came guilt. It was one thing to risk her own reputation, but should she also risk theirs? But how could she not? Garrick's life was at stake. Yet the doubts persisted.

You were not able to save your brother...what makes you think you can save the duke?

Tears welled up and Pru forced them back. She could not be sure what she was doing would be successful, but she knew she must try. Her love for Garrick was so strong now she would do anything she could to help him.

Fatigue finally overcame Pru. She fell into a deep sleep, only waking when Betty came in to rouse her, late in the afternoon. Her trunk had arrived from Brook Street while she was sleeping and she was able to put on a fresh gown before making her way back to Garrick's room at the appointed hour. Stow greeted her with relief.

'His Grace is growing restless, Miss Clifford. I have not seen him like this before.'

'Let us hope it is a good sign.' She laid a hand on the duke's brow. 'He has a slight fever. I will try the lavender water again.'

'Aye, ma'am. If it's all the same to you I won't leave yet,' said Stow. 'He is very strong and you might need me to help you, if he grows too fidgety.'

Pru sat down at the bedside, the bowl of water infused with lavender oil at her elbow. At first she feared Garrick would not respond. He moved his head from side to side as if trying to avoid the damp cloth, but gradually he grew calmer. She thought he had sunk back into unconsciousness when he suddenly reached up and caught her wrist.

'Prudence.'

Her heart leapt, but she replied as calmly as she could, 'I am here, Your Grace.'

She thought her words woefully inadequate but they seemed to calm him. He released her and his hand fell back to his side.

'Well,' breathed Stow, standing beside her. 'That surely indicates an improvement, doesn't it, ma'am?'

'I hope so, Mr Stow.' Trying not to tremble, she wrung out the cloth again and applied it gently to Garrick's brow. 'I hope so.'

The remainder of Pru's vigil was uneventful but Garrick's speaking her name was heartening. When Stow returned at midnight she did not want to leave. She wanted to stay with Garrick, to be at his side if he should wake again, but she knew that was foolish. Stow was perfectly capable of keeping watch and she needed to be fresh and alert to relieve him again in the morning.

When Pru returned to the sickroom soon after dawn, Stow informed her that Garrick had shown no signs of waking again during the night. She was disappointed, but summoned a smile and agreed that the duke looked better now he had been shaved and dressed in a clean nightshirt. Stow went off to seek his bed and Pru settled down to while away the morning with her embroidery.

By ten o'clock her spirits had not improved. Garrick remained unresponsive to her occasional remarks, although she had managed to coax a few drops of lemonade between his lips. Sighing, she picked up the book she had brought in with her.

'I have the Byron to read to you, if you wish.'

No answer, but what had she expected? She opened the book at the title page.

"'*The Bride of Abydos. A Turkish Tale.*'" Her eyes moved down to four lines of a poem. 'It begins with a quote from Robert Burns... "*Had we never loved so kindly, Had we never loved so blindly, Never met or never parted, We had ne'er been broken-hearted.*"'

Her voice cracked on the final line and she put the book aside. It summed up how she felt today. Broken-hearted. Pru gave a sob and put her hands over her face.

'Oh, Garrick, please don't die,' she whispered. 'Please don't leave me in this world without you.'

Hot, silent tears ran through her fingers and she dashed them away, appalled at her own weakness. She quickly searched for her handkerchief to dry her cheeks.

'I beg your pardon,' she said to the motionless figure in the bed. 'I must be very tired. I am not normally such a watering pot.'

Calming herself with a deep breath, she picked up the book again and turned the pages until she arrived at the first canto. Then she cleared her throat and began to read.

Pru was halfway through the second canto when she heard the door open. Thinking it was Stow, she carried on to the end of the stanza before looking up.

'Oh!' She almost dropped the book when she saw the lady in the doorway. A tall, upright figure dressed in black. She addressed Prudence in arctic tones.

'What in heaven's name are you doing with my son?'

Garrick's mother! Pru rose and curtsied.

'I am reading to him, Your Grace.'

She watched the duchess move closer to the bed. Pru thought she must have been handsome once, but her face was now pale and drawn, and the dark hair beneath the black lace cap heavily streaked with grey.

'But he is unconscious. What good will that do?'

Pru tried not to feel angry at the duchess's cold tone. She had not seen her son for ten years. Perhaps she was shocked by his appearance now.

'One never knows if someone in this state can hear anything, Your Grace,' she said calmly. 'But surely it is better to try than not.'

The duchess turned and Pru found herself staring into a pair of green eyes, so like Garrick's that she felt the breath catch in her throat.

'And what right have you to nurse him?'

Pru's chin went up. 'I have some experience of caring for persons with head injuries. My name is Prudence Clifford—'

'I know who you are.' The duchess cut her off. 'Stow has told me how you come to be here.'

'Nothing that has happened reflects badly upon the duke.' Pru was quick to assure her. 'Quite the opposite, in fact. He was being…recklessly brave.'

'I have never doubted his courage. Only his wisdom.' The duchess stared down at Garrick, her countenance impassive.

Pru said quietly, 'Mr Stow and I share the task of keeping vigil at his bedside. He might wake at any time.'

'And he might not,' retorted the duchess. 'Stow told me the doctor was not encouraging.'

'He was afraid of raising false hopes.'

'And how long do you intend to carry on this vigil?'

'I shall stay as long as it is necessary, Your Grace.'

'What of your family? Do they support you in this?'

Pru hesitated. 'They do not, ma'am. However, I am of age and they cannot compel me to leave here.'

But you could, Your Grace.

She waited, wondering if the duchess would order her to leave. After a long, nerve-racking silence, the older woman nodded. She looked around the room.

'Is that for my son?' she asked, indicating the tray bearing an empty cup and a plate of bread and butter.

'No, Your Grace. It was brought up for me to break my fast.'

'You did not want it?'

'I drank the coffee.'

Pru noted the duchess's frown and added quickly, 'Cook sends up nourishing broth for the duke. Stow tells me His Grace managed to swallow a little, tonight. We also keep lemonade and barley water for him, over there, on the side table. Stow and I administer a little every hour or so.' She added simply, 'It gives us hope.'

'Hope!'

The duchess looked unconvinced. She came back towards the bed and stared down at her son. It was impossible to read her countenance, but Pru did not think her uncaring. She suspected Garrick's mother did not like to display her emotions before a stranger. Finally, after another long silence, the duchess went out. With a sigh Pru sank down onto the chair and closed her eyes.

At noon, Stow came in to relieve her.

'Have you seen the duchess?' Pru asked him. 'Has she spoken to you about me?'

'Yes, ma'am, she has.'

'And…does she want me to leave?'

'Why no. Her Grace has requested your company at dinner.'

'Oh. I had not expected that! I would rather not…'

Stow coughed. 'If you will forgive my saying so, ma'am, I do not think it would be wise to refuse.'

'But I have to come back here at six o'clock this evening.' Pru was flustered. 'You cannot be expected to do it.'

'We can easily rearrange things, ma'am. Mrs Almond has said she will sit with His Grace while you are engaged this evening. She can summon me if needs be.'

'Very well.' There really was no choice. Pru realised the request from the duchess was in fact a summons. 'Perhaps you would help me turn the pillows before I go? I think it will make him more comfortable.'

The task was soon accomplished, but still she lingered, reluctant to leave.

'You should rest, ma'am.' Stow prompted her gently. 'You will need all your wits about you to dine with the duchess.'

'Yes. Yes of course.'

Chapter Twenty-Five

At the appointed time, Prudence was shown into the dining room, where she found the duchess already at the table.

'Forgive me if we do not observe the niceties of gathering in the drawing room beforehand,' she remarked as Prudence sat down to face her at the only other place laid at the table. 'I realise your free time is limited. I understand you mean to return to the sickroom after dinner.'

Prudence inclined her head, relaxing slightly. It appeared the duchess had accepted her presence in the house.

'That is my intention, Your Grace.'

'Very well. However, I insist upon you dining with me each evening.'

'Oh, but I cannot—'

She was interrupted.

'Stow tells me you only pick at the food sent up to you. You cannot nurse my son properly if you do not eat.'

Pru felt a smile tugging at the corners of her mouth and accepted defeat.

'You are quite right, ma'am.'

* * *

The meal proceeded. Prudence was subjected to what amounted to an interrogation by her hostess. She answered questions about her family, her friends and her visit to London patiently and truthfully, but she found it most dispiriting. Almost every sentence she uttered emphasised the difference between her own world and that of the Duke of Hartland.

Not that it mattered, she told herself as the covers were finally removed and dishes of sweetmeats placed on the table between them. Her only purpose was to convince the duchess that she was a fit and proper person to nurse Garrick back to health.

She braced herself for more questions as the duchess dismissed the servants.

'Stow tells me this is not the first time you have come to my son's aid.'

'No, ma'am.'

'Since the duke is clearly not able to tell me what is going on, I should be obliged if you would do so.'

Pru countered with a question of her own.

'May I ask first, why Your Grace is in town?'

In the brief pause their eyes met across the table. Pru had the distinct feeling she was being judged. She kept her gaze steady and at last the duchess nodded, apparently satisfied.

'I heard that my son is accused of treason. You look surprised, Miss Clifford. I may live retired in Devon, but I have friends here who keep me apprised of current gossip.'

'You may also know, then, of the other accusations that are levelled at the duke.'

'That he rejected the lady who has waited faithfully for him for the past ten years? That does not surprise me. His profligate ways have long been a source of dismay to me.'

'I do not believe he *is* profligate,' replied Prudence, surprised at her own daring.

'You presume to know him better than his own mother?'

'I know him to be a kind, brave and honourable man.'

'Do you indeed? Then you interest me, Miss Clifford. Pray explain yourself.'

'He has told me something of his earlier life.' How much should she say? 'His unfortunate *affaire* with a married lady—'

'Helene Conyers. Yes, I know of that!' The duchess interrupted her. 'If we are to discuss these matters then we should speak plainly, so there can be no misunderstanding.'

'Very well, ma'am. Lady Conyers seduced your son, as she had done with several young men before and still does. Her husband then gave Garrick the choice of paying a substantial sum to keep the affair from his family or facing him in a duel.'

'My son confided all that to you?'

The duchess looked shocked, but she had asked for plain speaking and Pru was not going to avoid it.

'Yes, although he was rather drunk at the time. I believed him then, and having since met Sir Joseph and his wife, I see no reason to doubt it is the truth.' She looked across the table at the duchess. 'Your son chose honour over extortion.'

'And was obliged to fly the country!'

'He told me he did not expect to hit his man. He believed *he* would be the one to perish.'

'Do you think his death would have been more acceptable to me?' exclaimed the duchess, high spots of colour appearing on her wan cheeks.

Prudence said gently, 'No, ma'am, but can you deny that he was reared to think the honour of the family of more importance than his life?'

She wondered if she had gone too far. The duchess reached towards the dish of sugared almonds then thought better of it and picked up her wine instead.

'You are quite right,' she said at last. 'Garrick has as much of the Chauntry Pride as any of his forebears. I can quite believe he risked his life to uphold the family honour. He broke his father's heart. And now he is going to break mine.'

Her voice shook. She dabbed at her mouth with her napkin and Pru felt a rush of sympathy for the old woman.

'He is not going to die, Your Grace, I will not let him.' Pru pushed back her chair. 'Now if you will excuse me, I had best return to my patient.'

Silence had fallen over the house. Pru heard the hall clock chiming the hours as she sat beside Garrick's bed. She had tried reading to him, but her mind was too distracted by her conversation with the duchess.

She had said she would not let him die and at that moment she had meant it, but now, sitting in the lofty, silent room, her conviction wavered. She could not see into the future. She did not know what state of mind Garrick would be in when he recovered. She could not even be sure that he *would* recover. But she must not think of that.

The eminent physician Sir Henry Halford arrived the following morning, summoned by the duchess, but his assessment was little different to that of Garrick's own doctor. There was nothing more to be done at present, and he could not fault the care the duke was receiving.

The days took on a familiar pattern. Stow and Prudence continued their vigil, both determined that one or the other of them would be on hand, should Garrick regain consciousness. Other members of his household were brought in when he needed to be moved while his bedding and nightshirt were replaced. Stow shaved his master at regular intervals, maintaining that the duke would not wish for anyone to see him looking less than his best.

'Especially now he is receiving visitors,' he added with a twinkle.

The only visitor was in fact Lord John, who called each day and stayed an hour talking with Garrick.

The duchess did not appear in the sickroom again, which saddened Pru until it occurred to her that the older lady might not be able to endure the sight of her only son lying still and unresponsive. Heaven knew it was hard enough for Pru! When they met at dinner each evening, she made sure she reported the duke's progress, or lack of it. Society manners prevailed in the dining room and, although their conversation was stilted at first, it gradually became easier. Pru grew more accustomed to her hostess's abrupt manner and was not afraid to disagree when she thought it necessary.

The duchess might not be pleased with her candid replies, but Pru saw no reason to dissemble. She was not trying to impress the older woman and there was no doubt it enlivened their discussions. Afterwards she would retire to her room, exhausted but well-fed, and sleep until she was roused in the early hours to sit with Garrick.

* * *

With a good meal each evening, Pru's energy and her spirits improved, although she still found the night-time vigil the most difficult. She stretched out on the daybed beneath the window, resting but alert for the slightest sound from Garrick. During the day she read to him, fed him with broth and teased drops of lemonade or barley water between his lips. She took courage from the fact that each day the bruises on his face were fading. He was looking better, but still he did not wake.

It was six o'clock on Monday morning and the household was already stirring when Prudence left the sick-room and returned to her bedchamber. In her pocket was the letter that had arrived late the night before and she had scanned it briefly, while sitting with Garrick.

Its contents had distressed her, but she had quickly hidden her anguish while she had tended Garrick. Now, however, in the privacy of her own room, she knew she must read it again.

It was from her Aunt Minerva, and after a brief hope that the duke was recovering she launched into the real reason for writing. The scandal had broken.

Heaven knows Lady B and I have not mentioned the matter to a soul, merely saying you were away on family business, but somehow word has got out that you are installed in Dover Street! It was the only subject on everyone's lips after morning service today, although no one was bold enough to quiz me directly about it.

The stories are wild and varied. Everything from the duke abducting you to be his mistress, to your being his nurse after he was fatally wounded in a duel and not expected to live.

My dear Prudence, I fear it is too late now to save your good name. All I can do is beg you to let me know as soon as you mean to quit Dover Street and I shall call for you. If I do not hear from you then I shall remain in London until the end of August, as planned.

Lady B is very good and insists I continue to live here as her guest. She still goes out into society, but I have quite given it up. Dear Jane is, of course, a diplomat's widow. She is accustomed to saying nothing and depressing pretension with a stare, but I cannot bear the sly looks and innuendo, for which I have no reply!

If you are still needed in Dover Street when I leave London, then you must come to me at Bath as soon as you can. Even if everyone there knows the scandal, I shall not desert you. From there we can write to your parents and arrange for you to go back to Melksham until this sorry business is forgotten…

There was more of the same. When she had first read it, Pru had shed tears for the hurt and disgrace she had brought upon her family. Word of the scandal could not yet have reached Dover Street, because the duchess had not mentioned it at dinner, and Pru was convinced she would not keep her thoughts on the subject a secret.

Pru was determined nothing should hinder a reconciliation between Garrick and his mother, but that could not happen until he regained consciousness. She could only pray she would be allowed to stay and nurse him until then.

* * *

Sleep was impossible, knowing that at any moment she might be summoned by an outraged duchess and thrown onto the street, and Pru merely dozed away the morning. However, by noon no such catastrophe had occurred and she took her place at Garrick's bedside. Stow went off after reporting that the duke had passed a peaceful night, which meant he had not stirred, there had been no sign of waking. And yet he breathed. She clung onto that one, fragile thread of hope.

Prudence sat down beside the bed. Her eyes were gritty from lack of sleep. She felt too tired to read and decided she would just sit there and keep watch. She reached out and took Garrick's hand—it was warm but unresponsive. Through the open window she could hear the traffic, the sounds of carriages rattling by, hawkers crying their wares, but in the room itself there was silence. Pru leaned forward and rested her cheek against Garrick's hand and closed her eyes.

'Pru.'

She heard him calling to her, very softly, and raised her head. He smiled, his green eyes warm with love.

'Come and lie with me.'

She walked around to the empty side of the bed and climbed in, measuring her length against him, sighing at the comfort it gave her just to be close to him.

'Darling Pru.'

He turned, folding her in his arms, kissing away all the pain and unhappiness. Desire stirred and her body came alive as his hands roamed over her breasts. They were both naked now, their skin touching, legs tangling. She moaned softly, her body aching with longing for him to hold her closer and feed the desire rippling through her.

A sudden crash and raised voices from the street jerked Pru to consciousness and her eyes flew open. She was still sitting beside Garrick's bed, still holding his hand and he was lying perfectly still, eyes closed. Dear heaven, it had all been a dream!

Yet her body was on fire for him. One night. One night she had spent in his bed and the memory was so strong it had infused her very bones! Tears of anguish and frustration welled up and Pru was obliged to blink them away. She went over to the wash stand and bathed her face. Was this what it would be like once she had left Dover Street? Would Garrick haunt her dreams as well as her waking hours?

I shall manage. I can live without him. Only please, please, let him recover!

She turned quickly as the bedroom door opened and the housekeeper bustled in.

'Well, ma'am, I beg your pardon for being so late with your refreshments today. The brewer's dray collided with a milk cart directly outside the door and the kitchen maid was too busy a-gawping at the mess to notice that the kettle had boiled dry. What a to-do! I hope the noise didn't disturb you or the master?'

'No.'

That must have been the crash that woke her. Pru looked at the motionless figure in the bed and her throat constricted.

'No,' she repeated. 'It did not disturb His Grace.'

Chapter Twenty-Six

By the time she had drunk a cup of tea and fed Garrick a few spoonsful of broth Prudence was once more in command of herself. Whatever the future held for her she would face it. If she could not return to Bath to live with Aunt Minerva then she would go back to Melksham and make a life for herself there with her parents. But for now, she must work at making Garrick well. She would read to him.

She had finished almost all of the books Lord John had procured for her. Having read several of Lord Byron's works and a rather improving tale by Maria Edgeworth she decided upon a three-volume novel handsomely bound in red leather.

'It is called *Pride and Prejudice*,' she told Garrick, keeping her tone cheerful. 'I think you were looking at it in Hatchards when I met you there with Lord John. Do you remember?'

She recalled that day only too well. How angry he had been with her and Jack for interfering. How she had found him later, beaten and bloodied. Pru quickly shook off that memory. She would not give in to any more melancholy thoughts today.

'I have heard good reports about this,' she went on. 'I hope we will enjoy it, Your Grace.'

It proved a good choice. The lively style and engaging character gripped Pru from the start. An hour flew by before she stopped and begged his pardon.

'My throat is too parched to carry on,' she told him, getting up and going across to the side table. 'The teapot is cold now…do you mind if I pour myself a glass of the barley water Mrs Almond brought up for you?' It had become second nature to carry on a one-sided conversation and she continued once she had filled a glass and taken a sip.

'Mmm,' she said, turning back. 'It is very good. I must ask her for the…'

The words died on her lips. Garrick's eyes were open and fixed upon her.

'Good day, Your Grace.'

Pru's cautious greeting was very much at odds with the ferocious pounding of her heart. She had longed for this moment, prayed for it, but now she did not know quite what to do. Garrick's eyes followed her as she started back across the room towards him.

'Pru.'

Her name. He murmured just the one word but it was her name! Relief and happiness flooded through her. It was a good start, but she must not be too complacent. She hurried over and took his hand.

'Yes, I am here.' His eyelids drooped and she felt a moment's panic. 'No, no, do not go back to sleep!'

She saw him frown a little, and although he did not open his eyes again, she felt the pressure as he squeezed her hand.

* * *

Over the next few days Garrick showed more signs of recovery. He was awake for longer periods and even managed to eat some of the succulent delicacies concocted by his chef to tempt his appetite. Between them, Stow and Pru watched him constantly, heartened by Sir Henry Halford's assurances that the patient was on the mend, even though he was dazed and confused, and only spoke the odd word.

Pru continued to read to him. The lively tale was so engrossing that at times she was even able to forget the weight of anxiety pressing down upon her spirits. She was halfway through the third volume, a few days after that first waking, when she looked up to find Garrick watching her.

Her heart leapt. Surely his eyes looked more alert this time.

She smiled. 'Are you thirsty?'

A slight nod. She picked up the glass of lemonade at the bedside and held it to his lips.

'Thank you.'

His voice was stronger, she thought, although as she turned away to put down the glass, she cautioned herself not to be too hopeful. Experience had taught her that indulging in fanciful imaginings only led to more pain. However, when she turned back, Garrick was holding out his hand and a surge of emotion rocked her. She could no longer deny the overwhelming love she felt for this man, nor the relief that he was awake and recovering.

She took his hand, saying as calmly as she could, 'What is it, Garrick, what can I do for you?'

His eyes closed and all her fears came rushing back.

She watched anxiously, desperate to stop him slipping away again.

'Would you like to talk, Your Grace?'

'No,' he murmured. 'Read to me. I am enjoying it.'

'There.' Prudence closed the book. 'That is enough for today. We have only a few chapters left and we shall keep them for tomorrow.'

He had not opened his eyes since she had started reading and she thought he was sleeping. It was something of a shock when he spoke to her.

'What happened to me? How did I get here?'

'You passed out in Lady Conyers's carriage.' She wanted to touch him, to pick up his hand and press her lips against it, or to gently caress his cheek, but it would not do. She was his nurse, not his lover. Instead, she straightened the sheet covering his chest. 'Do you not remember?'

'No.'

'No matter. That is often the case, I believe.' She studied his dear face, noting the faint crease in his brow. 'Shall I fetch Stow? He will be delighted to know you are awake—'

'No.' He reached out and caught her fingers. 'Not yet. What day is it?'

'Thursday, your Grace. You have been here for ten days.'

'And you were here all that time. Nursing me.'

'Yes.'

Nursing you, loving you, knowing our worlds are so far apart that this is all the time we can ever have together.

He was silent, but she thought he looked content and she was happy to sit down again, her hand snugly in his, storing up the memory for the dark, lonely days that stretched ahead of her.

The arrival of the duchess with her entourage had brought home to Pru the hopelessness of her situation. Garrick was a duke. His mother wanted a reconciliation and she would expect him to marry a lady of equal status, not an inconsequential spinster from Bath. Pru had no grand relations and no vast fortune to enhance the ducal coffers. If he had loved her, perhaps these things might not have mattered, but he did not. He liked her and he had taken her to his bed. He had even proposed to her, but that had been out of a sense of duty.

She hoped he was no longer in love with Helene Conyers, but there were other beautiful women in his world, women far more suitable to be his duchess than dull, plain Prudence Clifford.

The duke continued to be wakeful for the rest of the day and the following morning he insisted Stow should help him into a chair. He felt as weak as a cat and his mind was still fogged, but memories were returning. Stow fussed about him like a mother hen, banning all visitors except the duchess until Sir Henry had examined his patient and given his approval.

Garrick submitted meekly to everything, including the visit from his mother, who insisted on coming to see him shortly before the dinner hour. The meeting lasted only a few minutes, but it exhausted him. Not that they spoke much, mere platitudes, but there was true warmth in her eyes and she gripped his shoulder before leaving him and her touch conveyed a great deal. They both knew there was much to be discussed, but that could wait until he was stronger.

He felt too weak to argue with his man, except on one

point. When Stow suggested that Miss Clifford should return to Brook Street he refused to allow it. He persuaded Sir Henry to support him, when the physician called to see him later the same day, and that brought an indignant Pru into his room within minutes of Sir Henry's departure.

He was at least sitting upright in a chair, but his weakness frustrated Garrick. He managed a smile and waved a hand towards the garish banyan he was wearing.

'Forgive my informal dress, ma'am, and the fact that I am unable to rise to greet you.'

'It is time I went back to my aunt,' she said, ignoring his attempts at gallantry. 'I am no longer needed here.'

'You are wrong. *I* need you.' He smiled. 'Sir Henry agrees with me.'

'He does not. I asked Stow to tell me *exactly* what was said,' she retorted. 'Sir Henry advised that you were not to be upset.'

'Yes. It will upset me if you go now.'

'Nonsense. You have plenty of people to wait upon you.'

'But you have proved yourself a fine nurse.'

A becoming flush mantled her cheeks, but she shook her head.

'It is no longer necessary for you to have someone with you at all times. Mr Stow is quite capable of looking after you now. He is going to sleep in your dressing room, in case you wake during the night.'

His eyes searched her face. He said bluntly, 'Has my mother suggested you leave?'

'No. The duchess has been...most gracious to me.'

'I am glad of it. She can be rather outspoken.'

'I know it. I am only surprised she—' Pru stopped, giving her head a little shake before returning to her reason for being there. 'Sir Henry says you are recovering well. You no longer need me to nurse you, Your Grace. My work in the sickroom is done.'

He frowned. 'Is that all I ever was to you, a patient, someone to be nursed back to health?'

'Why, of course,' she said brightly. Too brightly in Garrick's opinion. 'Now I can go back to my life's work of helping the poor.'

She met his eyes; her gaze was steady, determined. Something was not right, although Garrick could not work out what it was. He must keep her at Dover Street a little longer. Until his faculties had recovered sufficiently for him to break through the barrier she had erected around herself.

'Give me your word you will not leave without telling me.'

'I must go today.'

'No! Damnation, you cannot go before I am on my feet again!'

Pru's heart ached for him. He looked so vulnerable, the black hair falling over his brow, his face still showing grey traces of the fading bruises. She wanted to stay with him. Not just until he was on his feet again but for ever. But it was impossible. Her reputation was already tarnished, it would be ruined completely if she remained in Dover Street. Garrick was still weak, but once he was stronger, he might want her for his mistress and she did not trust herself not to fall into his arms. To give herself up to the passions that she knew would be far stronger than her resolve.

The duchess never mentioned it, but she must know how Pru felt. Only last night Her Grace had talked about Hartland, which she had now vacated, having moved to the nearby Dower House. It was clear she expected the duke to marry soon and live at Hartland with his bride.

Pru guessed it was the duchess's way of warning her off. Quite rightly. Much better that she left him now.

'Excuse me,' she said at last, knowing she would not hold out if he continued to question her. 'I have arrangements to make. My aunt is anxious to return to Bath and I have to admit, I am, too. I miss my friends, and especially my work at the infirmary!'

It was not quite a lie. It might not be possible for her to remain in Bath but she could carry on her charity work in Melksham. The poor would always need her.

'No, stay.' Garrick's hands were gripping the arms of the chair. 'Stay and marry me.'

Chapter Twenty-Seven

Garrick held his breath. He had not wanted to utter those words until he was well again. Until his mind was sharp enough to refute any arguments she might come up with and he was physically strong enough to protect her from the world.

Pru was staring at him, horrified.

'I beg your pardon,' he said now. 'That was not right. What I mean is—' he put up a hand, raking back his hair. 'Pru—'

'I know exactly what you mean, Your Grace.' She was very pale, but she was calm enough, and at least she was smiling at him. 'This is not the time to discuss such matters. You need to rest.'

His mouth twisted. 'I have been *resting* for the past ten days!'

'Sir Henry said you must not overtire yourself.'

'I know, but.' He reached out to her. 'Pru, at least consider my offer.'

She came over and took his hand. 'I promise you I shall.'

She bent and placed a gentle kiss on his brow before turning and walking away.

* * *

It took an enormous effort but Pru managed to keep up the pretence until she had closed the door behind her. Then her smile disappeared. She felt quite sick. Jack Callater was coming up the stairs and she greeted him with relief.

'Lord John, the very person.'

'Good day to you, Miss Clifford. Stow had told me I may see the duke today.' He grinned at her. 'Veritable guard dog, ain't he? But what's this?' He looked at her more closely. 'Something has upset you. Has Garr taken a turn for the worse?'

'No, no, nothing like that. He goes on very well, but I would like a word with you, if you could spare me five minutes?'

'Yes, yes of course, ma'am.'

He followed her into the morning room and she invited him to sit down.

'I will, of course, but not if you are going to pace the floor,' he retorted. He took her hands and drew her down onto a sofa. 'We are good friends now, Pru, are we not? Tell me what is troubling you.'

'I…' Another steadying breath was required. 'I understand from my aunt that everyone knows I am living here.'

'Ah.'

Her throat felt constricted and she swallowed painfully. 'It is true, then. I am ruined.'

'No such thing,' he said stoutly. 'There has been the odd comment, but the official story is still that you have gone out of town. No one of any consequence has admitted to anything different.'

'I have not left the house since I arrived here with

the duke,' she said, slowly. 'But surely, if there is gossip, everyone in the household must *know*?'

'One would have thought so, yes. Except Garrick, of course.'

'I agree. Stow would not have mentioned it to him. But would the duchess be aware of it?'

He frowned. 'I cannot believe she does not.'

'Then why has she not said anything? Why has she not ejected me?'

'Possibly because she will do nothing to jeopardise Garr's recovery. The duchess loves him dearly, you know, although she would never say so. I think she now regrets keeping him away for all those years.'

'I am glad they have found each other again. I would not for the world have anything come between them.' Pru was silent for a while, then she smiled. 'Thank you, Lord John.'

'For what? I have done nothing.'

She fluttered one hand and shook her head, as if it was no matter. 'You should go to the duke now. No doubt you have news for him, about the Conyerses?'

'Aye. The home secretary now has them both clapped up. As if perverting justice was not enough, Stow and I also made sure they were accused of your abduction. I have taken the liberty of engaging a lawyer for you. He will need to speak with you soon.'

'Thank you.' Pru nodded, but did not linger on the subject. She would deal with that matter at a later date. 'Go and talk with the duke, my lord. You will see for yourself that he is very much recovered. He no longer needs constant nursing, whatever Sir Henry Halford might say. Perhaps you would be good enough to persuade him of that.'

'I shall do nothing of the sort. I certainly cannot go

against his physician.' Jack rose and stood, feeding the brim of his hat between his fingers. 'Garrick owes you a great deal, Pru. We both do, and—'

'Then you will repay me by saying nothing of this conversation to the duke.' She crossed to the door with him. 'Look after Garrick, Lord John.'

With that she slipped away to her room.

Garrick did not return to his bed until it was dark, when he fell into a deep sleep from which he did not wake until sunlight was filling the room the next morning. Who would have thought sitting in a chair could be so exhausting? However, for the first time since he had collapsed he felt hungry and was glad when Stow came in with his breakfast.

After that he submitted to being shaved and only when Stow had finished did he ask the question that had been on his mind all morning.

'Where is Miss Clifford?'

'I have not seen the young lady, Your Grace. If you remember, we decided last night that it was not necessary for anyone to sit with you during the night hours, now I am sleeping in your dressing room.'

'*You* decided that! But—' A knock at the door made him sit up eagerly. It was only a servant, announcing that Sir Henry Halford had arrived. 'Show him up.'

Garrick eased himself back in his chair. There was no time now to talk to Pru before he had seen the physician.

'Garr? Can I come in? I met Halford on the stairs and he said you were well enough to see me.'

Garrick opened his eyes. Jack Callater stood in the doorway, looking uncertainly across the room at him.

'Aye, Jack come in. I am feeling much better today and Sir Henry says I should begin taking a little exercise.'

Perhaps he would ask Pru to come for a drive with him in the park. The fresh air would do them both good.

'Excellent,' said Jack. 'We will soon have you back on your feet. And you will want to know what is happening with Conyers...'

Garrick listened, but he took little interest now he knew that Sir Joseph and Helene were no longer a threat. He had not seen Prudence this morning and his head was full of her. She thought she could fool him with her talk of charitable deeds, but he knew she cared for him, far more than she was admitting. He remembered her voice, when she had been sitting at his bedside. Not just reading to him. He had heard her weeping, begging him not to leave her. She had held his hand, too. Pressed her soft cheek against it...

He shifted restlessly in his chair.

'I am sorry to cut you off, Jack, but I need to see Pru. Now. Would you send for her?'

'Why of course, I'll go and find her.' He lounged out and Garrick waited impatiently. Something was nagging at his mind and he knew he would not be content until he had spoken her.

At last Jack returned, but one look at his face told Garrick something was wrong.

'She is gone.' Jack closed the door carefully behind him. 'She left while Sir Henry was here. Said she did not want you to be disturbed.'

'The devil!' Garrick pushed himself to his feet, swaying unsteadily and Jack quickly took his arm.

'Sit down, you fool, you are in no state to go after her.'

'But I must. I have to tell her.' He rubbed his temples. 'I made a mull of it, Jack. Yesterday. I asked her to marry me.'

'The devil you did.' Jack looked closely at him. 'Was that before my visit?'

'Aye. She was talking of leaving and I... Hell and confound it!' He looked up. 'Did you see her, Jack, did she say anything to you?' He frowned when he saw the consternation in his friend's face. 'Out with it, man!'

'She asked me about the rumours.'

'Rumours?

'Damn it all, Garr. She has been here all this time, nursing you. Tongues were bound to wag.'

'But that won't matter once it is known we are to be married.'

'I think it matters to Pru.'

'What do you mean?

Jack paused. Garrick could see he was choosing his words carefully. At last he said, 'I think Pru believes she is not worthy of you.'

'Nonsense!'

'Perhaps she thinks your mother would object to the union.'

Garrick waved a dismissive hand. 'And what if she does?'

'Something Pru said to me yesterday. About not allowing anything to come between you and the duchess.'

'Did I hear my name?

Both men looked up.

'Mama! Pru has gone,' Garrick barked out the words, trying to stay calm. 'Did you know of this?'

'No, but it does not surprise me.' She held out a letter. 'Mrs Almond found this in her room. It is addressed to you.'

Garrick snatched the paper and unfolded it, frowning over the script.

'She says she is gone back to Bath today, with her aunt. I am not to worry about her.' Muttering, he threw down the paper. 'How can I not worry? I must go after her!'

'Do not be so foolish, my son.'

'Is it true, then?' He glared at the duchess. 'You knew of the rumours about Prudence?'

'I had heard them, yes.'

'Of course.' He slumped back in his chair. 'She was already here when you arrived, was she not? She saved my life, but you have decided she is not the wife for me.'

'On the contrary,' retorted Her Grace. 'I think she is the *only* wife for you!'

Chapter Twenty-Eight

September had started with rain and it threatened to continue. Pru gazed out of the window and thought there was no place as depressing as Bath in wet weather.

She had been in Kilve Street for almost two weeks and would be here for some time yet. Her youngest sister, Jemima, was to be married at the end of the month and Pru had decided to postpone her return to Melksham. The presence of a prodigal daughter would cast a shadow over the nuptials and she had already caused enough upset to her family.

With a sigh she turned away from the window and went back to the little writing desk, where she was trying to compose a letter for Mama. She had been putting it off, but she needed to write now, as a matter of urgency, to explain why she would not be attending Jemima's wedding. Aunt Minerva was sure the gossip would not penetrate deepest Wiltshire, but Pru could not be so sanguine.

There was already speculation in Bath as to why Mrs Clifford and her niece had returned from London two weeks early. Soon other residents would be returning to Bath for the winter and some of them were bound to know the scandal surrounding Miss Prudence Clifford. Then there were the wedding guests. At least some of them would be from London. It could only be a matter of time before the rumours reached Melksham. Pru had made up her mind to write and tell her parents everything. They deserved to know the truth, however painful.

Her dismal thoughts were interrupted by the thud of the street door, then voices in the hall and a light step on the stairs. Moments later Aunt Minerva came into the room.

'My dear, how wise you were not to come to Milsom Street with me this morning. The rain was torrential and my dress is quite *sodden*! I am going up and change immediately, but a runner arrived with a note, just as I was giving my hat and pelisse to Norris, and I thought I would bring it up to you on my way.'

Pru took the sealed letter and stared at the unfamiliar handwriting.

'Who is it from, dear?' asked Minerva, pulling the muddy hem of her skirts away from her ankles.

'I do not know...oh!' Pru put a hand up to her cheek. 'It is f-from the Duchess of Hartland.'

Minerva gave a little shriek and ran over, her wet clothes forgotten. 'Let me see!'

'She is in Bath,' said Pru, handing her the letter.

'At York House.' Minerva nodded. 'And she has invited you to call. Today.'

'I cannot go!'

'You must,' replied her aunt. 'She is sending her carriage for you at four o'clock. Goodness me, that is only an hour!'

'Oh, heavens!' Pru jumped up and began to pace back and forth across the carpet. 'What can she want with me? Why will she not leave me in peace! I am sure I did not come away with anything inadvertently packed in my bags. I distinctly remember giving back the shift I borrowed from Mrs Almond!'

'My dear, I really do not think the duchess would be interested in that,' replied Mrs Clifford, regarding her with fond amusement. 'If she suspected you of stealing I am sure she would have engaged the runners to come after you.'

'Then what can it be?' Pru put both hands to her cheeks. 'Unless the duke has taken a turn for the worse.'

'Now stop that. You are working yourself up quite unnecessarily. You will only find out what Her Grace wants by going to York House, so you had best get ready.' She shepherded Pru out of the room, saying, 'What a pity you did not engage Meg as your dresser after all.'

'How could I, when I was leaving town in disgrace? It would hardly help the poor girl's prospects.'

'Well, no matter. Norris will have to look after you and I shall make do with the housemaid's services. I suggest you wear the new pelisse you bought from Mrs Bell. You wore it but once in London, the weather being so warm, but it makes you look quite dashing.'

'I do not want to look dashing.'

'Nonsense! If you are visiting a duchess, you want to look your best. And do not look so frightened, she cannot eat you. Now come along and get changed.'

When the duchess's carriage arrived in Kilve Street, Pru was ready in her new and fashionable Pomona green pelisse with the matching bonnet. The journey to York House was not long enough to calm her nerves and her knees felt dangerously weak as she followed a liveried servant up the stairs.

She was shown into an elegant sitting room where a small fire burned in the hearth. Not that the heat was needed, but it did add some cheer to the dismally wet day. The duchess, however, looked as cold and stern as ever.

'Thank you for coming, Miss Clifford. Please sit down.'

Pru obeyed, resisting the urge to perch on the edge of the chair, but she sat up very straight as she faced her hostess.

'You left London before we had an opportunity to talk,' remarked the duchess. 'Why was that? And pray do not give me any of the nonsense you gave my son about wishing to return to your charity work in Bath.'

'I was no longer of use in the sickroom. I thought it best to leave before—' she drew in a breath '—before I was asked to do so.'

'You thought that a possibility?'

'Yes.' Pru looked down and smoothed a crease from her skirts. 'Perhaps Your Grace is not aware of the gossip.'

'Of course I am aware of it,' snapped the duchess. 'Good heavens, girl, I am not in my dotage yet! I believe Garrick offered to give you the protection of his name.'

'He did, and I was very grateful for the offer, but—'

'But you could not bring yourself to accept a man with such a tarnished reputation, even to save your own.'

'No!' Pru looked up, shocked. 'That is not it at all.'

'Then tell me, truthfully, why you ran away, when you are clearly in love with him?'

Pru blushed. Was it so very obvious? She bit her lip.

'I am not of his world.'

'And yet you do love him.'

'Yes.' Pru did not hesitate.

'But not enough to fight for him.'

'I did not want to cause another rift between you.'

'Hmmph.' The duchess cast her eyes to the ceiling. 'I have no patience with you young people! In my day a duke would have carried you off and married you out of hand, none of this shilly-shallying. However, Garrick insisted I should come and speak with you first, to assure you I have no objection to the match. Of course, if you would rather not marry him, then I shall ensure no blame will be attached to you—you have my word on that. Now, I have said enough.'

She picked up a small hand bell resting on the table and shook it. Barely had the chimes died when a door behind her opened and the duke walked in.

Pru jumped to her feet and the duchess said, testily, 'Now pray do not run away again until you have spoken to my son. You owe him that, at least!'

Pru was rooted to the spot. She watched as Garrick held the door for his mother to withdraw, then he closed it gently and stood, looking across at her.

'Well,' he said at last. '*Will* you talk to me?'

She cleared her throat. 'Th-there is nothing to say.'

'When I saw you last, I asked you to consider my proposal of marriage.'

'I did consider it.' With an effort she turned away from his searching gaze and walked to the window.

'But you never gave me your answer.'

A hand fluttered. She said sadly, 'My leaving should have told you everything.'

'No. It raised a great many questions.'

She heard his soft tread coming closer and felt panic rising. What would she do if he pulled her into his arms? The small part of her brain that was still working said she must resist, but oh, how she wanted to give in! How she wanted to stop fighting and take the comfort she knew she would find there. Pru braced herself to be strong.

He did not touch her.

'Will you not sit down and take a glass of wine with me?' he said, politely. 'There is a rather fine claret on the tray that I would like you to try.'

'I know nothing about wine.'

'But you drink it, and I want to know your opinion before I stock our cellars.'

'I think it is your mother's opinion you need.'

'No, it is yours. I want to have the wine sent to Hartland before I take you there. As my duchess.'

'Pray do not tease me, Garrick!' She swung around to face him. 'You know I cannot marry you.'

'I know nothing of the sort,' he said smiling at her so fondly that she wanted to weep. 'Tell me why. Is it my reputation?'

'No, *mine*!' she hunted for her handkerchief and buried her face in it.

'Oh, my darling girl.'

Garrick's gentle endearment made the tears come even faster. He guided Pru to a sofa and he sat down with her, one arm about her shoulders.

'Here,' he said, handing her his handkerchief. 'That silly scrap of lace is soaked through.'

'Th-thank you.' She took the linen square he pressed into her hand and dried her cheeks. 'It is no good, Garrick. I have made up my mind not to marry you.'

'Even if I don't care a jot for your reputation? Why should I, when mine has never concerned *you*?'

'But it will concern our families,' she said, trying to make him understand. 'P-people will say I tricked you into offering for me, or that you were so grateful for my nursing that you felt you had no choice.'

'Does it matter what others think?' he asked as she gave her eyes a final wipe.

'Not in general, perhaps, but...' She was about to return his handkerchief, then thought better of it.

'But what?' he prompted.

Pru took a long breath.

'I am not the wife for a *duke*,' she said in a rush. 'Despite everything the duchess said, I cannot be the bride she had in mind for you! I w-would not have you fall out with her again when you have only just been reunited.'

Garrick was silent and Pru stared down miserably at the handkerchief clasped between her fingers, smoothing her thumb over the elegantly embroidered monogram. Could she keep it? A small, precious reminder of what might have been.

'So,' he said at last. 'You would have me marry a bride of my mother's choosing?'

'Yes!'

'Then let me tell you, my beautiful idiot, that is *exactly* what I am going to do.' His arm tightened around her shoulders. 'Why do you think she agreed to come to Bath with me? She is giving our marriage her blessing.'

'But, but she can't! I mean, everyone knows I was in your house alone with you...'

'As my nurse.'

'Many say I was there as your mistress,' she muttered, hanging her head.

This did not appear to shock Garrick at all, but neither did it appear to anger him, which it surely would, if he truly cared for her? She tried to shrug off his arm, but he tightened his hold.

He said, 'After you left town so precipitately, my mother went to see Lady Borcaster. They are both formidable women who know a thing or two about society. They have arranged everything between them.

'It is now common knowledge in town that you and I have been secretly engaged for some time, and that my mother was already in Dover Street the night you rescued me and brought me back there.'

'But—' She looked up and he laid a finger across her lips.

'It was the duchess who insisted that you stay to look after me,' he went on. 'Your aunt and Lady Borcaster were sworn to secrecy about the engagement, which led to a little embarrassment for them when the rumours began to circulate.'

His finger was tracing her lip and Pru felt a strong desire to kiss it. Instead she reached up and pulled his hand away. She needed to concentrate.

She said, 'But why should the duchess do this for *me*?'

'Because she wants you to marry me.'

That could not be right. And yet he looked and sounded perfectly serious.

'Mama told me herself she considers you the only suitable wife for me.' He paused. 'Of course, I realise that we have to consider your family, as well, which is why I stopped at Melksham on my way here.'

'M-Melksham?'

'Why, yes. I called on your parents and explained everything to them. They are up to their eyes in wedding preparations for your sister at present, but your father was good enough to listen to my proposal and give me permission to pay my addresses to you. He did suggest we should announce the engagement at your sister's wedding, but I thought that might overshadow her nuptials somewhat. I thought a special licence might be better. The ceremony to take place in Bath, as soon as possible.'

'Because you are ashamed of me?' she murmured.

'No! Damnation, Pru, because I cannot bear to live without you a moment longer.'

His hand twisted beneath hers and he gripped her fingers.

'If you want all the pomp and grandeur of a London wedding next year then it shall be arranged,' he told her, his voice ragged with emotion. 'The ceremony can take place whenever and however you wish it, my darling Prudence, only please say you will marry me!'

'For your mother's sake?'

'Because you love me.'

'I do, Garrick.' Hot tears threatened again. 'But do you love *me*?'

'Oh, my nonsensical darling, I love you more than life itself.' He pulled her onto his lap and kissed her, so deep and fierce that she was left breathless and dizzy.

'In fact,' he murmured as his lips dropped butterfly kisses over her cheeks, 'I do not think I can live without you.'

'Oh, Garrick!'

She caught his dear face between her hands and captured his mouth with her own, giving herself up to the pleasure of being in his arms, their tongues dancing together. She was filled with sensations new to her, but as old as time. He unbuttoned her pelisse, his mouth seeking out the bare skin of her neck as he pushed the cloth from her shoulders. Pru scrabbled with the buttons of his own blue coat and it quickly followed the pelisse to the floor.

Garrick was easing her down onto the sofa when she recovered her senses sufficiently to protest.

'Wait, wait! What if the duchess should return and find us like this?'

'My mother has gone to Kilve Street, to explain everything to your aunt. She has also given instructions that *upon no account* are we to be disturbed.' His eyes glinted. 'She would tell you herself that in *her* day, lovers did not have such namby-pamby notions of propriety.'

His face was so close, his forest-green eyes so dark that her insides were melting under their gaze. She tried to fight the rapid beating of her heart.

'I suppose these things are quite normal in ducal households,' she murmured.

'They will be in ours.'

The wicked smile that accompanied his words were Pru's undoing. The last shreds of resistance fell away. She pulled him down to her, closing her eyes as he lowered his head and trailed kisses over the column of her throat while his hands expertly freed her breasts from the muslin bodice, ready for his lips to continue their relentless onslaught. All the longing and desire that had been pent up since her one night in his bed exploded and Pru gave herself up to it. They discarded clothes as necessary to allow them to touch and caress each other.

Garrick had never known anything like it. Pru abandoned was a delight, swift to learn and eager to please. She was excited, wondering. Her soft fingers explored his body, repeating the lessons she had learned in his bed and rousing him to the very edge of ecstasy.

The sofa was too restricting and he eased her down onto the floor before running his mouth across the soft skin of her thigh, just above the garter. She moaned softly and he continued to kiss and stroke the soft skin with his tongue, gradually moving upwards to the warm hinge of her thighs. She was opening to him like a flower, offering herself to his touch. Garrick ignored the demands of his own body until she was almost thrashing beneath him, her fingers clawing at his shoulders. She began to buck wildly, sending the blood pumping through him, hot and urgent. He covered her, thrusting hard and fast until they both juddered with the final ecstatic release and clung together, bodies locked, gasping for breath.

Later, much later, they were sitting together on the sofa, Pru wrapped safely in Garrick's arms and with her head resting on his shoulder. He dropped a kiss onto her hair.

'You still have not given me your answer. Will you marry me, my darling Prudence?'

She chuckled, the soft, melodious sound filling him with hope.

'I believe I shall have to do so, or people will say I ran away from you, like poor Miss Speke.'

'Ah.' He settled her more comfortably against his shoulder. 'There has been an interesting development with the lady. It seems it was not just me that Annabelle was rejecting. She has renounced all men.'

'What? I do not understand.'

'Annabelle and her friend Miss Emily Undershaw have set up a permanent home together. They have both declared they have no intention of ever marrying. Upon learning of it, the Tirrills recently travelled into Wales to bring their daughter home, but she refused to leave.' He grinned. 'The best part, my darling, is that Annabelle admitted to her parents that she only remained faithful to me for all those years in order to avoid them making any other marriage plans for her.'

'But how can you know all that?'

'Lady Tirrill was angry and foolish enough to take her close friends into her confidence. Those same friends who spread the original rumours about me. Word has gone around London like wildfire, and society now believes that rather than being a jilt, I am well out of a bad bargain.'

Pru sat up and looked at him, her eyes searching his face. 'And you do not mind that?'

'Why should I? The match was suggested by our parents when we were children. We were friends, but I do not think we ever really loved one another.'

'And... Helene Conyers.' Her gaze shifted to somewhere below his chin and she began to fasten the buttons of his shirt.

'Ah, *la belle* Helene. She was my first real passion.' He brushed her hand away and drew her back into his arms. 'But that was mere boyish lust, not the enduring love I have found with you.' He kissed her. 'I do love you, you know. Beyond life itself.'

'Truly?' she asked, smiling up at him mistily.

'Truly. I want you here with me for ever. Dearest, loveliest Pru.'

'Oh,' she buried her face in his shoulder. 'That is so beautiful. Like something from a book.'

'It is. The one you never finished reading to me. I read it last night, when I could not sleep for fear you might reject me.' He added, 'You might still, since you have yet to give me your answer.'

'Do you doubt what it will be?'

'You are an independent and high-minded woman. I have no idea what you will do.' He paused. 'And I am still not strong enough to prevent you walking out on me.'

'Oh, I had quite forgotten your poor ribs!'

She tried to move away and his arms tightened. 'My poor ribs are doing very well, thank you. Although I am shocked that you should have forgotten so quickly.'

'You distracted me!'

'Did I?'

'You know you did,' she replied, blushing hotly. 'How can I think of anything else, when you are doing *such* things to me?'

'Think about it now,' he commanded. 'I must have an answer, madam.'

'Very well, then.' She lowered her eyes. 'If you are sure you want me for your duchess.'

'For my duchess, my wife, my lover and my friend,' he said, marking each word with a kiss. 'Now say it and put me out of my misery. Will you marry me?'

And Prudence, abandoning all reason, listened to her heart and gave him his answer.

'I will, Garrick. Yes, please.'

* * * * *

*If you enjoyed this story, be sure to pick up
one of Sarah Mallory's other great reads*

The Duke's Family for Christmas
Cinderella and the Scarred Viscount
The Mysterious Miss Fairchild

*And why not read her
Laird of Ardvarrick miniseries?*

Forbidden to the Highland Laird
Rescued by Her Highland Soldier
The Laird's Runaway Wife

Get 3 FREE REWARDS!

We'll send you 2 FREE Books plus a FREE Mystery Gift.

His Innocent for One Spanish Night — CAROL MARINELLI

PRESENTS

Bound by the Italian's "I Do" — MICHELLE SMART

FREE Value Over **$20**

Both the **Harlequin® Desire** and **Harlequin Presents®** series feature compelling novels filled with passion, sensuality and intriguing scandals.

YES! Please send me 2 FREE novels from the Harlequin Desire or Harlequin Presents series and my FREE gift (gift is worth about $10 retail). After receiving them, if I don't wish to receive any more books, I can return the shipping statement marked "cancel." If I don't cancel, I will receive 6 brand-new Harlequin Presents Larger-Print books every month and be billed just $6.30 each in the U.S. or $6.49 each in Canada, a savings of at least 10% off the cover price, or 3 Harlequin Desire books (2-in-1 story editions) every month and be billed just $7.83 each in the U.S. or $8.43 each in Canada, a savings of at least 12% off the cover price. It's quite a bargain! Shipping and handling is just 50¢ per book in the U.S. and $1.25 per book in Canada.* I understand that accepting the 2 free books and gift places me under no obligation to buy anything. I can always return a shipment and cancel at any time by calling the number below. The free books and gift are mine to keep no matter what I decide.

Choose one: ☐ **Harlequin Desire**
(225/326 BPA GRNA)

☐ **Harlequin Presents Larger-Print**
(176/376 BPA GRNA)

☐ **Or Try Both!**
(225/326 & 176/376 BPA GRQP)

Name (please print)

Address   Apt. #

City   State/Province   Zip/Postal Code

Email: Please check this box ☐ if you would like to receive newsletters and promotional emails from Harlequin Enterprises ULC and its affiliates. You can unsubscribe anytime.

Mail to the Harlequin Reader Service:
IN U.S.A.: P.O. Box 1341, Buffalo, NY 14240-8531
IN CANADA: P.O. Box 603, Fort Erie, Ontario L2A 5X3

Want to try 2 free books from another series! Call 1-800-873-8635 or visit www.ReaderService.com.

*Terms and prices subject to change without notice. Prices do not include sales taxes, which will be charged (if applicable) based on your state or country of residence. Canadian residents will be charged applicable taxes. Offer not valid in Quebec. This offer is limited to one order per household. Books received may not be as shown. Not valid for current subscribers to the Harlequin Presents or Harlequin Desire series. All orders subject to approval. Credit or debit balances in a customer's account(s) may be offset by any other outstanding balance owed by or to the customer. Please allow 4 to 6 weeks for delivery. Offer available while quantities last.

Your Privacy—Your information is being collected by Harlequin Enterprises ULC, operating as Harlequin Reader Service. For a complete summary of the information we collect, how we use this information and to whom it is disclosed, please visit our privacy notice located at corporate.harlequin.com/privacy-notice. From time to time we may also exchange your personal information with reputable third parties. If you wish to opt out of this sharing of your personal information, please visit readerservice.com/consumerchoice or call 1-800-873-8635. **Notice to California Residents**—Under California law, you have specific rights to control and access your data. For more information on these rights and how to exercise them, visit corporate.harlequin.com/california-privacy.

HDHP23

Get 3 FREE REWARDS!

We'll send you 2 FREE Books plus a FREE Mystery Gift.

FREE Value Over **$20**

Both the **Romance** and **Suspense** collections feature compelling novels written by many of today's bestselling authors.

YES! Please send me 2 FREE novels from the Essential Romance or Essential Suspense Collection and my FREE gift (gift is worth about $10 retail). After receiving them, if I don't wish to receive any more books, I can return the shipping statement marked "cancel." If I don't cancel, I will receive 4 brand-new novels every month and be billed just $7.49 each in the U.S. or $7.74 each in Canada. That's a savings of at least 17% off the cover price. It's quite a bargain! Shipping and handling is just 50¢ per book in the U.S. and $1.25 per book in Canada.* I understand that accepting the 2 free books and gift places me under no obligation to buy anything. I can always return a shipment and cancel at any time by calling the number below. The free books and gift are mine to keep no matter what I decide.

Choose one:
- ☐ **Essential Romance** (194/394 BPA GRNM)
- ☐ **Essential Suspense** (191/391 BPA GRNM)
- ☐ **Or Try Both!** (194/394 & 191/391 BPA GRQZ)

Name (please print)

Address   Apt. #

City   State/Province   Zip/Postal Code

Email: Please check this box ☐ if you would like to receive newsletters and promotional emails from Harlequin Enterprises ULC and its affiliates. You can unsubscribe anytime.

Mail to the Harlequin Reader Service:
IN U.S.A.: P.O. Box 1341, Buffalo, NY 14240-8531
IN CANADA: P.O. Box 603, Fort Erie, Ontario L2A 5X3

Want to try 2 free books from another series? Call 1-800-873-8635 or visit www.ReaderService.com.

---

*Terms and prices subject to change without notice. Prices do not include sales taxes, which will be charged (if applicable) based on your state or country of residence. Canadian residents will be charged applicable taxes. Offer not valid in Quebec. This offer is limited to one order per household. Books received may not be as shown. Not valid for current subscribers to the Essential Romance or Essential Suspense Collection. All orders subject to approval. Credit or debit balances in a customer's account(s) may be offset by any other outstanding balance owed by or to the customer. Please allow 4 to 6 weeks for delivery. Offer available while quantities last.

Your Privacy—Your information is being collected by Harlequin Enterprises ULC, operating as Harlequin Reader Service. For a complete summary of the information we collect, how we use this information and to whom it is disclosed, please visit our privacy notice located at corporate.harlequin.com/privacy-notice. From time to time we may also exchange your personal information with reputable third parties. If you wish to opt out of this sharing of your personal information, please visit readerservice.com/consumerschoice or call 1-800-873-8635. **Notice to California Residents**—Under California law, you have specific rights to control and access your data. For more information on these rights and how to exercise them, visit corporate.harlequin.com/california-privacy.

STRS23

HARLEQUIN
PLUS

Try the best multimedia
subscription service for romance
readers like you!

Read, Watch and Play.

Experience the easiest way to get
the romance content you crave.

Start your **FREE TRIAL** at
<u>www.harlequinplus.com/freetrial</u>.